F[...]

"They're the most [...] [...] ever seen," Ashley gasp[...] [...] the glittering emerald necklace, bracelet, and earrings. "I have never possessed anything so lovely. Are they family items?"

"No, most of the Shandal jewelry is made of diamonds. These are yours alone." He smiled. "With your eyes, my dear, you must have emeralds."

"But the expense!"

Shrugging, he laughed. "Don't concern yourself with price, Ashley. I don't! So do you like them?"

"I adore them!" Shyly, she leaned forward and dutifully kissed his cheek. "Thank you."

The marquess caught her chin with his fingers. "Is that the way a bride should kiss her bridegroom?"

Ashley trembled when his mouth descended on hers, gently but firmly parting her lips. Her heart pounded wildly, her pulse rising to her throat, as his thumb caressed her jawline. Her whole body seemed to flush with warmth.

"There," he said softly, "that is better."

Ashley stared into his vivid blue eyes, her flesh aglow from her first, true adult kiss, and her mind reeling with a strange desire for it to go on and on . . .

*** *** ***

Praise for Cathleen Clare's *An Elusive Groom:*

"A delightful romp full of great characterizations. The witty dialogue and spicy and humorous situations make this a must read."

—*Rendezvous*

". . . a sparkling comedy of manners . . ."

—*Romantic Times*

LORD SCANDAL'S LADY

Cathleen Clare

Zebra Books
Kensington Publishing Corp.

http://www.zebrabooks.com

ZEBRA BOOKS are published by

Kensington Publishing Corp.
850 Third Avenue
New York, NY 10022

First Printing: March, 1997
10 9 8 7 6 5 4 3 2 1

Printed in the United States of America

For Carol and Leon Garlinghouse,
with love

One

"Well, Jane, at last we're on the ground again." The young lady alighted from the coach, resisting the shocking temptation to stretch her travel-weary body. "In the future, we shall journey much more comfortably. I am certain that my aunt's carriages must be of the very finest quality."

"Hm!" her servant snorted, disdainfully stepping from the odorous public conveyance. "You should have been able to use your own carriage. The very idea of a nice young lady having to travel with the likes of them!" She jerked her head towards the remaining passengers, lifted her chin, and looked down her nose at them. "And to be set down at a place like this with no one 'ere to meet her! It's not right!"

"Oh, it isn't so terribly bad. This inn looks rather attractive. Think of it all as an adventure, Jane! Do not fret. Aunt Sheldon will send someone for us as soon as she receives my message."

Green eyes sparkling, Miss Ashley Madison cheerfully glanced around the bustling courtyard. Even a naive, country girl could see that this establishment was different from a great many of the common inns that dotted England's highways and byways. Located on the major thoroughfare between London and Bath, the Horn and Hunter, a large, rambling half-timbered hostelry, was a busy place after the social Season in the city ended. Well-known for its hospitality, cleanliness, and excellent country cuisine, it had become a favorite stopping place for the *ton* as they fled London's oppressive summer heat.

Additions to the building had been added through the centuries as the inn had prospered, creating a jumble of ells outside and a labyrinth of passages inside. Fortunately the current innkeeper had drawn it all together with a coat of whitewash and dark brown trim, making the structure very pleasing to the eye. Rising above a bricked yard, it looked sturdy, solid, and most welcome to the weary traveler.

Still, their arrival at what appeared to be a very decent inn had not mollified the young lady's maid. "It's just not proper!" Jane grumbled.

Ashley shrugged indifferently. "Lady Madison had need of the carriage. Remember, it isn't mine. It belongs to my brother. In his absence, his wife must make the decisions."

"Mark my words, she won't use it. She's mean and spiteful! Lord Madison would never have let you travel in a public coach."

"Perhaps not, but he had no say in it. Please find the landlord, Jane, and arrange for a chamber so that I may freshen myself while we wait."

"Yes, Miss Ashley," the girl said dutifully, but the resentment remained in her voice. "I hope this inn is cleaner than the one last night."

"From its appearance, I believe it will be. But we shan't be here long, anyway."

"A good thing that is! No matter how clean it is, it is no fit place for a young lady," she proclaimed as if she were much older than her twenty-five years. Imperiously, she elbowed aside a hostler and stalked into the inn, the rigid set of her shoulders expressing her displeasure at the whole episode.

Shaking her head slightly at her abigail's disgruntled behavior, Ashley remained in the yard and watched carefully to see that all of her baggage was unloaded. None of it was worth a great deal, but it represented most of her worldly possessions. She knew that her country-made clothing was not of the first stare of fashion, and Lady Madison, at the last moment, had taken the best of her paltry jewelry, claiming that they were family pieces and thus belonged to Deron. Ashley sighed, remembering the small ruby pendant, a gift from her grandmother, hanging around the neck of her sister-in-law as she bid her farewell. How could Deron have married such a woman? Worse still, why had he sprung her without warning upon his sister? Sometimes her brother could be perfectly unforgivable!

Deron, Lord Madison, in his usual spur-of-the-moment fashion, had taken a leave from the Army and arrived in London, bent upon spending his time away from the troops in a grand style of celebration. He'd set aside only the last few days to visit his sister at Oakwood Manor, his ancestral estate. Gadding about the city with his former schoolmates, he, in quick succession, met, fell in love with, and married the pretty widow, Eve Trehorne, who was two years his senior and caught in the throes of several ill-mannered moneylenders. With his pockets to let from paying her debts, he terminated the lease on her London house and took her to the country. He overcame her protests with concern for her well-being during his absence, further hinting that she might spend her time restoring his fine old house to its former glory.

Deron had spent two nights and one day at home before returning to the Army, but in that small amount of time he had absolutely overturned his sister's life. No longer was Ashley the mistress of the estate, as she had been for the three years since their parents had died. Now his lady wife was in command, and she proceeded to make things quite unbearable for everyone around her. Sweetly kind while Deron was there, she had impressed Ashley with her London manners and stylish attire, but when he left she immediately began to rule with a heavy hand and a cutting tongue.

The lady had constantly degraded Ashley for a lack of polish, beauty, and suitors, reminding her daily that she, at the age of twenty-one, was destined to be an old maid if she did not set herself to rights. She complained about the servants, bullying and ordering them about as though they were devoid of any sense whatsoever. She began to redecorate, boasting of the fine parties she would have and the notable guests she would receive, when "this horrid ruin is transformed into a home of taste."

Within a short time, Ashley could stand it no more. The growing surliness of the servants, the expenditures which would certainly bring Deron into heavy debt, and the slurs upon herself were too much to bear. In desperation she wrote to her aunt, Lady Sheldon, whom she had scarcely seen above two or three times in her life.

The letter bore fruit. Dear Aunt Rose wished her niece to come to her as soon as possible. Now that her daughters were married, she missed not having a young lady in the house. They would have such fun together during the London Season!

Ashley was uncertain about coming out in Society. She had seen enough of what that had to offer in Lady Madison. But she was happy to leave her overturned home, and if she must act the role of a society miss to please her aunt, she would do so. Nothing could be as distasteful as her life at Oakwood Manor had become.

"Miss Ashley!" Disturbing her mistress from her unsettled thoughts, Jane emerged from the inn, followed closely by a plump, jolly-faced woman. "I've got the room," she said with satisfaction. "This is Mrs. Bennett, the innkeeper's wife. She'll show us the way."

"How do, Miss Madison," her hostess said effusively. "Welcome to the Horn and Hunter. We've a good room for you."

"Oh thank you, Mrs. Bennett." Ashley smiled gratefully. "I did so dislike the idea of meeting my aunt in this deplorable condition. The innkeeper last night was not . . . not at all interested in meeting my requests."

"You won't find that at the Horn and Hunter, miss. We take pride in serving our guests. Why, all the gentry stop here! Meeting your aunt, y'say? Might she live nearby?"

"Yes, though I am not sure how far. I shouldn't think it to be too great a distance. My aunt and uncle are Lord and Lady Sheldon. Perhaps you know of them?"

" 'Pon my soul! The Sheldons' niece!" twittered Mrs. Bennett. "My Lord and Lady Sheldon are well-respected in the neighborhood. Now you just come with me, dearie. We'll care for you proper!"

"I do so appreciate it." Ashley exhaled with relief. "I'd like to send a message to my aunt, if that is possible? And to bathe?"

" 'Course it is! I'll bring paper and pen, and you can write whatever you want while you're waiting for your bath. The Hall's not far away. I'll have the note taken there in a jiffy!"

Ashley allowed herself to be escorted grandly into the inn, through the noisy common room, and up the stairs to a sunny, sparkling-clean chamber. She paused at the door, mentally comparing this cheery prospect to the dingy, damp quarters of the night before.

"Does this room suit you, miss?" The landlord's wife made a great show of fluffing the pillows. "It's one of our best. I'm happy that it was available. We're busy this time of year with everyone coming to the country. They all plan to stay here on their way! They know we'll take care of 'em proper."

"It is very pleasant, Mrs. Bennett. Thank you so much."

"Ah, you're a sweet miss, that you are." She winked. "I say it won't be long before you do all your traveling with a husband!"

Ashley's cheeks grew pink, knowing that a match for her would soon become Aunt Sheldon's foremost goal.

Mrs. Bennett chuckled. "Now you rest and I'll fetch you paper and pen, and arrange for your bath." Still laughing, she exited the room.

Ashley looked longingly at the bed. "Oh, Jane, I didn't realize how weary I am."

"Do you wish a nap, miss?"

"No, there isn't time. I want to be ready when they come for me." Removing her bonnet, she wandered across the room and gazed into the mirror. A tired and slightly haggard young woman stared back. "Dear me, I look a fright!"

"Of course you don't," the maid scoffed. "You're a pretty young lady!"

Ashley stared at the reflection. "Am I? I seem so pale!"

"You're just overtired, miss. You've usually got pretty color."

"I wish I had it now. All this black hair makes me look as if I'm in mourning." She peered closer. "I look like a witch, and I did so hope to impress my aunt!"

Jane laughed. "You'll be happier after you bathe. You'll have roses in your cheeks again, and if you don't, just remember Mrs. Bennett's talk of husbands. That'll do it!"

"I'll be lucky to find a husband," she said sarcastically, "at my age."

"Now don't you heed Lady Madison! That one was jealous of your pretty looks." The abigail answered a tap at the door and admitted Mrs. Bennett with her writing materials, her servants following with a tub and pails of water.

"Here we are!" the landlady nodded. "Write your letter, miss, and send your girl down with it. It'll be at Sheldon Hall in no time."

"You are very kind, Mrs. Bennett." As her hostess departed, Ashley sat down at the table, composed a short message and handed it to her maid. "There, it's finished! Now I'll have my bath and be all ready to meet Aunt Rose."

She took down her long dark hair and stood, allowing her maid to assist her undressing. "Perhaps, Jane, when you take the letter down, you could fetch me a cup of tea? Also, take my purse and settle with Mrs. Bennett. I don't wish to keep my aunt's carriage waiting."

"Yes, miss. I shan't be long. Have you everything you need?"

"I think so." She stepped into the bath and sank down into the warm water, drowsily laying her head against the back of the tub. "Ah, I almost feel fresher already! You needn't hurry, Jane. I could stay here forever. Get yourself something to eat. We've time enough for that. I suppose we shouldn't have skipped luncheon, but that inn was so filthy."

"Shall I bring you some food, Miss Ashley?"

"No, I'll wait till I get to Sheldon Hall. But do have a bite. We don't know what sort of schedule the servants keep there."

"Thank you, miss. You're sure you'll be all right?"

"I'll be fine. Go along now." Ashley shut her eyes and tried to imagine how lovely and comfortable Sheldon Hall would be. She knew that her aunt and uncle were quite wealthy, so they probably had no need to practice strict economy, as she had done for so long at Oakwood Manor. It would be wonderful to have a fine variety of food to eat and to buy pretty new dresses, as her aunt had promised in her letter. She would surely become very spoiled.

Yet, it was hard to banish Oakwood Manor from her mind. With Deron in the Army, she had been both its master and its mistress for the past three years. Although it had been a struggle, she had turned the estate around until it gradually began to reap a profit. Of late, she had even been able to pay small amounts towards retiring the tumultuous debts against it. Now it was certain that Deron's new wife would plunge it deeper in the suds than it had ever been.

She sadly shook her head. Her brother simply must sell out, come home, and take charge. She hoped that the letter she had written would jog some latent sense of responsibility in him. At any rate, she was gone from Oakwood Manor and must stop worrying over what happened there. She had done her best, and that was all anyone could do. It was time to think of herself and to enjoy being young and trouble-free. At Sheldon Hall, all would be well.

Brandon Havard, Marquess of Shandal, alighted from his curricle and looked with aggravation at the damaged wheel.

" 'Tis broke bad, my lord," his groom pronounced darkly. "Nothing we can do for it."

"Yes, it appears to be beyond our means of repair." The marquess shrugged his broad shoulders. "Well, it is our good fortune that it happened so near to the Horn and Hunter."

"Yes, sir. Shall I ride there for help?"

"You do that." He glanced up at his valet, who had

remained in the vehicle. "Lindsey? You may ride with him and arrange for rooms. I'm sure we'll be there overnight."

"But, my lord, we can't leave you alone by the side of the road!"

"Nonsense!" he scoffed. "It's a perfectly civilized stretch. Besides, I don't want to soil my clothing."

"Neither do I," the valet said under his breath.

Shandal overheard, and laughed. "Lindsey, I daresay you are becoming more of a dandy than I am! Go along now!"

"Yes, sir." The fastidiously attired servant stepped down, eyeing the horses with distaste. "I hope I'm not thrown."

"I wouldn't worry about it. The horses were growing tired. They'll put up with you! Now help John unhook them and be on your way."

" 'Twill give you a good chance to practice your horsemanship," the groom said cheerfully, pressing a set of reins into the valet's hands. "You ride like a sack a meal! I'll give you some pointers as we go along."

"Kindly keep them to yourself," Lindsey haughtily proclaimed, looking down his thin nose. "My profession does not require equestrian skills."

"A good thing, that! You would never—"

"Hurry along!" the marquess commanded sharply, interrupting their continual feud. "The sun is hot!"

Seeking shelter under a tree, he sat down, stretched out his long legs, and watched his minions set off down the road, John moving gracefully with his horse, while Lindsey bounced painfully beside him. It was truly a good thing that the Horn and Hunter was so close. Dasher would not stand that pounding to his kidneys very long before tossing the valet into the ditch.

The marquess must have dozed, because it didn't seem long before John and a groom from the inn arrived, driving a wagon and a gig. Standing, he brushed off his trousers and languidly walked forward to meet them.

"Lindsey stayed behind, my lord," the groom explained, "making ready for your arrival. If you'd like to go ahead with the gig, we'll take off the wheel and bring the baggage later."

"Yes, I shall," he agreed, yawning. "I've need of a good brandy."

It was a shorter distance to the hostelry than he had realized, and though the horse was a simple country nag and poorly mouthed, they arrived quickly at a brisk enough trot. Pulling up in the yard, Brandon tossed the reins to a hostler and, placing a coin in the boy's hand, went inside.

He found Lindsey in the common room, drinking a tankard of ale and presiding in grandeur over those present. Surprised at his master's early arrival, the valet detached himself and moved at once to serve him.

"I've brandy in your room, my lord. The private salons are in use at present, but we'll have one soon."

"Excellent. Go back to your ale, man; I can find my own way, and I won't be needing you for a while."

"Thank you, sir. Your chamber is at the top of the stairs."

"Enjoy yourself then, Lindsey. It's been a long day. Just don't get foxed!"

"No, sir. Of course not!"

Shandal started up the stairs, aware of all the eyes staring at him. It was a familiar occurrence. Even if he had not been a wealthy peer, he was so handsome a man that he would always be the center of attention wherever he went. Well, he wouldn't be the prime attraction at Lady Alicia Milton's manor tonight, and she would be furious. He smiled cynically at the thought of it. Of late, his mistress had been growing a bit too possessive. He wouldn't send her a note to advise her of what had happened. His unexplained absence should make her pause to consider her actions.

In fact, he wouldn't visit her at all. He'd go on to Bath. His mother, who was staying there, had recently written to him and seemed most anxious to see him. That should put Alicia in her place.

Reaching the first floor, he saw that there were two doors nearby. Frowning at Lindsey's poor direction, he chose the one that appeared to be the closest.

The marquess, entering the chamber, immediately spied a screen, from behind which protruded the edge of the bathtub. His valet, as usual, had thought of everything his lord might wish for. He might be tiresome in his bickering with John and overly fond of his own consequence, but no one could see to his master's comfort as well as Lindsey.

Glancing around the room for the bottle of brandy, he saw a woman's dress lying across the bed, and realized that he had selected the wrong room. Though his comfort quite often included women, his servant wouldn't go to the extreme of providing him with one. Brandon began a quiet retreat.

"Please hand me a towel," a dulcet voice echoed from behind the screen. "I have soap in my eyes."

He paused, grinning.

"Do hurry!" the voice entreated.

Nodding to himself, he crossed the room, picked a towel off the screen, and turned the corner.

A very pretty, and very naked, raven-haired young lady sat dripping wet in the tub, her arm outstretched and her eyes tightly closed. The marquess put the towel in her hand, his gaze sweeping the soft curves of her body and alighting on her firm, pertly uplifted breasts.

"Thank you, Jane." She rubbed her face and looked up, horror spreading across her interesting features.

"Who are you!" she shrieked, hastily shrinking into the water and covering herself as best she could. She stared angrily at him. "How dare you! Get out of here at once!"

"Your servant, miss." He bowed mockingly, glanced away from her silky legs, and looked into her furious green eyes. "Please accept my apologies. I seem to have entered the wrong room."

"Damn your apologies! Just go away!" she cried.

"As you wish." Laughing lightly, the marquess departed. What a spirited girl, he thought. She had not only kept her wits about her, but she had cursed him, and would, very likely, have landed him a facer if he had come any closer. Most other young ladies would have either screamed their heads off or would have been frozen into speechless huddles of shocked femininity. Lady Bathtub had spunk.

Still chuckling, he entered the neighboring chamber, saw the waiting bottle of brandy, and knew that this time he'd guessed right. But he certainly wasn't sorry for his previous error. As a man well-known for his conquests of women, he recognized outstanding beauty. The scintillating female next door possessed more than her share of comeliness. From her long, supple legs to her full, luscious breasts to the satiny locks of her midnight-dark hair, she was something very special.

It was too bad that he probably would never see her again, but even if he did, a dalliance would be out of the question. Despite her interesting reaction, she was much too young for him and the games of love he enjoyed. Her delectable, youthful body was destined for a marriage bed, not for a marquess's mere pleasure.

Ah, such were life's disappointments! Brandon popped the cork of the bottle of liquor, poured himself an ample amount, and settled down in a chair. Grinning in remembrance of the little minx, he proceeded to wash the journey's dust from his throat.

When the door clicked shut behind that rogue, Ashley leaped from the tub, wrapped herself in the dripping towel, and dashed across the room to secure the lock. Weakly, she leaned against the wall, her heart pounding frantically. Good Heavens! The nerve of the man! Had he no sense of honor? Oh, Lord, what he must have seen!

Blushing furiously, she returned to the bath screen, dropped the wet towel over the edge of the tub, and hurriedly dried herself with a fresh one. Pray God she would never see that horrid beast again! If she did, perhaps he would not recognize her. But, oh my, she would always know him. She could never forget those blue, blue eyes, that guinea-gold hair, his rakish smile. He was overwhelmingly handsome . . . and just as dangerous.

She dressed quickly, scarcely caring for her appearance. She only wished to have clothing on her body as soon as possible. There would be time enough for primping at Sheldon Hall.

She gasped as a light rap sounded on the door. What if he had come back? What would she do?

"Y-yes?" she stammered.

"Lady Sheldon," an imperious voice announced.

"Aunt Rose! Thank God!" Ashley ran barefoot across the room to throw open the door. "Dear Aunt Rose!"

She would have flung herself into the lady's arms if she hadn't suddenly felt enormously intimidated. Lady Sheldon, dressed to perfection in a dark green gown and spencer, her fluffy white hair tucked under a stylishly matching bonnet, exuded such dignity that Ashley could only curtsy respectfully. She was, however, permitted to kiss a cool pink cheek.

"How do you do, Ashley?"

"Much better, ma'am, since you have come to my rescue." Next to her aunt's modishness, she became conscious of her own dishevelment. "Please come in. I'm sorry to greet you in such disarray, but I did not expect you so soon."

Lady Sheldon nodded elegantly, studying her niece. "I had been visiting the vicar and was intercepted on my way home." Finishing her perusal of her niece, she glanced about the room. "My goodness, have you no maid? Surely you cannot have traveled alone!"

"Jane is in the kitchen, Aunt," Ashley assured her.

"Thank goodness! My," she said, twitching her nose, "what black hair you have!"

"My papa's grandmother was Spanish, ma'am. It must come from her."

"Well, we shall have it cut and crimped. Short, curly hair is the fashion."

Ashley frowned slightly. "I . . . I like my hair the way it is."

"Blondes are the style," Lady Sheldon went on as though her niece hadn't spoken. "Still, maybe he won't mind. Your eyes are quite fine."

Determined to allow no scissors near her head, Ashley eyed her warily. "Who won't mind?"

Her aunt seemed briefly surprised by the question, then burst into genteel laughter. "Of course you don't know! How could you? Don't tell me that I am becoming a forgetful old woman!" She cheerfully embraced her. "You're to be wed, Ashley. We've already found you a husband!"

Two

Wed! To whom? What sort of nonsense was this?

Ashley had not had time to recover from her shock nor to question her aunt before Jane had returned. In a flurry, she'd been properly dressed, and her hair done up. With orders given for Jane to follow with the baggage, Ashley soon found herself seated beside Lady Sheldon in the earl's luxurious carriage, and on her way to Sheldon Hall.

She cast a surreptitious glance at the attractive lady, who had so kindly offered her a home. Had this been Aunt Rose's intention all along? To rid herself of her niece as soon as possible?

"Aunt," she began, "what is this matter of my marriage?"

"Why, it is all arranged! I cannot believe our good fortune!" The countess's eyes glowed with pride. "After your letter arrived, I had a guest in my home, an old and dear friend with a very eligible son. Immediately, we settled everything."

"It is impossible!" Ashley gasped.

"Oh no, not at all. I remembered seeing you as a young girl, so I was sure you would be pretty enough for him. My goodness, Mandy and I have been friends for years! She trusts my judgment."

"But what about her son? Surely he has something to say in the matter."

"He trusts his mama," she confidently replied. "When Mandy finally brought him to believe that it was time he set up his nursery, he gave her leave to find him a suitable bride. You, my dear."

Ashley set her jaw. If Lady Sheldon expected her to participate in this farce, she was very much mistaken. "Aunt, I fear you have wasted your time," she said firmly. "I shall not marry a man I don't even know, and I won't marry anyone who cares so little for his future wife that he lets his mother choose her for him. I won't do it!"

"Of course you will," said Lady Sheldon, just as stubbornly. "You have no other choice."

"Oh yes I do! I can become a governess or a companion to an elderly lady."

Her aunt laughed merrily. "You are too young and too pretty for either of those positions. No lady would hire you as a governess. You would be too much a temptation to her husband or an elder son. No one would hire you as a companion because you are too young. No, Ashley, you will marry Lord Shandal."

"I will not," she repeated.

Was she never to be rid of problems? First her parents' deaths, then Deron's defection, and now this. Marriage was the goal of every young lady, and Ashley was no exception. She wanted a husband and a family, but she wanted to choose her mate herself, and she wanted him to love her. This man selected by her aunt didn't care whom he wed. Perhaps he was such an antidote that no one would have him.

Her aunt broke in on her thoughts. "You must trust me, my dear. Shandal is a great catch."

"If so, why hasn't someone else caught him?" Ashley asked bluntly.

The lady winked slyly. "Because he has escaped them all."

"Then why me?"

"It is a matter of being in the right place at the right time. I don't like the tone of your voice, Ashley. It isn't becoming. Nor do I care for your insinuation that your uncle and I don't know what we are doing. We arranged our own daughters' marriages very successfully."

Ashley colored. "I'm sorry, Aunt, if I seem rude. You must admit that you have quite overset me. You may, if you please, send me back to Oakwood Manor, for I do refuse to go along with your scheme."

"Oakwood Manor! Ha! I don't think you wish that! Tell me of Oakwood Manor. Are things there still as bad as you told me in your letter?"

"They'll probably become worse," she was forced to admit. Though the subject was distasteful, it was better than the previous one. Perhaps if her aunt felt sorry enough for her, she would not persist in planning the marriage. "At least when I was there, I was somewhat able to curb Lady Madison's spending. She is determined to turn the house into a showplace, and there simply isn't the money to do it. I cannot understand why she was under the impression that we were wealthy."

"Perhaps Deron led her to believe so."

"He would do no such thing!" she protested loyally.

Lady Sheldon lifted her thin, well-bred nose. "Men who are out to make a conquest are often very irresponsible in what they say."

"But surely not Deron!"

The countess shrugged. "I had a slight acquaintance with Eve Madison in London. It was well known that she was looking for a man of title, wealth, and good looks."

"Deron is certainly handsome, and he has a title. Perhaps with those two qualities, he swept her off her feet."

"I doubt it," Lady Sheldon said dryly.

"Aunt, from the tone of your voice, I daresay you share my dislike of the lady."

"Lady? Ha! It is Deron's good fortune that a divorce, though scandalous and difficult to obtain, is not unheard of today. He will soon tire of her objectionable ways. Now tell me how she treated you."

"Very shabbily." Ashley shook her head. "We quarreled frequently. When I left, she predicted that I would become England's greatest ape leader."

"Fustian! She was jealous."

"That is what my abigail said."

"The girl was right. You are a very attractive young lady, Ashley. Once that woman hears of your betrothal, she'll eat her words."

Ashley sighed heavily, pushing back a lock of hastily arranged hair. "I was so very happy to be away from Oakwood Manor and starting a new life of my own," she murmured sadly, "and now it is all to be ruined."

"Ruined!" Her aunt laughed. "Don't be foolish. Your life is anything but shattered! You will see."

Ashley drew herself up, squaring her shoulders. "I must repeat, ma'am, that I have no intentions of wedding this man. It was so kind of you to take me in, and I knew you would wish for my eventual marriage. But not like this! Please try to understand."

"Child," Lady Sheldon confided, "my own marriage was arranged by my parents. I didn't know Raymond, yet we have been so very happy together."

"You were lucky."

"Perhaps, but there is more to life than love," she insisted. "There is position, security. There is comfort!"

"I wish to love the man I wed," Ashley said softly.

Her aunt chuckled. "Maybe you will do so. Shandal is charming and handsome. He seems to have no trouble making the ladies swoon. Aren't you the least bit interested in learning more about him?"

"Very well." Her curiosity was piqued. Why should a charming, handsome man allow his mother to choose his bride? Either he didn't care, as she had previously decided, or he was a mama's boy.

"His first name is Brandon. He is the Marquess of Shandal."

Ashley raised a dark eyebrow.

The countess caught the gesture. "Exactly so! You will be a marchioness! And what is more, your future husband is very wealthy, has a beautiful house in London, and several fine estates. His lineage is impeccable. He is a prime catch!"

"Then why has no one caught him? What is wrong with him, Aunt? What are his faults?"

"I have told you, Ashley, that he has escaped the traps laid for him." She looked vaguely uncomfortable.

"Are you hiding something?" she prodded. "No man can be so perfect."

"I'm sure he has some faults. Everyone does. Oh look, Ashley, here is Sheldon Hall."

Aware that her aunt had deliberately turned the subject, she gazed obediently out the carriage window as they swept through a set of ornate iron gates and trotted smartly through a large grassy park. The house, a magnificent brick of the eighteenth century, loomed ahead on a low, elegantly landscaped rise. What a fine home for her it would have been if only she hadn't been faced with this dilemma!

The carriage deposited them at the door. Immediately after they had removed their bonnets, Lady Sheldon escorted her to the library to meet her uncle. Looking more like a country squire than an earl, he rose to greet them jovially.

"I am delighted," he said, cheerfully kissing Ashley's cheek. "What a taking miss you are! With a little town bronze, you'll be a real Beauty!"

"She'll need a new wardrobe immediately," Lady Sheldon announced. "Finances have not been good at Oakwood Manor."

"I'll stand the toll. Wouldn't want her to go dowdy to Shandal."

Ashley stiffened.

"Something wrong, young lady? Hasn't your aunt told you of your good fortune?"

"I have." The countess went to the sideboard and poured them each a glass of sherry. "Sit down, Ashley." She handed her the drink and turned to her husband. "She doesn't wish to marry him."

Her uncle laughed. "A case of bridal nerves, no doubt. Any chit would give her right arm to marry Shandal!"

"I wouldn't," Ashley murmured.

He frowned. "This is an unexpected turn of events."

"Perhaps she will listen to you," Lady Sheldon muttered dismally.

"Hm." He returned to his seat behind the desk and thoughtfully sipped his sherry. "We've known the young man's family for years. Very fine people! I wouldn't have hesitated to have my very own daughter marry into them, Ashley."

"I know that you and Aunt wish only the best for me, Uncle, but . . ."

"Is it his reputation?" he asked kindly. "Don't worry yourself over his little . . . er . . . peccadillos. Shandal is a gentleman! He won't embarrass you."

"So that is what is wrong with him!" Ashley cried, unable to keep from looking accusingly at her aunt. "He is a rake!"

"No no, not that! I have never heard of him drinking or gambling to excess."

"That is true," Lord Sheldon agreed hastily. "His nickname probably doesn't even suit him."

"What is it?"

"Thank you, Raymond," his wife muttered irritably. "You would tell everything you know."

"If she is to wed him, she should know as much as possible about him," the earl grimly insisted.

"What is his nickname?" Ashley demanded.

Lord Sheldon took a deep breath. " 'Lord Scandal'," he admitted.

Ashley gaped. "But, Uncle, if he does not overindulge in gambling or drink, then . . ." She gasped. "Women! He is a . . . a . . ."

"Now that is only hearsay!" her aunt said briskly. "I am certain that his . . . ah . . . prowess . . . is highly exaggerated."

"Whatever it is, I know he will be discreet," her uncle soothed.

"You would marry me to a . . . a . . . womanizer." Ashley slumped back in her chair. In her wildest imagination, she would never have dreamed of anything like this. Good Heavens, what was she going to do about it? She caught the inside of her lower lip between her teeth and nibbled nervously. She must think of something! She could never wed a man known as *Lord Scandal,* no matter how handsome, wealthy, or exalted he might be! What would such a beast expect of *her?*

"Ashley," warned her aunt, "do cease twitching your mouth. It makes you look like a rabbit. Lord Shandal would not be impressed."

"Good! Then if I ever suffer the misfortune of being in his presence, I shall do it continuously!"

"Now, now, my dear ladies," her uncle interjected. "Let us think or speak no more of this matter. Things will look better tomorrow, after a good evening meal and a night's rest."

For you, maybe, Ashley thought. *For me, one night will only bring me that much closer to my doom.*

Shrugging, Lord Sheldon gave up trying to cheer her and largely ignored her, engaging his wife in mundane gossip of estate events.

Ashley's restlessness did not allow her to sleep late into the next morning. Her horrible dilemma had completely overset a good night's rest in the most comfortable bed she had ever lain in. Unused to calling Jane for anything but a minimum of personal service, she got up, washed with last night's tepid water, dressed herself and her hair without assistance, then left the room in search of breakfast. After the disasters of the previous day, which had quite taken her appetite, she was ravenous.

The breakfast room was empty, but a buffet had been set on the sideboard. Delicious odors arose from candle-warmed silver chafing dishes of bacon, ham, eggs, and assorted hot breads. Fresh fruits, butter, marmalade, and coffee completed the tempting ensemble. Delighted, she picked up a thin china plate and helped herself to a sample of all, remembering the scant meals at Oak-wood Manor.

She had just begun to eat when her aunt entered the room, looking about with pleasant surprise. "Good morning, Ashley. How delectable everything looks!"

"Good morning to you." Ashley watched curiously as the lady inspected all the offerings and sat down without choosing any of them.

"It all looks tempting, but I suppose I shall stick to my usual."

Almost at once a footman appeared, setting a cup of warm chocolate before Lady Sheldon.

"Do you wish chocolate too, Ashley?" her aunt asked kindly.

"No, ma'am. I like my tea."

Her aunt nodded the servant away. "Is your breakfast good, dear?"

"It's delicious."

"I'm so glad. Only Raymond comes down for breakfast, and he isn't a very good judge of food. If there is plenty, he is suited; it doesn't seem to matter how it tastes. I feared that Cook might have become a bit careless."

"Your cook is excellent, but, Aunt Sheldon, there is more than plenty here. Who eats all this food?"

"The servants?" She shrugged. "I confess I do not know. Perhaps the dogs or the pigs."

Ashley looked with awe at the large quantity of leftovers.

"Don't concern yourself with it, my dear," Lady Sheldon said gently. "I know that you were forced to practice the strictest economy at Oakwood Manor, and it was admirable that you contrived to do so, but you need never trouble yourself with it again. Shandal is a very wealthy man."

"I shall not," Ashley said with finality, "marry a man I don't know, especially one with such a reputation! It is outside of ridiculous."

"Who cares how he behaves? He is a marquess, and a handsome one at that, with plenty of money."

"I care! Uncle said he was a scoundrel!"

"Your uncle said nothing of the kind. He simply admitted that Shandal was a ladies man. You'll be a marchioness, you foolish girl!"

"With a husband around whom no woman is safe? No, ma'am! I shall not! I'll return to Oakwood Manor!"

"Oh? Will Lady Madison welcome you with open arms? I think not."

"She cannot turn me away," Ashley retorted angrily.

"Well, we shall never know if that is true, because I won't permit you to do it," Lady Sheldon said with just as much force. "Neither will your uncle, nor the marquess, permit it! I doubt very much that Lord Shandal would take kindly to his bride running away from him. He may be a rake, but he has a great deal of pride. Remember that!"

"I shan't marry him!" Tears sparkled in her green eyes. "I do appreciate the kindness you and Uncle have extended to me, and I am sorry to disappoint you, but I won't do it!"

"Don't you wish to marry at all?" Lady Sheldon cried, exasperated.

"I wish to marry someone I care for."

"Do you prefer to be a spinster in the servitude of Lady Madison and her yet-to-be-born brats?" she went on relentlessly.

"I like children. I would be a caring aunt."

"Wouldn't you rather have children of your own?" Ashley hesitated. "Yes, but . . ."

"Then don't throw it all away!" The countess leaned forward intently and took her niece's hand, squeezing it encouragingly. "You must use your head and not your feelings. There are many benefits to this match."

"Such as a husband who spends his evenings with his mistresses instead of his wife?" she asked cynically.

"Many men have mistresses. Shandal may frequent the bedrooms of others, but you will be his marchioness. It just might save you the bother of certain unpleasant marital duties. You would have only to preside over his drawing room and be the mother of his heir. And you will have his respect."

"But not his love," she sighed.

"We do not know that. Perhaps in time, you shall love each other very much. For now, if you will honestly consider the facts, I believe you will find that the good far outweighs the bad. I beg you to trust me. I know what I am talking about! At the very least, you could meet him before deciding."

Temples throbbing from the constant battering, Ashley set her elbows on the table, wearily leaning her head on her hands. "I don't know," she said softly.

"Ashley, please, it is only fair!"

"Very well," she yielded.

Lady Sheldon exhaled a pent up breath. "Mandy has been sent word of your arrival. Naturally Lord Shandal will be anxious to see you. By the time of his arrival, I know that you will have come to a favorable decision."

Ashley stood her ground. "I have promised to meet him, not to marry him."

"My word, gel, you are headstrong!"

"When it comes to my future, yes ma'am, I am very stubborn."

"But you will think about it?"

She unhappily nodded. "I will think about it."

Ashley excused herself and went out into the garden. Strolling along the brick paths edged with carefully trimmed hedges, she considered her situation. Without money, she was a virtual prisoner of her aunt and uncle. Only with their largess could she return to her home, and Lady Sheldon had made it plain that she opposed the idea.

Eve Madison would not help her. She would enjoy her sister-in-law's dilemma. She wouldn't spend a shilling or lift a slender finger to aid her.

Deron could not assist. Even if he were in England, he possibly would side with her aunt and uncle, or he might even ignore her plight altogether. Much as she loved him, she had to admit that her brother was irresponsible.

There was no one to turn to. Or was there? Perhaps the marquess himself would help! Surely he could have no desire to marry a lady who didn't wish to marry him. Together they could cry off.

She breathed a sigh of relief. The scheme might work. No one would be angry if they stopped proceedings by mutual agreement. She could go on living with her aunt and uncle, and when Aunt Rose introduced her into Society, maybe, just maybe, she would find a man that she could love.

Brandon alighted from his curricle, tossed the reins to his tiger, and entered the Pump Room at Bath. He crossed the floor, aware of all the eyes immediately turning to him. Nodding to acquaintances, he glanced over the company until he found the object of his pursuit. He bent over her shoulder and kissed her on the cheek. "Hello, Mama."

She startled. "Oh my goodness, Brandon, you frightened me!"

"Unaccustomed to having gentlemen sneak up to steal a kiss?" he drawled.

"Certainly!" She lightly tapped his wrist with her fan. "For shame!"

He dragged a chair up beside her and sat down. "You appear to be in fine fettle, Mama. Surely not from drinking the waters." He glanced pointedly at her scarcely touched glass.

"Oh, but I do drink it! It improves my health. You should try it, dear."

"No thank you. My health is already excellent. Besides I find brandy to be more bracing. You would too if you weren't such a hypocrite."

"Brandy is a man's drink," the Marchioness of Shandal proclaimed.

"All right, I shan't tease you." He smiled fondly at her.

"I shall never see *that* day!"

"Probably not," he said dryly, "but tell me, Mama, what is going on? Your summons was quite emphatic."

"Summons?" she cried. "Oh dear boy! You make it sound like a royal decree. I would never so summarily . . ."

"Mama?" he prompted.

"Brandon," she whispered, leaning towards him, "I do think we should conduct this discussion elsewhere. It is a rather private matter."

"Very well. Shall we go then to your house? I am terribly curious."

"If you are ready to leave," she agreed.

"Mama, I was ready to leave when I came. I am not a great advocate of Bath." He stood and offered her his hand.

Lady Shandal rose and tucked her arm companionably through his. "My, but you are creating such a stir here! Look at all the young ladies, their hearts afluttering! Any one of them would wish to take my place in your attentions. I am much flattered."

"My lady, surely you know that none could supplant you in my attentions *or* affections," he vowed.

She mischievously cut her eyes at him. "Sir! Do you trifle with me?"

He laughed. His mama was perfectly outrageous. He had never seen any mother attempt to carry on flirtation with her son. And to succeed! Miranda Shandal was an original when it came to that. She enjoyed it, and so did he. In fact, she had taught him a great deal about pleasing the opposite sex. She was an absolute darling.

Escorting her grandly from the building, he raised a hand to his servant. John quickly brought the curricle forward and leaped down, bowing respectfully to the dowager.

"Your curricle?" she asked incredulously. "I could not!"

"Of course you can, Mama. Why not?"

"I'm too old," she whispered into his ear. "Really, Brandon!"

"Nonsense! You are not. Shall you step in gracefully, or shall I toss you in like a load of baggage?"

Lady Shandal lifted her chin. "I shall step in. Under protest!" She barely hid the laughter in her voice. "You are beyond all belief!"

"I know." He assisted her into the vehicle and hopped in beside her, taking up the reins. "Hold on, Mama. Here we go!"

He started the horses but, instead of springing them, moved them forward at a decorous pace. Lady Shandal, preparing for the worst, had gripped his arm and held onto her hat. "Are you frightened, Mama?"

"Hm!" She cast a sardonic look at her handsome son. "You are bamming me."

"That is not my intention! Do you wish more speed?"

"No! I am quite satisfied."

Brandon neatly threaded his way through the busy streets of the city until he reached her townhouse. "There! I have delivered you in one piece."

"But of course," she sniffed. "I never doubted it."

Together they entered the house. Lady Shandal removed her bonnet and gloves, ordered refreshments, and drew him into her salon with a word to the butler that she would not, under any circumstances, receive callers while she was closeted with her son. Wondering at her exclusiveness, Brandon went to the sideboard and poured himself a glass of brandy.

"Mama, you are being mysterious."

"I've found her, Brandon," she announced with excitement, plopping down on the edge of the sofa.

He lifted an eyebrow. "Found whom?"

"Your bride, of course!"

He stared at her. "What?"

"You know the conversation that we had? Concerning the fact that it is time you set up your nursery?"

Rotating the glass in his hand, he walked across the room and sat down beside her, letting the words sink in. "Yes, I remember, but I didn't expect it to be so soon."

She anxiously turned toward him. "You did ask my assistance."

"Yes, in a way, but . . ."

"You asked me to arrange it," she insisted.

His mind quickly reverted to that day two months ago when she had confronted him with his bachelorhood. Astutely, she had pointed out that he wasn't getting any younger, and that he was responsible for getting heirs to continue the line. It wasn't right for him to depend upon his younger brother.

Brandon had admitted that she was right. Much as he loved Jamie, he had enough pride to wish to have a son of his own to inherit the title and the vast Shandal fortune. He was thirty years old. It was time that he married.

He'd asked her assistance for he trusted his mother implicitly. She was shrewd, and she was a fine judge of character. She would be able to sift through the number of candidates and knowledgeably choose him a suitable wife.

He didn't really care who it was. A wife was a tiresome necessity. Wives didn't have the magical thrill possessed by ladies of certain persuasions. His marchioness would be his hostess and the mother of his children. Her behavior would be perfect, and he would respect her. Perhaps he would become fond of her. Little else mattered. It was a thing he must do.

So now his mama had found her. It was quicker than

he had expected, but perhaps that was just as well. He could marry her and get on with his life.

"Who is she?" he asked. "Do I know her?"

"I doubt it. Due to her parents' deaths, she was not introduced into Society. Her name is Ashley Madison, and she is the niece of Lord and Lady Sheldon."

"Lady Sheldon, your best friend?" He grinned knowingly. "Are you not being prejudiced, Mama?"

"Certainly not!" she bristled. "I trust Rose. If she recommends the gel, I must believe her."

"What does this young lady look like?"

"She is pretty, of course," Lady Shandal said vaguely. He narrowed his eyes. "Have you seen her?"

"Well . . . no . . . but if Rose says she is pretty, I'm sure she is. Brandon, my friend would not lie to me! And she assures me that the gel is perfect in every other way too."

He thoughtfully sipped the brandy. "Tell me more."

"Although she is unknown to Society, I'm sure her manner is impeccable. I remember her mama, a very beautiful and graceful lady. And without having been influenced by the *ton*, you can mold her however you please. Her lineage is entirely suitable. You know the Sheldons. No one can find fault with them."

"High sticklers, if I recall," he mused.

"No more than any well-bred family. You see, Brandon? She is perfect." Lady Shandal sat back cheerfully, pleased with herself.

"I wish you had seen her yourself," he murmured doubtfully.

"But I do trust Rose! She would not, under any circumstances, attempt to push an antidote off on us."

Brandon shrugged. "No, I suppose not. Did you make an offer?"

"Yes, I did. Of course they accepted."

So it was done. His future was joined with that of

Miss Ashley Madison. He hoped that she would be content to accept his way of life. She might be his marchioness, but she would not change his delight in pursuing excitement, particularly that which was offered by experienced, willing females.

"She is now in residence at Sheldon Hall," his mother continued. "I know that you will wish to meet her as soon as possible, and that she will be anxious to meet you."

A servant entered with a tray of refreshments and set it down before her mistress. Lady Shandal offered her son a cup of tea, which he refused, pouring himself another brandy.

"Brandon, I am glad that you have decided to take this step, but you should consider other aspects of your life as well."

"Why? I'm rather pleased with it."

Lady Shandal sighed. "You know what I mean. Alicia Milton should be tossed out with all the rest of the rubbish."

He grinned lopsidedly, helping himself to a small sandwich. "You shouldn't know about her."

"But I do, and so does everyone else. Start your marriage with a clean slate. I do believe that woman actually considers herself eligible to become your wife! It is unimaginable!"

"Just so, Mama." He winked mischievously. "But she is very entertaining."

Lady Shandal lifted her nose expressively. "I should not grace that statement with a reply, but I am your mama so I will take the privilege to give advice. Let little Ashley entertain you from now on."

He laughed. "I doubt that that will happen. I imagine that you have chosen me a most suitable marchioness, but a lady who will entertain me? I hardly think so!"

"You must give her a chance."

"Oh I'll give her that, Mama, but don't expect to see me living in her pocket. I intend to go on much as I have before."

"Brandon, no," she begged. "There is a great deal of adjustment to be made when two people wed. Don't complicate matters. You should devote your complete attention to your bride, or the damage could be irretrievable."

"I disagree," he said coolly. "At our first meeting, I intend to tell Miss Madison exactly how things will be. There will be no surprises."

"You will hurt her!"

He shook his head. "In a marriage of convenience? I think not. She knows, just as I do, that this is not a love match."

"She may decide that she doesn't wish to marry you," the dowager warned.

He laughed. "But how could she? It's all settled. She wouldn't dare refuse!"

Three

Ashley, seated in the pillowed window seat of her bedroom, witnessed the arrival of the Marquess of Shandal to Sheldon Hall. The distance was too great for her to make out his features, but she could tell by the easy grace with which he drove his horses that he must be an excellent horseman. A man like that would probably have a fine stable of blooded horses. If she married him, perhaps there would be one for her.

Horses had been her passion for as long as she could remember, but she had never had a good one of her own. By the time she had graduated from ponies, there had been no money to buy a well-bred horse for the daughter of the house. Deron had always had one though, and when he was in a particularly good mood, he had let her ride his. It had been like riding on a cloud compared to the stiff-backed, thick-legged cob that served as her mount.

A smile touched her lips. As she had been told, there were advantages to being the Marchioness of Shandal. How surprised her aunt would be if she told her that she would marry the marquess for his horses!

Her humor swiftly faded. Marry him? How could she even address it in jest? Her aunt's daily harangues must be muddling her mind.

Standing, she went to the mirror and studied her

appearance. "He's here," she murmured. "Do I look well enough, Jane?"

"You look very pretty, miss. You always do."

Ashley frowned. "The dress seems tight. Has it shrunk?"

The maid chuckled. "You're filling it out. Your figure is becoming more womanly."

"I do not seem overweight?" she asked anxiously.

"No, miss, you're still slender. Your curves are in the right places, that's all. They're *curves*, not fat!"

Ashley looked at the softly rounded tops of her breasts and shook her head. "We shall tuck some lace, Jane. This dress exposes too much of me."

"Very well, Miss Ashley," the abigail murmured, her mouth slightly tugging downward at the corners.

As they were finishing the task, Lady Sheldon entered the room and paused to survey her charge. "Lord Shandal has arrived and is in the library with your uncle."

Biting the inside of her lip, Ashley took a final glance at herself. Her hair was shiny and neatly done up. Her lips were a maidenly pink, but her cheeks were too pale, making her eyes look enormous and very dark. The sprigged muslin dress with its green riband trim was country-cut. All in all, she looked like a prim vicar's daughter, pretty perhaps, but not at all the type to catch the eye of a man of the town. Well, wasn't that what she wanted? She certainly didn't want to attract him! In fact, she hoped to do just the opposite. Her appearance was simply a matter of pride.

With a sigh, Lady Sheldon shook her head and clicked her tongue. "Get rid of that lace," she ordered, "and fetch me some rouge."

"Aunt, I shall be bare without the lace!" Ashley cried.

"Yes," Lady Sheldon agreed. "Get rid of it."

"What will he think of me!"

"Believe me, Shandal will think much more of you

without the lace." She herself applied the lightest touch of rouge to her niece's cheeks.

"This is scandalous! I have never used color on my cheeks," she gasped with horror.

"Then it is time you did. You are too pale, Ashley. You look like a starving child." She stepped back. "There! See what an improvement I have caused?"

Ashley would never have believed what a difference a bit of paint could make. It brought sparkle to her eyes and set off her delicate nose. "You were right about the rouge, Aunt, but the dress!" Ineffectively, she tried to tug the bodice higher.

Her aunt ignored her. "Come along. We have done as much as we can. Let us not keep the marquess waiting."

"Aunt . . ."

"Prepare yourself to fall in love!" Lady Sheldon interrupted cheerfully. "Lord Shandal is even more handsome than I remembered him to be."

"I shall dislike him intensely! He is the root of all my trouble, and I will not marry him!" she declared.

"Don't start up again, Ashley," Lady Sheldon warned. "You will marry him, and you will be happy to do so." Taking her hand, she fairly pulled her from the bedchamber, down the stairs, and into the drawing room. "Compose yourself. You look like a convict on the road to the gallows."

"That is exactly how I feel."

"Then feel it, but don't look it. I am running out of all patience with you! I've a great notion to box your ears."

Ashley choked.

"Ungrateful child!" the countess lectured. "I was not close to my sister, your mother, but I am certain that she would deplore your behavior. Do you not realize that the Sheldon honor is at stake? Yes, and the honor of your parents as well!"

Further words were silenced as the door opened. Ashley caught a glimpse of her uncle and a rather tall gentleman before she quickly lowered her eyes. In a daze, she acknowledged the introductions and made her curtsy.

"Well then," her uncle said jovially, "now that formalities have been observed, we shall leave the two of you for a short while to become acquainted. Under the circumstances, I believe that such privacy is acceptable."

"Yes," seconded Lady Sheldon. She leaned close to her niece's ear. "How proud your parents would be," she whispered in reminder. "How pleased they would be to know that your future is secure." Almost painfully squeezing Ashley's hand, she made her departure.

Numbly, Ashley stood in the center of the floor where her aunt had left her, her eyes fixed unseeingly on her toes. No one really cared for her. Her aunt and uncle were only concerned with ridding themselves of her, not of the way she felt. They didn't mind throwing her to a vulgar wolf who chased women. Her parents couldn't possibly be pleased, could they?

The marquess broke the silence. "I am not generally considered bad to look at, so is it altogether necessary that you stare at the floor?"

Biting her lip, she lifted her head, loath to face the instigator of her horrible dilemma, but try as she might, she couldn't help gaping, stunned by his imposing appearance.

The Marquess of Shandal was dressed in a neatly tailored coat of bottle-green. His pantaloons were cream-colored and fitted as tight as a second skin, descending down long legs into boots so shiny that she could have seen her face in them. At his throat was a snowy cravat, enhanced by an emerald stickpin.

His face alone was enough to melt the heart of any woman and excite the envy of any man. His uplifted chin and well-chiseled nose proclaimed his aristocratic lineage, but his sensual mouth hinted at another role in life. His hair, as gold as a newly minted coin, begged to be touched, but his deep blue eyes were aloof.

Golden hair? Blue eyes? Ashley stifled a wail. It was him! It was the man who had seen her in the bathtub at the inn! Merciful Heavens, what if he recognized her?

"Miss Madison?" he drawled, interrupting her wild recollection. "Have you finished your perusal of me?"

She blushed furiously. "Forgive me, my lord," she stammered. "I was extremely rude."

A cynical smile played at the corners of his mouth. "In our situation, I believe your curiosity to be entirely natural. Any lady would wish to study the appearance of her bridegroom. Then too, I do have the advantage. As I recall, I have seen a great deal more of you than you have of me."

He knew! Ashley whirled her back to him, pressing her hands against her burning face. "How could you say that?" she cried. "You must be aware of how mortified I am!"

"*Lady Bathtub.*" He laughed. "I do beg your forgiveness for my outspoken, fond remembrance. Shall I promise not to tease you? No. Teasing ladies is one of my most enjoyable pastimes." He lightly laid his hands on her shoulders and turned her around. "If you are to be my wife, you will grow accustomed to it."

His touch sent delicious tremors rushing through her body. Naive as she was to such disturbing feelings, Ashley knew instinctively that if she looked up at his breathtaking face, she would be in danger of falling right into his arms. Instead, she stared blindly at his pristine cravat.

The marquess looked down on her shining blue-black hair. "Do you like my pin?"

"It is very pretty, my lord."

"I'm glad you like it, but if we are to talk, I would prefer you to look at me." He slid his fingers under her chin and lifted it. Her wide, fearful eyes met his dancing ones. Her parted pink lips trembled. "Has anyone ever kissed you?"

"My parents . . ."

"I was referring to an unrelated male."

"Oh, no, my lord," she whispered, her eyes continuing to be hopelessly locked with his.

"Shall I?" he wondered out loud. "You are asking me to."

The hypnotic spell broke. Ashley drew back her arm and swung her hand towards his cheek, but the marquess parried by catching her wrist.

"You despicable man!" she spat.

"My, my." He grinned. "Not a moment before, you would have received my kisses."

"Sir, you are quite mistaken!"

"I think not," he said swiftly. "Perhaps, Miss Madison, you are too naive to realize it."

"You beast!" She tried unsuccessfully to pull free of his grasp.

"Surely not that," he protested mockingly. "Really, Madam, this is a terrible way to start a life of wedded bliss."

Ashley trembled uncontrollably. Painfully wrenching her wrist from his hand, she fled across the room to the window. "Sir, I do not wish to marry you."

The distance between them gave her strength. She gazed out into Lady Sheldon's lovely rose garden and tried to calm herself. "Lord Shandal," she began, trying to make her voice as matter-of-fact as possible, "this is all quite ridiculous. I do not wish to marry you, and I doubt that you wish to marry me. It is not necessary to carry out this farce."

"Whom would you wish to marry?" he asked, coming up behind her. "Is there someone else?"

"No, but that is of no concern of yours. I wish to marry someone I love."

He chuckled. "You certainly are an innocent little girl."

"I am not a child!" Ashley snapped. "I am twenty-one years old!"

"Well, at that great age, you should be able to view our situation more realistically," he proclaimed, humor glittering in his eyes.

"That, I am trying to do!" she countered. "We wouldn't suit. It would be better never to marry, than to engage myself in misery for the rest of my life."

"Do you truly believe it would be that?" His voice was silky, seductive.

It hinted at matters of which she had no experience, and because of that, it infuriated her all the more. Her temper raged. "I am convinced of it! Any man, with so few scruples as to spy on a lady in her bath, would make a most disagreeable husband!"

He grinned. "You did ask me for a towel."

"You *knew* I thought you were my maid!"

"Yes," he admitted, "but really, Miss Madison, no red-blooded male could refuse such a delectable request."

"I do not wish to hear your excuses! I will not marry you, and that is final! With that in mind, surely you cannot want to marry me, so the matter is closed," she stated with an emphatic nod.

"But I do wish to marry you. I have a great admiration for you." He lay his hand on her shoulder. "Come now, catch hold of your temper so that we may rationally discuss this."

"I am in control of myself!"

"Are you?"

His finger massaged the little, ticklish place where her neck joined her shoulder. Ashley's heart tripled its beat. Her breath grew short. Ripples of strange emotions coursed through her body. Her conscious mind told her to make him stop, but she was powerless to do so. He had placed her under his spell.

"Am I so undesirable?" He paused his persuasive gesture. "Tell me, Miss Madison, do you not find me attractive?"

"You know you are well beyond that," she answered breathlessly.

"Yes I do, but do *you* find me so?"

"Of course," she murmured. He was now standing so close to her that his breath was ruffling her hair. Weakness swept over her. Faintly, she sank down onto the window seat and escaped his hand. Her equilibrium slowly returned.

"Do you like children?" he asked abruptly.

"I adore them," she said, glancing up with surprise.

"What else do you like?"

"I like to ride." She blushed, remembering her foolish fantasy of marrying him for his horses. "I like to read. Really, my lord, what are you about?"

"Miss Madison, you cannot imagine how distressed I was at the idea of marriage. Not just to you, but to anyone! However, I must marry sometime, so I considered the possibilities and asked my mother's assistance in choosing a proper lady. Although I did not doubt her judgment, you have answered several questions for me."

She shook her head. "I cannot think of it so coldly."

The marquess studied her with an expression of supreme patience. "Consider, Miss Madison, just consider. You do not find me unattractive, so you couldn't mind having my children, whom you would adore in any case. As to the rest, I have excellent horses and a

large library. You haven't mentioned else, but I also
have a house in London, several fine estates, and
enough money to buy you pretty things and to make
you comfortable for the rest of your life. I can give you
a great deal, as you can see."

Ashley bent her head, focusing on her slender hands
clasped together in her lap. The temptation was great.
If she married him, she could escape poverty, Aunt Sheldon, and Lady Madison. Another man might not come
her way. But could she bear to be wed to a man like
Lord Shandal?

"I don't know," she said softly.

Frowning, the marquess propped his leg on the window seat and, leaning on his knee, gazed thoughtfully
out the window. Ashley wondered what Lady Sheldon
would think of his boot resting on her powder blue
upholstery and decided that her aunt would think the
marquess too grand to worry about a smudge.

"Why do you allow your mother to choose your
wife?" she asked curiously.

He laughed. "I trust her judgment better than mine
when it comes to *proper* ladies."

"But if you did choose for yourself, what would you
look for in a wife?"

"She would be attractive and mannerly, come from
a good family, be young enough to bear my children,
and her reputation would be beyond reproach. There
would have been no other man in her life, nor would
there ever be," he said without hesitation.

"I am surprised."

"At what?"

Ashley made a small shrug. "I would have thought
that you would want your wife to be dashing and exciting and beautiful beyond belief."

"I was describing my marchioness, not my mistress,"
he said sardonically.

She flushed deeply. She had requested blunt truth, and she had gotten precisely that.

"Suffice it to say, Miss Madison, that I believe you possess the necessary attributes to be my wife."

She could see her face in his highly polished boot that rested so casually on the window seat. His casual disregard for the furnishings bothered her. More than that, his trim leg so close to her face was decidedly unsettling.

"Lord Shandal?" she queried cautiously.

"Yes?"

"Would you please remove your foot from the upholstery? It worries me."

He gave a shout of laughter. "You already sound like a wife." Obeying her request, he reached out his hand. "Let us sit on the sofa."

She allowed herself to be drawn along with him. He sat down beside her, keeping her hand in his.

"Ashley, I think we should do quite well together. You will give me what I have mentioned, and I can give you a great deal in return."

"But not your love!" she blurted, feeling the trap close around her.

"No, not my undivided love, but if all goes well, we shall probably become quite fond of each other." His voice grew hard. "I like women, lots of them, and I don't intend to give them up, not for you or anyone else. That is something you must understand."

She looked up at him and once more was lost in his devastating handsomeness. How could one man arouse in her such a myriad of tangled emotions? "You will give me your kindness?" she heard herself say.

"I shall endeavor to do so."

She took a deep breath. Her aunt was right. It was folly to refuse such a splendid offer. "Very well then."

"I beg your pardon?"

"I shall try to be a good wife to you," she announced quickly before she could change her mind.

"You are sure?" he asked incredulously.

"I cannot fight everyone and everything."

The marquess raised an eyebrow. "That is a strange thing to say."

She sighed. "Perhaps someday I shall explain it."

"Then we are betrothed." He removed an ornate ring from his pocket and placed it on her finger. His lips touched hers in a brief, chaste kiss.

Ashley felt again the strange emotions tingling, once more, through her body. Unless she could make him love her, he would break her heart. She was certain of it. But she couldn't turn him down. Could any woman? And there, indeed, lay the problem.

The days following Ashley's meeting with Lord Shandal passed by in a relentless flurry. Unable to procure a London modiste, Lady Sheldon hired a local dressmaker, who with her assistants moved into the Hall to hasten the fashioning of a wedding gown and trousseau. They worked long hours and required frequent fittings so that Ashley, wishing she could take a long mind-clearing ride on one of her uncle's fine horses, was forced to remain nearby at their beck and call.

Still, it was exciting to be getting new clothes. Despite her lack of enthusiasm for the wedding gown, she was pleased with the other dresses and felt that she would look quite stylish in them.

Her aunt, however, dismissed them as being only passable. "You must go as soon as possible to Francine in London and order a complete new wardrobe. You will find that her taste in fashion and the quality of her design are unexcelled."

"Wouldn't it create a great deal of expense for the

marquess?" Ashley asked doubtfully. "I do not wish to be a financial burden for him."

"Shandal is wealthy. Enjoy yourself, and spend his money! He'll never miss it."

Ashley shook her head. "I shall dress well, but I shan't be extravagant. He said that I would live comfortably. In my opinion, that statement does not give me *carte blanche* to his purse. In fact, I intend to economize. I cannot abide waste."

"Poor Shandal!" Lady Sheldon laughed. "He has never economized in his life! His world will be turned upside down."

"No, it won't! I shall take great care that he is not discommoded at all, and he will have no cause to complain about my spending. To the contrary, he will be impressed."

"We shall see. The lackluster marchioness! Hm . . ."

"Don't tease me, Aunt." Ashley was unable to refrain from smiling. "You know I shall always contrive to be presentable."

"I should hope so, but seriously, child, you must do much better than that if you wish to capture his attention."

"I am not altogether sure that I want it," she avowed, but she knew that her aunt was right. Deep inside, she did want the handsome marquess to be attracted to her, but she remembered what he had said. He liked lots of women, so it would probably be impossible for only one to have his love. Perhaps he would grow quite fond of her, but she knew that her face alone wasn't enough to turn his head. She would have to dress stylishly too.

"Did you say that Francine was the best modiste, Aunt?"

"I did. Shall I write down her address for you?"

"If you please, and there is one other matter upon which you must advise me."

"Of course, my dear."

"It's Lady Madison," she said worriedly. "I don't want her at my wedding. But if I invite her, I know that she will come."

"Yes, that one wouldn't miss the opportunity to social-climb."

Ashley sighed. "It would be a direct cut to ignore her, wouldn't it? And I don't wish to make Deron unhappy."

"Her attendance cannot be avoided." Lady Sheldon shuddered. "It would be most improper to exclude her."

"I suppose so. But what will Lord Shandal and his family think of her? I don't wish them to think that I am like my sister-in-law."

"They will not. Believe me, Miranda Shandal already knows all about your family, including Lady Madison, but she would be the first to admit that most families have some member of whom they are embarrassed. Mandy and I were girls together. She is a dear friend. I know she would never judge you by that woman's behavior, and neither will her son."

With the invitations sent and the wedding approaching, Ashley's nerves grew raw. She wished she could back out of the whole thing. Thinking of the marquess's imposing appearance and his reputation, she had to admit that she was afraid of him. That she would soon be solely under his control was almost more than her wits could bear.

But there was an uncanny fascination that made her long for his presence. She couldn't forget the effect he'd had on her, and she wondered if she would feel that strange and confusing excitement when she saw him again. It was not surprising that women pursued Lord Shandal, if he ignited that same emotion in all of them.

A week before the wedding, the guests began to arrive. The first to come were the Sheldon daughters and their husbands. It was Lizzie, the closest to Ashley's age, who brought up the subject of the intimacies of marriage.

"Mama thought someone should mention to you the . . . uh . . . let us say, a wife's duties to her husband."

Ashley laughed. "So you were chosen."

Her cousin giggled. "I'm known as the outspoken member of the family, but now I confess that I don't know what to say!"

"I trust you are not referring to being a hostess to his guests?"

"No." Lizzie's cheeks grew pink. "Don't tease me, Ashley. It isn't easy to discuss such things."

"Then say no more. Remember? I managed my brother's estate. I am aware of what is expected of me."

"You are so confident," her cousin said admiringly.

"Not at all! Shandal frightens me out of my wits," she admitted. "Perhaps I simply hide it well."

"He would frighten me." Lizzie stood and walked to Ashley's bedroom window. "The side of marriage Mama wished me to speak to you about is not very pleasant, cousin. Still . . ." She brightened. "No one ever died from it! And Shandal does have his mistress. Perhaps he won't bother you overmuch."

"Tell me what you know of his mistress," Ashley asked curiously.

Her cousin's cheeks grew brighter still. "I should never have mentioned her. Mama would *murder* me!"

"Please, Lizzie."

"Well, after all, it is scarcely a secret. Her name is Alicia Milton. She is a widow."

"A beautiful widow?"

She nodded uneasily. "Ashley, I should never have told you. If Mama knew . . ."

"I shall never tell." She felt a strange urge to cry. She knew that her future husband had a mistress, but learning her name made it so very real.

"Many men have mistresses," Lizzie soothed. "Do not give it a second thought. Instead, congratulate yourself for landing such a prize catch."

"That remains to be seen," she said cynically.

"Perhaps he shall make a good enough husband. He's a marquess; he's wealthy; and he is so very handsome."

"Yes, he is that." Ashley sighed.

Her cousin looked at her sharply. "You aren't in love with him, are you?"

"Certainly not!" she flatly denied.

Lizzie smiled sympathetically. "Maybe he'll fall in love with you."

"Yes, and maybe the sky will fall. If it weren't for family pressures, he wouldn't look at me twice."

Her cousin shrugged. "Maybe so, maybe not. You're quite pretty, you know."

"Let's not talk of it further," Ashley said uncomfortably. "I want to put it all out of my mind for as long as I can."

That, of course, was impossible with the house plunged into the last-minute turmoil of wedding preparations.

Four

Two days before the wedding, the marquess arrived, accompanied by his mother and his brother, James. Even at her advanced age, the marchioness was a lovely woman, making it easy to believe that she had been a Beauty in her youth. She was kind to her future daughter-in-law, and in return, Ashley liked her and felt that she would have a friend in her husband's mother.

James, called Jamie by the family, was delightful. A younger image of the marquess, he had a much more artless personality than his brother. His humorous stories and outrageous flattery soon had Ashley dissolved in laughter and even drew a fleeting grin, now and then, from the unusually somber bridegroom.

Lord Shandal was moody and subdued. He held himself detached from the others, making only short, polite replies, and looking as if he didn't know what was happening to him. It secretly amused Ashley to see him so nonplused. She wondered if he had ever, in all his life, behaved as such a dullard.

Lady Madison arrived the day before the event. After greeting her host and hostess, she freshened herself in the room assigned to her and immediately went in search of her sister-in-law.

Ashley was in the garden with her future husband. Sitting on a stone bench, a novel in her lap, she was relating to him an amusing passage from *Pride and Preju-*

dice by Miss Jane Austen. The marquess was smiling, but Ashley wondered if it was more from politeness than genuine interest.

"There you are!" Eve glided into view with outstretched arms. "I've searched and searched! Really, Ashley, couldn't you have contrived to be nearby to welcome me?"

"I am sorry. No one told me of your arrival." She submitted to the lady's cold embrace and dutifully kissed her cheek, turning to the marquess. "My lord, this is—"

"Lord Shandal and I are well acquainted." Eve extended her hand. "How good to see you again, my lord, and on such a felicitous occasion."

He bowed over her hand, but he didn't actually touch his lips to it. "You are looking well, Lady Madison."

"Indeed I am in fine fettle, though I wonder why I am not close to exhaustion. I'm overseeing the remodeling of my new home, an absolute barn of a place. Such a wearying pastime!"

Ashley stiffened. Remodeling? How could she! There was no money for such a thing.

She resisted the impulse to question Eve. What his wife did and what she spent was Deron's business. His marriage had ended her responsibility.

"I'm sure you ladies have much to discuss, so I shall leave you to it." The marquess kissed his fiancee's fingertips and strode down the walk as if he were glad to escape.

"Well," said Eve, sinking onto the bench and looking after him. "You certainly have done well for yourself. I didn't realize that the Sheldons had so much influence. The Shandal family is very *haute ton*. I suppose your aunt and uncle must have supplied you with a very large dowry to attract their attention."

"I don't know if there was any dowry at all," Ashley replied honestly.

Her sister-in-law shook her head. "Impossible. Your looks alone would not tempt such as he, and your manner . . . You are such a little country mouse! Ashley, we at least must do something about your appearance or you will never hold his regard. Shandal has a veritable stable of mistresses. His current favorite, Alicia Milton, is particularly exquisite so you will face tremendous competition. As a beginning, you must allow my maid to bob your hair."

"I like my hair as it is," Ashley declared. If she had defeated her formidable aunt in the same endeavor, she would certainly not bow to Eve.

Her sister-in-law groaned. "But it is so unfashionable!"

"I don't care." She set her jaw.

"Why must you be so stubborn? Don't you realize that you are in the position to gain all sorts of favors if you please the marquess? Diamonds . . . emeralds . . ."

"That sort of thing doesn't matter to me." She proudly lifted her chin. "I didn't wish to marry him in the first place."

"Didn't wish to marry him!" Eve gasped. "Have you taken leave of your senses? Think of what a man like Shandal can do for you! For *all* of us!"

"All?" Ashley asked suspiciously. "What do you mean, *all*? I fail to see how this effects you and Deron."

Eve's face stiffened, rendering her void of expression. "Why, it will lend great consequence to the family," she murmured offhandedly.

"Perhaps." She stood. "But now I really must go back inside. I have a great deal to do."

"Of course," her sister-in-law said cheerfully, "and I shall help you!"

She truly did assist, to a small extent, but by evening

Ashley and the entire party were totally weary of Lady Madison. She monopolized every conversation, managing neatly to turn any subject to herself. She exaggerated her own importance, and that of her husband, and described Oakwood Manor in terms more suited to a princely palace than to a sadly impoverished estate. She openly flirted with the marquess and his brother.

After supper, when the gentlemen had finished their port and joined the ladies in the salon, she began to talk of how dearly she cared for Ashley and how greatly she missed her delightful little sister.

Lady Shandal, who had been trying all day to converse with her future daughter-in-law, turned on her. "Is that so?" she asked coldly, raising a perfectly formed eyebrow. "Then I am quite surprised that you left her to the care of her aunt. It appeared to me that the two of you were not close at all."

Lady Madison's pretty pink lips were left agape. Her eyes darted first to Ashley, then to Lady Sheldon, and back to Lady Shandal. "I believed that Ashley would be better guided by a lady of greater age and experience."

"Wise," Lady Shandal nodded, "and of course, Lady Sheldon does have the respect of the *ton* and *entrée* to all the finest gatherings."

Eve Madison set her jaw at this hint of disparagement to her character. "That was of no concern. I myself have enjoyed London society for a number of years."

"Have you indeed? I must apologize! I hadn't noticed you, my dear." Lady Shandal smiled, her voice sparkling with artificial kindness.

"I was acquainted with your son, madam," Eve archly declared.

Her attention diverted to the battle of wits, Ashley glanced sidelong at her sister-in-law and unhappily wondered if Eve had been one of Shandal's paramours. It was entirely possible. She was a very attractive woman.

"I have two sons," the marchioness said, her nose rising slightly higher.

"I am referring to the marquess," Lady Madison told her smugly. "Would it not have been surprising if I, and not Ashley, had been his bride?"

The marquess choked on his tea, and his mama burst into laughter. "Oh, I hardly think that would have happened! You are not his type. Perhaps it was only a dalliance." She turned her attention to her son, who was engaged in a fit of coughing. "Brandon, are you quite all right?"

Eve stood, her face flushed with unbecoming anger. "I respect your distinction, Lady Shandal, but even though you are a marchioness, you have no right to accuse me of unseemly conduct. I shall not listen to any more. I shall retire to my chamber!" Encompassing Ashley with her look of disgust, she swept from the room.

Lady Sheldon collapsed into laughter. "Mandy, you were marvelous! I confess that I did wonder how long it would continue."

The marchioness chuckled. "It did take above average to send her on her way."

"You gave her quite a setdown, Mama," Jamie grinned.

"Indeed I did! I have been wishing all day to talk with my soon-to-be daughter-in-law!" Lady Shandal squeezed Ashley's hand. "Now we shall have a comfy chat and I dare anyone, even you, Brandon, to interrupt us!"

The wedding day dawned foggy, but before the assembly had reached the church, the sun blazed forth. The ceremony went as well as could be expected, given the circumstances. Ashley, pale, though delicately pretty in her pearl-seeded white gown, glided on the arm of her uncle down the aisle to meet her bridegroom. Her voice, as she promised to love, honor, and obey him, had been soft but steady, and though her hand had trembled when he slipped the ring in place, only he could have noticed.

The marquess himself was the nervous one of the pair. After a quick, cursory glance at her as she approached him, he engaged for the rest of the procession in looking beyond her to the door. He mumbled his responses and at one point, forgot her name, necessitating a prompt from the vicar. At the close of the services, he escorted her so speedily out of the church, that he nearly pulled her off her feet.

His restlessness continued throughout the wedding breakfast. He exchanged few words with the guests, and immediately following the meal, he called preemptively for his carriage.

Taking her place beside her lord, the new Marchioness of Shandal, eyes downcast, sat quietly as the handsome conveyance rolled smartly down the drive from Sheldon Hall. It had been a long day and was far from over, but she was limp with exhaustion. The marquess must have experienced a similar lethargy for he leaned deeply into the plush upholstery and put his feet on the opposite seat. Ashley waited to see if he intended to take a nap, but when his cool, blue eyes remained open, she advanced a question.

"My lord, I am curious to know where we are going."

"Now that we are married, Ashley, it would be perfectly proper to address me by my given name. In fact, it would have been permissible to do so before now."

"I shall try . . . Brandon." She smiled. "It is all so very new."

He vigorously nodded agreement. "To answer your question, we are going to London. It will be late when we arrive, but the servants are expecting us."

"I see."

"You are displeased?" he asked shortly.

Hastily, she shook her head. "No, I am merely surprised. I thought most people spent this season in the country, or at one of the watering places."

"They do. It is because of you that we are going to London."

"Me?"

"Yes, I must buy your wardrobe."

Ashley colored. "That is not necessary, I assure you. My aunt had dresses made."

"Country fashions," he dismissed. "I like my women to . . . er . . . I want my wife to be well dressed."

The slipped allusion to other women rankled. "They are pretty gowns," she replied archly. "There is nothing wrong with them, whatsoever."

"Good! You may wear them in the country, when I am not at home. You dress like a debutante. I shall clothe you as a woman."

She eyed him with misgiving.

He met her gaze. "You distrust me?" he asked coolly.

"I shall not wear the clothes of a doxy!" she pronounced.

His jaw hardened. "Good God, wife. How could you believe that I would do such a thing? Furthermore, a lady does not discuss such women with her husband!"

"I do not believe that a gentleman, when conversing with his wife, makes reference to his mistresses!" Ashley heatedly returned.

"Please accept my apology, madam," he drawled. "It was an unfortunate error. I do tend to forget your juvenile sensibilities."

She flushed. She knew she had gone too far. Her own words had embarrassed her. If he would only cease provoking her! She would have to endeavor very hard to keep from rising to his bait.

"I apologize," she stated softly. "What I said was very

rude. I can only plead fatigue. The past days have been difficult for me, as I'm sure they have been for you."

"Indeed. It is hard to become accustomed." Without further comment, he shut his eyes and appeared to drop off into a doze.

Ashley, too, fell into a fitful sleep, to be awakened at dusk by her new husband. "Are we there?"

"No, we have reached an inn. I thought it best to stop now for dinner."

"I must look a fright." Hastily, she smoothed her mussed dress and rearranged her hair, staring in awe at her sadly crumpled bonnet. "Oh, why did I sleep in that? I have ruined it!"

The marquess's eyes rolled heavenward. "You shall have another. Come, my dear, I've already bespoken dinner."

"But I haven't a hat to wear!"

"It doesn't matter." Tossing the ruined headgear onto the opposite seat, he escorted his rumpled little marchioness inside.

Ashley was pleased to see that her husband's nap seemed to have refreshed him and put him in a more pleasant mood. He ate heartily and took particular pleasure in the wine they were served. Though still feeling desperately weary, she made an effort to match his growing cheerfulness and finally caught a glimpse of the charm her aunt had referred to.

After dinner he called for brandy and laid a polished wooden box in front of her. "I neglected to give you your wedding gift."

"I did not expect . . . but, thank you!" Smiling, she unfastened the tiny clasp and lifted the lid, gasping spontaneously at the glittering emerald necklace, bracelet, and earrings lying within. "Oh, my lord," she breathed, "you should not have done this."

He frowned slightly. "You don't like them? Ah well, they can be exchanged."

"No!" Ashley quickly protested. "They're the most beautiful pieces of jewelry I've ever seen! I have never possessed anything so lovely. Are they family items?"

"No, most of the Shandal jewelry is made of diamonds. These are yours alone." He smiled. "With your eyes, my dear, you must have emeralds."

"But the expense!"

Shrugging, he laughed. "Don't concern yourself with price, Ashley. I don't! So you do like them?"

"I adore them!" Shyly, she leaned forward and dutifully kissed his cheek. "Thank you."

The marquess caught her chin with his fingers. "Is that the way a bride should kiss her bridegroom?"

Ashley trembled when his mouth descended on hers, gently but firmly parting her lips. Her heart pounded wildly, her pulse rising to her throat, as his thumb caressed her jawline. Her whole body seemed to flush with warmth.

"There," he said softly, "that is better."

Ashley stared into his vivid blue eyes, her flesh aglow from her first, true adult kiss, and her mind reeling with a strange desire for it to go on and on.

"My God, you are such an innocent," he continued in the same gentle tone. "What am I to do with you?"

The question didn't seem to require an answer, but the next one did.

"Ashley, do I frighten you?"

"A little," she murmured breathlessly.

He studied her thoughtfully. "Well then," he said, rising and extending his hand to her. "We must be on our way. We still have some distance to travel."

It was the middle of the night when the carriage at last stopped before Shandal House. Although the rest of the neighborhood was darkened, a welcoming light glimmered from the mansion's windows, as the marquess had ordered. His bride, fast asleep, did not notice. A few miles from the inn, she had fallen into a sound, heavy slumber. Brandon, suspecting that she hadn't rested so well in a long time, had pitied her cramped position and pulled her down onto his lap. Sighing, the exhausted young marchioness had snuggled, quite unselfconsciously, against him, tucking her feet up onto the seat. There she had remained until they had arrived in London.

"Ashley?" He lightly shook her shoulder. "We're home."

"Um?"

"We are in London. Wake up, my dear." He sat her up in the seat. "Come now, it won't be long before you're in your own bed."

"But I am so very comfortable here," she murmured, sagging toward him.

"Yes, I know, but you must come now." Giving up on arousing her, he stepped out and drew her after him, carrying her into the house, where his drowsy butler and housekeeper awaited them. "I'm afraid you must meet your new mistress tomorrow," he smiled. "She is quite overcome."

"Poor lady," Mrs. Briggs cooed sympathetically. "It was a long trip for her and a big day too."

"Yes, it was. Please go to bed now. You've been kind to wait up." Followed by Ashley's sleepy maid, he carried his wife up the wide stairs and into the bedchamber adjoining his. "Care for your mistress, girl, and see that she isn't awakened tomorrow until she is ready." Depositing his light burden onto the bed, he departed through the connecting door.

His valet didn't bother to suppress a yawn as he

helped the marquess out of his coat. "I'm sorry, sir. It's been a lengthy day."

"Longer for you, I daresay."

"I doubt that, my lord."

"Still bemoaning the end of my bachelorhood?" He grinned. "Don't! All will be well. Pull off my boots, Lindsey, and go to bed. I'll finish undressing myself."

Lindsey heaved off one of the shining Hessians. "Her ladyship was a pretty bride."

"Was she? I confess I was too terrified to notice."

"You, sir?" His valet snorted. "With your way with women?"

"Yes, me!" He shrugged wearily. "I've enjoyed numerous women, but none quite so young or so innocent as the new Lady Shandal."

"You'll do, my lord." The second boot joined the first. "Women are women, no matter what their age, or experience, or station in life. All they think about is love."

"All? Well, we'll see about that! What do you think, Lindsey, of having a mistress of the house?"

"If that is what you want, sir," he answered, his face a mask.

"That is what I've got!" The marquess laughed easily. "I'm not at all sure it's what I want. Oh, go on to bed! You won't give me your opinion anyway."

"Are you sure that is all, sir?"

"Yes, I shall have a glass of brandy and then retire. Goodnight."

"Goodnight, sir." Tired though he was, Lindsey managed an impudent wink. "And good luck!"

"I shall probably need it." Brandon chuckled as the door closed. Pouring himself a glass of brandy, he was acutely conscious of his lady's nearby presence. Soft movements still sounded from behind the connecting door to her bedchamber. Removing his limp cravat and unbuttoning his shirt, he sat down, sipping slowly on the drink until all grew quiet.

By now his marchioness would be sleeping again, perfectly oblivious to the upheaval she had caused in his life. He had pretended to himself that he could go on as he always had, racing his horses, attending parties, visiting his mistress, but that wasn't really true. He was responsible for someone else now. He could simply leave her in the country on one of his estates so that he could go about his own pleasurable pursuits, but she would still be a part of his world.

Undoubtedly, they would have children, adding to his responsibility. He couldn't quite visualize himself in the role of a father. His own father had performed it quite easily, but then he had been a family man like his brother would be. It wasn't hard to picture Jamie romping on the floor with a passel of offspring, but he couldn't see himself doing it. Still, he hoped he would have a son. As much as he loved his sibling, and as much as he ignored certain conventions, he wanted his title, his lands, and his fortune to pass to his own child.

The marquess sighed, drinking deeply of his brandy. He had a wife, and now he must get used to the idea of it. He must grow accustomed to her. Standing, he stripped off his clothes and tossed them in a heap, then climbed into his big four poster bed. In the morning, he would start his career as a husband.

Five

Ashley slept far into the morning and awakened with a start to a bright sun shining through her window. Sitting up, she studied her new surroundings. Obviously newly redecorated, the chamber was a large one, much bigger than her room at Oakwood Manor, and very feminine with its rosy walls and fabrics. The tent bed, with its rose silk canopy, was the most impressive piece of furniture. Made of walnut, it was delicately styled, with rambling roses entwined on the headboard. The same design was found on flanking bedside tables. Before the hearth stood a floral chintz sofa and winged chair, fronted by a tea table. Nearby were a card table, two side chairs, and a desk.

The pictures on the walls were of pastoral landscapes, no doubt especially chosen for a room of repose. Carpeting the floor was a large floral Aubusson, its muted colors dominated by a dusty rose. The whole room suggested the kind of tasteful, subtle luxury found only in the homes of England's very old and very wealthy families.

Again, Lord Shandal had surprised her. Because of his reputation, she had expected the bedroom prepared for his wife to be somewhat bold, perhaps even vulgar. Instead, he had surrounded her with understated elegance. Who was he inside? Rakehell or gentleman? Or could a man truly be both?

Ringing the silk bell rope for her maid, Ashley snuggled down into the featherbed and thought of her husband. Last night, he had given her a very expensive gift, one he had chosen especially for her. Then he had kissed her. Her cheeks grew pink at the memory of it. Only in her wildest imagination had she ever dreamed of owning such magnificent jewelry and being kissed by such a handsome, lofty peer. The fact that he was her husband was even more of a fantasy. She, an impoverished viscount's daughter, had become a marchioness!

She wished that she could forget the reasons for their marriage and pretend that he had chosen her for love. If that were so, how much easier this change in her life would be! Then he would always be hers alone, and she would not be so fearful of him and the future.

A soft tap sounded on the door, interrupting her reverie. Jane, with vivid dark circles under her eyes, peeped in. "You're awake, miss . . . er . . . my lady?"

"Only just now." Ashley stretched. "From your looks, you should have stayed in bed longer too."

"Oh no, ma'am. Mrs. Briggs, the housekeeper, seems very strict. I must be up early to await your ring."

"Then I shall give orders for you to nap this afternoon. You have been so good to me, Jane, that I won't have you treated shabbily."

"I believe she knows I'm not really a lady's maid, and that I've had no training to be one."

"Don't let her intimidate you," Ashley counseled with a confidence she herself didn't feel. "You are my personal maid, and I shall have no one else." She swung out of bed and wiggled her toes in the silky carpet. "Isn't this a beautiful room? Is the rest of the house as pretty?"

"As much as I've seen of it, ma'am. 'Tis a fine house!" Jane poured a ewer of hot water into a pink flowered basin. "I'm to ask what you want for breakfast. It's late, so you'll be served here in your room."

"Is it almost time for luncheon?"

"Yes, ma'am." Jane smiled.

"Oh, dear, I did sleep late! Whatever will they think of me?" she wondered worriedly.

"You're the marchioness. I believe you can do what you want."

"Yes, I suppose so." Ashley brightened. "No more Oakwood Manor, Jane! No more Lady Madison! Isn't it good fortune for us both?"

"I hope so, my lady."

"Let us not be so formal when we are in private," Ashley begged, "and also, I shall continue to value your opinion. Of late, I haven't heard it. What do you think of all this?"

"It will all be wonderful if he grows to love you as he should."

Ashley shook her head. "I don't know if that will happen. Nor do I know if I will fall in love with him. But he is so very handsome, it will probably be hard not to do so!"

"Yes, and he is well aware of it," the servant blurted.

She laughed. "Now that sounds like the Jane I am accustomed to!"

" 'Tis true what I say." The maid giggled. "Also, ma'am, you are very pretty, and you should be aware of that too!"

"Oh, I could not compete with him," she declared.

"But you are pretty inside as well!"

"Thank you. That was a very kind thing to say." Ashley took a cloth and began to wash her face. "Is he at home?"

"Lord Shandal went out. They expect him, however, for luncheon."

"Then I'd best hurry, so as to be ready for anything.

Please fetch me some tea, but nothing to eat. I shall wait for luncheon. I'll dress while you are about that errand."

"Please wait, my lady," Jane begged. "It is my job to help you. Mrs. Briggs wouldn't like your dressing yourself."

"Mrs. Briggs is not the mistress here," Ashley said firmly. "Don't you dare make me too dependent!"

The abigail laughed. " 'Tis time you had some spoiling."

"That may be, but allow me some measure of competence," she insisted.

As Jane left the room, Ashley dried herself on the thickest towel she had ever seen, dressed carefully in a simple pale yellow round dress, and brushed her long, silky hair. She would wait for Jane to style it.

Crossing the room, she peered out the window to the street below. It was quiet of traffic, and all the imposing houses bore signs of being closed for the summer. Still, she could picture how grand a square it must be when the owners were in residence. There would be a bustle of horses and carriages, and fine ladies and gentlemen coming and going. There would be balls and routs, and she, the Marchioness of Shandal, would be a part of it all. That is, if he allowed her to.

Another knock, more firm than Jane's, sounded on the door. "Come in please," she called gently, watching it swing open to reveal a short, plump, matronly woman, carrying a tea service on a silver tray.

"I am Mrs. Briggs, the housekeeper, my lady," she announced in a formal tone of voice. Curtsying, she set down the tray on the tea table and looked pointedly at Ashley's flowing hair. "Your maid will be along at once, but I did feel that I should make your acquaintance as soon as possible."

"I'm glad that you did, Mrs. Briggs. I am most pleased

to meet you." Ashley smiled sweetly. "I do hope I haven't inconvenienced the staff by sleeping so late."

"Certainly not!" the woman cried, horrified. "You shall sleep whatever hours you please! We will accommodate your wishes, madam."

"Thank you." She, too, began to experience Jane's feeling of intimidation and tried to push it away. "There is one thing I desire," she ventured.

"Yes, my lady?"

"I am not knowledgeable of the protocol of this house, but I do insist that Jane, my personal maid, will take her orders directly from me. She has been with me a long time and knows my requirements. Indeed, she is as much companion as servant."

"Yes, madam, of course." The housekeeper's lips tightened ever so slightly. "If I have intervened too much this morning, it was done through thoughtfulness for your comfort."

"I understand, and I do appreciate your concern," Ashley said kindly. "I fear I must rely a great deal on your abilities. My family was not well-to-do, so they were unable to maintain an establishment such as this. After my parents died, I was forced to practice the strictest economy. So you see, I shall need your expertise! I have lived quite informally."

"You may depend on me, my lady," the housekeeper assured her, seeming to warm to her new mistress.

"Thank you. You know my lord's likes and dislikes much better than I. If I run counter to them, I hope that you will correct me. Forgive me, but the tea smells so delicious that I must have a cup." She moved to the sofa. "I wish you had brought one for yourself. Please do so in the future."

Mrs. Briggs looked rather surprised. "You are very kind, madam. I shall do my best to advise you properly. I've brought the evening menu, and one for tomorrow's luncheon, for your approval. Under the circumstances, I took the liberty of planning today's luncheon myself."

"Certainly!" Ashley laughed. "Do sit down." She glanced quickly over the lists. There seemed to be entirely too many offerings for only two diners, but not knowing Lord Shandal's tastes, she approved them both, glancing up to see the housekeeper perched on the veriest edge of a chair. "I must take care not to gain weight. Everything sounds so delicious!"

"I believe that you will be pleased. Duval, your chef, is French, and quite exceptional at his art. You will, of course, wish to meet him and the rest of the staff, and to inspect the house."

"I am most anxious." Ashley could barely suppress her curiosity. "When would it fit your schedule?"

Once again, the woman seemed surprised. "My schedule is yours, madam."

"Do make a suggestion," she begged. "I shouldn't like to disrupt your established routine."

Mrs. Briggs permitted herself a chuckle. "I'm afraid my routine hasn't gone well today. The staff is so anxious to meet the new marchioness that they haven't accomplished much."

Ashley flushed with guilt. "Someone should have awakened me earlier."

"Oh, no, it was the marquess's express desire that the house be kept quiet so you could sleep as long as you pleased."

"Is there time before luncheon?" she asked eagerly. "I can be ready very quickly."

"There is time," Mrs. Briggs assured her. "Shall we say forty-five minutes? Will that rush you?"

"That will be fine."

"It will give us time to tour the main floor unless Lord Shandal arrives home earlier than expected. He informs me that he intends to take you to Madam

Francine, the dressmaker, this afternoon, so we shall see the rest of the house on another day."

"He wastes no time," Ashley mused.

"He is anxious to go to the country."

"Does the staff accompany us there?"

"No, ma'am. Each of Lord Shandal's homes has its own staff, so that it may be available for his visit at a moment's notice. We will close this house and take our holiday when you leave."

"Oh, dear," Ashley murmured worriedly, "have I kept everyone from their time away?"

"We are too fond of his lordship and too happy that he is married to think of that, madam. Also . . ." She winked conspiratorially. "He has given us a sizable addition to our wages in honor of the event!"

Ashley smiled with her, but felt sorry for the marquess, whose marriage was costing him so dearly. She herself would have position and comfort for the rest of her life, even if he never grew to love her. All he required of her was an heir. It was truly a small price to pay for this luxury. After all, the kind of love she dreamed of probably existed only in novels.

Ashley had met the curious staff and had toured most of the main floor when a flurry of activity in the entrance hall heralded the marquess's arrival. He found her in the formal drawing room and favored her with a light kiss on the forehead as Mrs. Briggs quietly withdrew.

"How has your morning been, my dear?" he inquired politely.

"I have met the staff and seen part of the house. It's a beautiful home!" she enthused. "You must be very proud of it."

"I am, and I hope you will be too."

She sighed dreamily. "Yes, indeed. I would never have imagined that I would live in a marvelous place like this."

"You sell yourself short, Ashley," he chided.

"I must sound like a naive fool," she admitted. "Oakwood Manor, too, could have been beautiful, if there had been any money. Most of the nice things were sold before I was old enough to appreciate them. I suppose the estate would have been gone, if it had not been entailed. Things aren't at all the way my sister-in-law portrayed them to be."

The marquess nodded. "I confess that I do have some questions about Oakwood Manor and your family, if you don't mind my asking."

"No, my lord," she said slowly, "I'll answer whatever you wish to ask."

They were interrupted by the summons to luncheon, but the marquess returned to the subject as soon as they had been served. "I observed that you seemed rather distant with Lady Madison."

"I am ashamed to say that I dislike her intensely," she admitted. "I cannot understand why Deron married her. Of course, I wrote to him about my leaving Oakwood Manor, and of our marriage, but I don't expect to hear from him. He's probably not very happy with me."

He eyed her curiously. "Why?"

"I'm sure he thought I would keep managing his estate, but Eve made it impossible. Most likely, Deron won't understand that. He'll think I have been very irresponsible."

"You?" Brandon spoke quietly, but his meaning was uncomfortably clear.

"Please don't judge Deron by this. He was never required to be reliable. He doesn't know how." Embarrassed, she lowered her eyes. "I love my brother. I was pleased to help him, even though I felt he should have sold out and come home when Papa died."

"I apologize if I have distressed you."

"No, you have a right to know," she said firmly. "Perhaps my marriage will make Deron stand on his own two feet. Oakwood Manor is now making a small profit, or it was when I left. He can take it from there."

The marquess nodded. "Let us hope that he does."

A new and frightening thought assailed her mind. Before the wedding, Eve had hinted that the marriage would be beneficial to them all. What if her family applied to her husband for money? How humiliated she would be!

"Whatever happens, you must certainly not concern yourself," Ashley stated. "Deron must come home now and take care of his own affairs."

Francine Dubonnet was one of London's most fashionable dressmakers. Although her success came primarily from her outstanding artistic skill, she had to thank the Marquess of Shandal for bringing her work to the attention of the *haute ton*. Some years ago she'd had a brief affair with him, which had lasted no more than a few tempestuous weeks, but had left her wealthier by one fine diamond brooch. Shortly after their amicable farewell, his mother had come into her shop and ordered a dress. The marchioness had liked it so well that she had made Francine her only dressmaker, thus providing cache with the upper echelon of the *ton*. The modiste had no doubt that the marquess had pointed his mama in her direction, and she was very grateful to him. Now, she had received word that she would dress his lady, too.

She was anxious to meet the new marchioness. A female with the ability to snare Lord Shandal must be a very beautiful and exciting woman. It was almost beyond belief that someone had actually accomplished the feat. The new marchioness would probably become a style-setter, and she would do it in Francine Dubonnet's gowns. The little Frenchwoman fervently hoped that the lady would have the figure to appear in some of her more *nouveaux* designs.

Five minutes before the appointed time, a carriage emblazoned with the Shandal crest drew up in front of the shop. His lordship stepped out and turned to assist his lady.

Francine was nearly struck dumb. The new marchioness was pretty enough for any man, but she was not the resounding Beauty that one would expect a man like Shandal to choose. And she was most unfashionable in her ill-cut clothes, which didn't suit her figure and looked too young for her. There was too much trim and too many ruffles for her classical countenance, and that insipid yellow clashed with her complexion. It was no wonder that the marquess desired Francine to dress her in entirety. The new marchioness must have no fashion sense at all!

Watching the couple walk toward the door, their movements stiff with each other, the modiste realized that this was not a love match. The marriage had undoubtedly been arranged. Poor lady, Francine thought, to be married to a woman-loving man like Shandal and not to be thought attractive by him.

As her doorman opened the door, she dropped a low curtsy.

"Good afternoon, Madame Dubonnet," the marquess said smoothly. "My dear, this is Mama's dressmaker."

"How do you do?" the marchioness murmured politely. "My aunt, Lady Sheldon, has also mentioned your skill."

"Thank you, my lady. I have made several dresses for her ladyship. Won't you come and sit down? *Pardon,* if I seem to stare, but I must assess which style will suit you best." She led the way to an elegant brocade sofa and glanced at the marquess. "You will be staying, sir?"

"For awhile." He favored Francine with his breathtaking smile.

Seeing a mischievous glint in his eyes, she wondered if he was remembering their times together in her bed. She couldn't help shooting him a naughty look in return.

The young marchioness witnessed the exchange and tried unsuccessfully to look the other way.

The modiste turned immediately to her. "First, I shall show the designs that we have already made up, then we'll look at fashion plates and fabrics." Excusing herself, she went to summon her assistants, who were clad in the lovely gowns that she had personally designed.

Returning, Francine proudly watched her own expensive fashion show. "Many of these gowns, madame, would be most fashionable for a lady of your style and figure. Also, I have in my mind a style of ball gown that I should like to be permitted to make for you." Seeing the confusion in the young lady's eyes, she glanced at Shandal, who was standing over the lady's shoulder.

"She shall have it," he said, "along with any other style she may inspire in your talented mind, Madame. You have my *carte blanche.*"

Her expression betraying her shock at his largess, Lady Shandal stared numbly at the parade of beautiful clothes and then at the fashion plates Francine handed her. Her husband and the modiste made all the selections until Francine showed her a view of a riding habit.

"I do like to ride. Remember?" She glanced hopefully at her husband.

"Yes I do." He nodded to Francine. "Perhaps three for summer, and two for winter."

"I shouldn't need that many!" the marchioness protested, but they embarked upon a discussion of the relative merits of two styles of bodices and ignored her protest.

It was the same way when the fabulous fabrics were brought out on display. The marquess and the dressmaker chose while the young marchioness sat quietly, seemingly overwhelmed by the rich quality and the sheer number of the beautiful goods. Again, discussions arose over various types and colors until the selections were made. The new Lady Shandal ventured no comment.

After this, Lord Shandal left for his club, going on foot so that the carriage would remain waiting for her.

"My lady is fortunate," Francine complimented, serving her a cup of tea. "You have a husband who is interested in what you wear. I am surprised that he did not wait for the lingerie selection. That is usually all that men are interested in!"

The marchioness flushed. "He probably knew that it would mortify me!"

The dressmaker laughed and handed her an assortment of drawings. "Let us begin."

Lady Shandal sorted through the cards, shocked at the almost nonexistent bodices and sheer fabrics. "I cannot sleep in these! They are too . . . too revealing! Is there no such thing as a plain linen gown, such as I have been used to wearing?"

Francine nodded, biting back a chuckle. "A high-necked, long sleeved gown worn by girls and grandmothers? Of course there is, but you cannot want that."

"But these are almost indecent! What does my lord's mama wear? Or my aunt?"

"You are not his mama, my dear," Francine said gently.

"I would slide right out of these!" She shook her head. "No, the style is impossible. I would look like a courtesan."

The dressmaker drew a deep breath. "Forgive me if I go too far, but with a husband such as yours, my lady, you cannot wear a plain linen gown."

The marchioness eyed her sharply.

Francine smiled kindly. "I assure you that these are the favored fashions for all the young married ladies. Perhaps I could raise the necklines just a little, *non?*"

Lady Shandal sighed. "Very well, but they shall be in whites or pastels. Nothing vivid."

"As you wish." She was swept with relief. Shandal would never have forgiven her if she had turned out his wife in such modest nocturnal attire. In turn, she felt sorry for the sweet little marchioness. How was the innocent lady to cope with her husband's sensuous appetite? The poor girl was in for some difficult times. But on the other hand, the marquess might only do his duty to her and leave his pleasure to the ministrations of women like Lady Milton. Either way, it was not Francine's concern. She had only to dress his lady for him, and she had accomplished that.

Six

With most of the *ton* either in the country or at one of the fashionable watering places, the company at White's was thin. There was a minimum of card players. Several members sat at the famous bow window and made caustic criticisms of the passersby. But all were older men—widowers and old bachelors.

The marquess ordered a glass of brandy and leisurely read the collection of daily newspapers, then quickly found himself bored. Consulting his timepiece, he estimated that Ashley had probably finished at Francine's and returned home. Perhaps she would enjoy a drive about the town.

Taking his leave, Brandon strolled home and found his wife re-exploring the rooms she had been shown that morning.

"Finding changes you wish to make?" he asked, startling her from her study of a Chinese rose medallion vase.

"Oh, no!" Ashley hurriedly returned the vessel to the mantel. "It is all so very perfect! I don't know how anything could be improved upon. Did your mother do the decorating?"

"She did."

"She has such excellent taste." Her voice contained a slight tone of awe. "She must have spent many happy hours assembling and enjoying these beautiful things."

"Actually my parents spent as little time as possible in London. They preferred Havard Hall. My father may have been a marquess, but he was a country squire at heart."

"But not you?" she queried.

"Not hardly! I enjoy the country, especially during this season of the year, but I would greatly miss not spending most of my time in London."

She smiled. "Well, you certainly have a lovely home to spend it in. I hope you don't mind my wandering about admiring its treasures?"

"You forget something," he chided gently.

"What is that?" Ashley turned wide nervous eyes toward him, looking for all the world like a child who had been caught pilfering a biscuit.

Brandon suppressed a chuckle. "You are the mistress of this house. You can do whatever you wish." Crossing the room, he lightly laid his hands on her shoulders.

Nibbling her lip, she slowly looked up at him. "I confess I don't feel like your marchioness yet."

"You shall." With his forefinger, he lifted her chin and lay his thumb over her mouth, stilling the fidgety little mannerism. "You shall, very soon."

Cheeks pink, Ashley lowered her gaze. "You must give me time to grow accustomed to . . . to everything, my lord," she murmured.

"I am all patience," Brandon drawled, lowering his lips to hers and drawing her close against his hard masculine frame.

Timidly, she began to respond to him, slipping her arms around his waist, her fingers smoothing the lush fabric of his coat. In return, he kissed her harder, his mouth bearing down firmly to part her lips. His caressing hand slid down her back, gently pushing her even closer against him.

She stiffened, drawing her mouth away from his.

"Don't be afraid, Ashley." He frowned with concern at her troubled face and refused to let her back away from him.

"But you shouldn't . . ." She shook her head. "I know you have the right and the authority, but . . ." Her voice trailed off.

"I believe that you are making too much an issue of this part of our relationship."

"That is easy for you to say! You are no stranger to it!"

Brandon laughed softly. "I am glad that one of us is experienced. I do wonder what would happen if neither of us were! But I daresay we would come to some sort of a conclusion. After all, madam, you are so eminently touchable."

She looked at him in confusion. "You promised me your patience."

"So I did." He smiled enigmatically and reluctantly let her go. Nothing would be gained in rushing his skittish wife, although he was beginning to doubt that she would welcome his intimacies in as short a time as he wished. He walked to the sideboard and poured himself a glass of brandy.

"Much as I would like to continue my advances," he smiled, "I did come home to ask you if you would like to take a short drive around London. Would you enjoy that or are you too tired from your outing to Francine's?"

Her eyes sparkled with relief. "I would like it above all things!"

"Then I shall order the carriage. Can you be ready in half an hour?"

"Oh, yes! Even sooner, if you wish."

"Half an hour will be fine." He returned to her and dropped a light kiss on her forehead. "I shall await you in the library."

"Thank you. Thank you so much!" She fled from the room.

Shaking his head, Brandon departed for the library. His bride was asking a great deal of him. Some patience was reasonable. She was so innocent and naive. But even the greenest country girl must recognize her duty and realize that she must perform it.

He sighed, sitting down behind his desk and idly swirling the liquor in his glass. It was too bad that he was such a connoisseur of feminine attributes and could not assume an indifference to her. But all too well he remembered how she looked in that bathtub, and he longed to caress her silken skin. How long could he be patient?

Brandon found himself biting his own lip and took a sip of brandy. Patience! What a damnable quality! Surely, she wouldn't ask him to wait much longer. She was driving him mad in just this short a time.

He gave his head a swift jerk to clear his jumbled emotions. Perhaps by tonight she would be willing to accept her wifely duties. If she was not . . . well, he firmly believed in his own practiced powers of seduction.

The carriage moved smartly through the city streets, pausing before the fascinating historic sites that the marquess deemed to be of interest to a newcomer to London. Brandon surprised himself in his ability to give his lady a brief but thorough description of the highlights of events that had taken place in each one. Never a dedicated scholar, he realized that his tutors had managed to drill a surprising amount of his country's history into his head, in spite of his preference for more active pursuits.

Also, it was interesting to see the familiar scenes

through Ashley's eager eyes. She had a bright, quick mind and several times, aided the travelogue with her own knowledge. He discovered that his new wife was not just a simple country girl. Probably, if the truth be known, her limited scholarship equaled or surpassed his own. Someone in the impoverished viscount's household had educated her well.

At one point, when he was describing a sixteenth-century ancestor who had lost his head on Tower Green, her enthusiasm bubbled over to the point that she thrust her arm through his, squeezing excitedly. "Have you a portrait of this lord?"

"Yes we do. In the gallery at Havard Hall." He covered her hand with his. "Remind me to show it to you."

"I shall. It must have been very frightening to lose one's head." She shuddered. "I would die of terror before I even reached the block."

To his surprise, she didn't draw away from him, but remained close, her arm still linked in his.

"I wonder how his wife felt," Ashley mused, "to have such a terrible thing happen to her lord? I wonder if they loved each other?"

"I'm sure I don't know." Brandon grinned. "Perhaps you can sort through the family muniments and find out something about them."

"May I? That would be beyond all enjoyment!"

He laughed. "More likely it would be beyond all boredom. There must be thousands of papers, all ill-assorted."

"You should hire a librarian or archivist to catalog them," she advised.

"Maybe I shall. Each marquess has always made some sort of contribution to the family seat. Perhaps that could be mine."

"An excellent idea!" she enthused. "Especially if I can help? Please do so!"

"Very well, Ashley. I'll see about it."

If she became occupied with that form of activity, it would release him from the growing feeling that he must entertain her. It hadn't been bad today, but he knew he would soon tire of it. Only her newness and his aching desire to possess her kept his attention at the moment. He would weary of her just like he did all the others.

There was also the matter of Alicia Milton. He wasn't at all ready to discard her yet. He hadn't seen her since his earth-shattering visit to his mama in Bath, but if he didn't attend her soon, she might become irritated enough to turn to another. He must send her a short note and enclose enough money to keep her dangling. In a few weeks he would have settled Ashley in the country and satisfied his hunger for her. Then he could return to his experienced, pleasure-driven mistress and leave his wife to her own devices.

After a delicious supper in which Duval proved his genius as chef, Ashley excused herself and retired to her room. Weary from her long, full day, she entered the dressing room and put herself in the hands of her maid. "I am simply exhausted, Jane. I shall fall asleep as soon as my head touches the pillow."

Her abigail gave her a curious glance and moved quickly to assist her.

Ashley raised an eyebrow at her maid's strange expression. "Is something wrong?"

"I thought that perhaps his lordship . . . well . . . it was so late last night that . . ."

"He has promised me his patience in certain matters. We shall become thoroughly acquainted before . . . before anything else," she said, blithely holding up her arms as Jane divested her of her gown. "Do not look so disbelieving! For all the gossip, I have come to consider Lord Shandal to be quite civilized."

The maid shrugged. "I'm sure you know best, my lady, but . . ."

"Yes?"

"He is a man, ma'am, a newly wed one."

"Is that all you have to say?" She laughed. "Fetch me my nightgown. I am going to bed."

Jane did as she was bid, returning with the sheer silk negligee that Lady Sheldon had forced Ashley to have.

"No, not that! My usual one, Jane. I won't sleep in that tonight."

"As you wish." Laying aside the wafer thin garment, the maid doubtfully produced the high-necked, long-sleeved linen one, helped her mistress remove her chemise, and slipped it over her head.

"That's better." Ashley sat down at her dressing table while Jane removed the pins from her hair, brushed it thoroughly, and braided it neatly into one long plait. "That will be all. Sleep well, Jane, you still look tired."

"Thank you, ma'am. Are you sure . . ."

"Yes. He won't come tonight," she replied kindly.

"Very well, my lady. Good night."

As the maid left her room, Ashley splashed her face with warm water and cleansed her teeth. Satisfied with her simple ablutions, she made her way from the dressing room toward the soft, inviting bed. A door closed quietly. Turning, she saw the marquess, splendidly clad in a shimmering blue dressing gown and carrying a bottle of brandy and two glasses.

He frowned. "Is this what you're going to wear? You look like a farmer's wife."

Her heart fluttered in her throat. "Do you speak from experience, my lord?" she asked impertinently, nearly choking on the words as soon as they had left her mouth. Why, oh why did she bait him whenever he was uncomplimentary and she was nervous? It only made matters worse and this was a time when she could ill afford his anger. She gritted her teeth, waiting for a scathing retort, but Shandal only looked mildly at her. His gaze slid to the white silk negligee still lying across a chair.

"I see that your maid had set out something different for you to wear."

"Yes, but . . . it didn't fit," she stammered.

He set down the bottle and glasses, picked up the garment, and held it out to her. "Please put it on; I shall judge."

Ashley's cheeks flushed a deep pink. She thought of the diaphanous night gowns she had ordered only hours before and of Francine's gentle admonition to her. Acceptance of the reality of her situation had been much easier in the modiste's cheerful shop than here, in her own bedroom, standing before England's most notorious rake.

Her stomach cramped. Oh why had she married him? Anything would have been preferable to this! "Sir," she began, "it is not too late for us to obtain an annulment. Immediately in the morning, I'll cancel the order with Francine, I'll give you back the jewelry, and I shall repay every shilling you have spent on me! We both know that we do not suit. We are so very different!"

His cynical smile barely touched the corners of his mouth. "You would be making a very grave mistake, and we would become the laughing stock of England. All this because an innocent young lady is afraid of a perfectly natural act? I think not, Ashley. I shall not allow it." He walked around her and began to unbutton her unfashionable nightdress. "Come now, let us dress you in a manner befitting a bride."

Her bare skin burned where his fingertips brushed

it. "No, please!" She whirled away from him. "Please," she murmured, lifting her chin, "I shall do it."

Wordlessly, he handed the gown to her.

With as much dignity as she could summon, Ashley took the flimsy nightrail, brushed past him into her dressing room, and disappeared behind the screen.

The sheer fabric slid smoothly over her body, clinging seductively to her curves. Looking down at herself she saw that its thinness would leave nothing to his imagination. She cringed, suddenly realizing that she had not brought her dressing robe. Peeping from behind the screen she saw it lying across her bed, very far away in her bedroom. In between was her husband, staring that moment at the ceiling.

"Lord Shandal?"

"Yes, my dear?"

"I have forgotten my dressing robe. Could you . . . ?"

"Of course."

"It is on the bed."

Instead of laying it across the screen, he came around and stopped, his eyes slowly raking her up and down. "My God," he breathed, "you are beautiful."

Trembling visibly, she shook her head, catching her lip in her teeth.

"You don't believe it?"

"I suppose I am well enough."

"Whoever told you that wasn't a man." He gazed fixedly, unable to take his eyes off her.

Ashley flamed with embarrassment at his perusal. Her heart pounded frantically and nerves writhed in the pit of her abdomen. Tears sprang to her eyes. "It is too much!"

Her plea jolted him. Thrusting her robe into her hand, he retreated to her bedroom and sat down on the sofa, pouring them both a glass of brandy.

Ashley came fearfully from behind the screen, her

robe securely sashed around her. Pausing at the door, she studied her husband's burnished blond head bent over his brandy. He was, after all, only a man. A very handsome one, but just a man! As Lizzie had said, women did survive these encounters. Living in the country, she was not a stranger to the fact of procreation. However, with the marquess, it would probably be far different from any simple act. If only it were not for his reputation, which had caused her to conjure up the wildest fantasies!

He lifted his head. "I have poured you a glass of brandy. Come sit with me."

"I have never tasted brandy," she whispered, seating herself as far away from him as possible.

"You shall try it tonight." He glanced down the length of the sofa. "You sat closer to me in the carriage. Yesterday, in fact, you even slept with your head in my lap."

"I don't remember."

"No." He reached for her. "Come here. You do remember this afternoon? You weren't afraid of me then."

Shivering, she obeyed.

"Are you cold?"

"No, not at all."

He slipped his arm around her. "Try the brandy."

Taking a sip, she erupted into a spasm of coughing as the fiery liquor burnt her throat.

"Too strong." He grinned. "I daresay I did the same thing when I first tried it."

"You?" When he smiled that way, she couldn't help warming to him. "I cannot believe it."

"I wasn't born knowing how to drink brandy, dear. I did have to grow up."

It was hard to picture that he wasn't always the way he was now. She set the drink aside, drawing a deep breath. "The women . . ." she said carefully, "the women you are acquainted with . . ." She pressed her hands to her hot cheeks. "I'm sorry! I shouldn't mention it!"

"What is it you wish to know?"

She stole a sideways glance, finding him with a perfectly agreeable expression on his handsome face. "They are experienced?"

"Yes."

"I see."

He sipped his brandy, his fingers idly toying with her silky braid.

"These women give you great pleasure?" she asked softly.

"Ashley!"

"I'm sorry. I know I shouldn't ask. Please forgive me. It is my abominable curiosity!"

"I shall answer, if it will help whatever it is that is bothering you." He sighed. "Yes, I suppose they do."

"I cannot do as they do! I don't know how."

He relaxed. "Is that all that is bothering you? I know, dear, that you are inexperienced. I don't expect you to respond like a courtesan. Love-making with you will be a new experience for me, too. I want it to be a pleasure for us both."

"Can it be?"

"I believe so."

"When we don't even know each other?" she asked incredulously.

"We are beginning to know each other. This is just another part of it." Lowering his head, he kissed her sweetly.

Ashley tensed. As he deepened the kiss, she tried to pull away, but his hand on the back of her head kept her face against his. Nerve endings in her mouth began to tingle vibrantly until it was almost more than she could bear. She melted into his arms, shyly slipped her arms around his neck and finally, heart pounding, she caressed his guinea-gold hair.

Slowly, his lips never leaving hers, the marquess picked her up and carried her to the bed, lowering her onto her back and loosening her sash.

Ashley's return kiss ceased. Fear knotted her stomach. "Lord Shandal, please . . ."

"You are so very lovely," he whispered huskily. Reaching down, he inched up the skirt of her gown.

"No!" She tried to wrench herself away from him. "Oh please, no!" Wildly, she shoved him away, drawing her knees to her chest.

"Damnation!" he shouted angrily. "What is wrong with you?"

"I'm sorry."

"Not nearly so sorry as I am!"

She burst into tears. "I didn't mean . . . I only wanted . . ."

"Oh, be still," he said grimly, getting out of the bed. Returning to the sofa, he reached for the brandy. "Don't you know anything?"

"I know a great deal!" she sobbed. "I know you promised to be patient! I know that!" Wrapping herself in her robe, she wiped her eyes on its sleeve.

"Well if you know so damn much, pray enlighten me on a wife's duties to her husband." He tossed down the liquid and refilled his glass.

She lowered her head, wiping her eyes on a corner of the sheet. "I told you that you must give me time."

"Oh, must I?" he asked sarcastically.

"Please, my lord," she whispered. "Everything has happened so quickly! I want to be a good wife to you, but I can't do it all at once, and sir, I do know the 'duties' of a wife."

"Well then, you had better refrain from feeling sorry for yourself and become accustomed to doing them!"

"I shall. Please don't be angry with me."

He favored her with a look of pure frustration. Standing, he picked up his glass and the bottle of brandy and returned to his own room, shutting the door between with a loud snap.

Ashley buried her face in her pillow. Why hadn't she gritted her teeth and let him have his way, instead of letting her fear overcome her? Anything would have been preferable to his anger.

Muffling a sob, she clenched her fists. It had been such a nice day, a promising start for their future together. He had promised her his patience. Didn't he know what that meant? Why couldn't he have given her more time to get to know him?

And now what would she do? Go to him, make a proper apology, and promise that she would never again behave in such a manner? Or should she ignore what had happened and wait for him to approach her again?

Either way, she would do nothing tonight. He was too angry. She would rise early and meet him at breakfast, hoping that the night's sleep had put him in a better humor. Then she would assess the best way to remedy the situation.

Seven

Awakening at eight o'clock, Ashley rang for Jane and began to dress rapidly. Ignoring the questioning look in her maid's eyes when Jane saw the white negligee, Ashley remained silent throughout the morning routine and as soon as she was satisfied with her appearance, hurried downstairs to the dining room.

Her heart sank as she saw the note and the purse lying on the table. Her husband was gone. And if he had left her money, he might be planning to be away for some time. Pouring herself a cup of tea, she sat down to read what he had written.

My dear Ashley,
  I shall be out for the day. If you wish to go shopping, I have left you an amount of money. Not knowing if it is enough, I ask you to contact Charles, my secretary, if you desire more. He will supply you with however much you need, or simply have the bills sent to me.
                                           Brandon

So she was left alone and miserable, and through no fault but her own. If she had been sensible last night, she was sure they would have been dining comfortably together this morning. Well, she would have been as comfortable as any lady could be in Shandal's presence.

Instead, she had behaved like a foolish schoolgirl and now must reap the rewards of her own folly.

Had he gone to his mistress? His wife had been unwilling to fulfill his needs so he had turned to another? Damn! If he had only given her more time! But thankfully it appeared that he had gone only for the day.

She crumpled the letter and looked into the purse. He had left her a substantial amount of money. Ashley was forced to smile at his wondering if it would be enough. At Oakwood Manor she could have lived for a year on that sum! Obviously, no matter how great his anger or disappointment, the marquess did not wish her to live on a pittance.

She sipped her tea and made a resolution. Her husband did not intend to stay away for long. When he returned, she would steel her nerves and submit to his desires. She would be duty and kindness itself, and never again give him cause to be angry with her.

The door clicked softly open and Pym, the butler, stood before her, stiffly bowing. "You have a caller, my lady, Lord Madison."

"My brother!" she cried. "Is it Deron?"

"I believe so, my lady."

"Do send him in at once!"

"To the dining room, my lady?"

"Yes, for if I know Deron, he hasn't breakfasted."

She was on her feet when her tall, handsome brother dashed into the room. "Deron! Oh, dear, dear Deron! You can't believe how happy I am to see you!" She flung herself into his arms.

Lord Madison laughed at his sister's exuberance and enveloped her in a breathless hug that lifted her off her feet.

"Deron, you have missed my wedding! Did you get my letter?"

"I did, but I couldn't have come any sooner. I've sold out, Ashley. I'm no longer in the army."

"I'm so glad. Oakwood Manor needs you."

"Yes, with you gone I'm sure it does. Eve too, I daresay. That lovely lady wouldn't know the first thing about managing an estate."

"No, but come, Deron, have you breakfasted?"

"Only a bite. I'll be glad to partake of your hospitality."

She released him and escorted him to the buffet. "Eat it all! I have never seen such a shocking waste of food as there is at this house or at Aunt Sheldon's, for that matter."

"I suppose the marquess has no need to concern himself with waste," Deron remarked, "nor do the Sheldons either. I was at Sheldon Hall yesterday. Finding that I had missed you and Eve both, I came posthaste to London. I must see my man of business before I go to Oakwood Manor and of course, I hoped to see and congratulate you and the marquess. Is he at home?"

"Not at present."

"Unfortunate." Deron helped himself to a heaping plate from the buffet and joined her at the table. "But since I intend to beg quarters from you during my stay in London, perhaps I shall become acquainted with him later. It's good to be back in England! You were right to implore me to sell out, although I shall miss the military life."

"Poor Deron, you should have been born a second son."

"Perhaps." He settled down to the business of eating. "Tell me about your new husband, Ashley."

She smiled. "I hardly know what to say. He is very handsome, and I think he will be kind to me."

"It appears that he is quite wealthy."

Ashley's eyes fell on the purse still lying on the table.

"Yes, so it seems. I don't really know. One does not discuss finances with one's bridegroom."

Deron laughed. "Well I've heard it all from the Sheldons. You have had very good fortune, my dear. According to Uncle Sheldon, Lord Shandal is very wealthy. To tell the truth, I could not imagine you being swept off your feet by any man, no matter how handsome or titled, but I do know that you have a head for business."

"I did not marry him for his money," she protested. "I shall not entertain any such notion!"

"Don't ruffle your feathers, little sister. I am only congratulating you on this piece of luck. I'm sure the marquess will make you a good husband or you wouldn't have married him. Now bring me up-to-date on the situation at Oakwood Manor. I would like to hear your side of things before I see Jenkins this afternoon."

Her remembrance of his estate seemed very distant, but she managed as best she could to describe its financial standing and to hint that all might not be as well as when she had left it. Deron took it in good stride and even thanked her for her careful guardianship.

"It's too bad that Papa left it so encumbered," she said wistfully, "but I have proved that in time, things can become better. It is merely an exercise of economy."

"Perhaps. But of course there will no longer be my income from the Army."

Ashley had seen precious little of that. "It doesn't matter. It can still be done."

"I hope you're right. I'm a family man now and that gives me a great many added responsibilities."

"You can do it," she encouraged. "I have proved that it is possible."

"Yes. Well, we shall see." He eyed her almost speculatively for what seemed like a *very*, very long time.

* * *

When Deron left to visit his man of business, Ashley took the opportunity to explore the parts of the house she had not yet seen. In activity, she was able to turn her mind from her rift with her husband.

Her brother returned, pale and much cast down. "It's not good, Ashley. Not good at all. In fact, I scarcely know what to do."

She seated him in the salon and poured him a hefty glass of brandy. "It cannot be as bad as all that. I, too, wondered what to do, when I began to manage the estate. But once you are there and begin to assess the situation, you will see how matters can be improved."

"Eve has begun redecorating. Didn't you know that? Why did you not advise her against it?" he said quarrelsomely. "There was no money for that sort of thing! Now, if you would see the tradesmen's accounts!" He shook his head. "When the bills began to come in, Jenkins himself visited Oakwood Manor. Eve could understand nothing of what he was talking about. She has no financial sense. Why, Ashley, did you not stay there until I came home?"

"How did I know that you would come home as quickly as you did?" she cried.

Ignoring her, he settled heavily into a winged chair. "I am facing ruin."

"I'm heartily sorry, Deron, but you gave me no indication that you were intending to sell out. If you had, I would surely have waited. But you didn't! I had to get on with my life. Can't you understand?"

"No, I don't! I don't understand any of this! First you fly away and leave my new wife, whom I entrusted to your care! Next you are married to a man I have never met! What is this business, Ashley? Have you taken leave of your senses?"

"I have not!" she snapped. "And you most certainly did not entrust Eve Madison to my care! She is an adult, has been married, widowed, and married again! I am certain that she would highly resent being left in the trust of anyone!"

"She was helpless with no one to advise her. You should have realized that!" He tossed down the contents of his glass and held it out to be refilled. "I depended upon you!"

"Don't you dare blame her foolish spending on me, Deron Madison! I tried to stop her, but she refused to listen. What could I do? Nothing!"

"You could have explained our financial situation."

"I did!" she defended. "You must have led her to believe that you were wealthy, for she merely laughed at me and called me penurious. It is your fault and I shall not allow you to heap the blame on me!"

"So it's all my fault? Poor little Ashley, so mistreated and put upon!"

"I blame you for nothing." She shook her head. "I was glad to manage the estate for you, but can't you see that everything changed when you married? You began a family, so Oakwood Manor was really no longer my home. It solely became your responsibility. I tried to tell your wife what to do, but she certainly didn't wish to hear it from me! Perhaps she will listen to you."

"If it is not too late." He leaned back his head and closed his eyes. "If only you had waited."

Ashley bit back a retort. If, after all this, he continued to blame her, there was nothing more she could say that would change his mind. "I'm sorry, Deron, truly I am, but when you go to Oakwood Manor, look over the accounts and speak honestly with Eve. Perhaps you will see a way to overcome this."

"I see a way right now," he said quietly. "You have married a wealthy man. You could lend me the money."

The blood drained from her face. "You cannot ask

me to do that. Indeed, I could not do it without Lord Shandal's approval.''

"Surely he has put you in possession of money of your own.''

"Not such a sum as that! Deron, I could not ask him to pay Eve's bills! Not unless you were absolutely destitute! You haven't tried yet. I am sure that if you stop the expenditures and live frugally, all will be well.''

"So you won't help me?''

"It is a matter of pride.''

"Whose? Yours or mine?" he asked shortly. "I would care none for mine if its loss would let me out of this situation.''

"That may be, but would your wife think less of you if you continued to depend on me?''

"Perhaps." He sighed. "Very well, Ashley, I shall do as you suggest, but if things do not work out, I shall apply again. After all, Oakwood Manor was your responsibility when I was away.''

The Marquess of Shandal did not come home to dinner. Mortified in front of her brother, Ashley tried to put on a casual front, but inwardly she was trembling with worry. What if he didn't come home at all tonight? What would Deron think if her husband was still absent in the morning? He must be curious even now. New husbands simply did not leave their wives alone in the evening.

No matter Deron's thoughts, what about her marriage? It was failing before it even got started. Why could Lord Shandal not have been patient with her and why, oh why had she been so missish? Tonight she had dressed with care in one of her pretty new dresses, hoping to placate him. But he wasn't even here to see it.

The dinner went on interminably as course after

course of delectable food was presented. Duval had out-
done himself for his marchioness's brother. With a nonexistent appetite, Ashley tried to do justice to it to keep
from insulting him.

Deron, however, gave his meal his undivided attention. He was still irritated with her and spared her few
words as he concentrated on his food. But at least he
didn't strike up an argument in front of Pym and the
footmen.

At last it was over and Ashley stood. "I shall leave you
to your port and await you in the salon."

"Why should I want to sit here alone? Can't I have
my port in there?" he asked querulously.

"Of course, Deron." She stiffly led the way. "I'm
sorry that Lord Shandal was unable to join us."

"Unable or unwilling?" he laughed. " 'Lord Scandal'
is probably seeking more interesting amusements!"

Ashley swallowed. "I don't know what you are talking
about."

"I think you do. Your husband has quite a reputation.
Don't ever try again to make me believe that you didn't
marry him for his money."

"I did not! Deron, why must you be so nasty?"

"Because you have access to enough money to save
me and you won't let me have it!" he bitterly burst out.
"My own sister!"

She sat down helplessly. "First you yourself must try.
Then, if you do not succeed . . . I will ask him."

"If he ever came home, I might ask him myself."

"Deron, please!" she cried, panic stabbing her breast
at the thought of her brother begging her irritated husband for money.

"Despite his colorful reputation, I doubt that the
Marquess of Shandal would wish to see his brother-in-
law go to jail."

"It cannot be that bad!"

"Not just yet. Your marriage to a rich aristocrat has raised my credit."

"Then that will give you time to get on your feet!" Ashley snapped, falling silent as Pym brought the tea tray. Why had she never realized how selfish her brother could be? It was true that their parents had spoiled him. He had had everything he wanted, whether there was money for it or not. Now it was frustrating him beyond all reason.

But he was still her brother and she loved him. She supposed that no matter what he did or how he acted towards her, she always would. However, she could not allow him to threaten her tenuous marriage.

"Deron?" She took a deep breath. "You know that my marriage was one of convenience, and I fear that all is not going well with it, at the moment. I can't ask the marquess for money now. I just can't! He . . . he isn't very pleased with me just now."

He immediately dropped the quarrel and became the sweet brother she loved. "I'm sorry, Ashley. Is there anything I can do?"

"I don't think so," she said miserably. "We have started off wrong and it's all my fault. I begged him to be patient, but . . . Deron, I don't know what to do. I want to be a good wife, but I'm afraid of him!"

"Has he hurt you?" he demanded.

"No, nothing like that. He has been very kind, but last night we had a terrible difference of opinion."

He narrowed his eyes. "Good God, Ashley, have you refused him a husband's rights?"

She lowered her gaze.

The viscount began to laugh. "You refused 'Lord Scandal'? Oh Lord, that's rich! It's probably the first time in his life that has happened to him! And from his own wife!"

"It isn't funny, Deron! He became angry."

"Fancy that!"

"I'm sorry I even mentioned it," she said irritably. "I only thought to explain why you must not ask him for a loan! And I hoped you might give me your advice."

"Allow him his rights, Ashley. I cannot believe you are so damn naive!"

"Oh yes, you do make it sound easy."

"It is! You're making too much of it!"

"That's what he said."

"He's right." He took her hands. "Come now, I've never known you to be afraid of anything."

"The marquess can be very intimidating."

"That may be, but I wonder if he hasn't met his match."

"What do you mean by that?"

He shrugged and smiled fondly at her. "Just an idle thought."

Ashley sighed. "Well then, Lord Shandal gave me some shopping money. He was very generous. I will give it all to you, but you must promise me something."

"Pin money?" he asked doubtfully.

"I assure you that I could have lived on it for a year at Oakwood Manor."

He nodded shortly. "Go on. What must I promise?"

"You must promise not to go to my husband for money without asking my permission. You must use this money wisely and try hard to get yourself out of debt. I firmly believe that with proper management and economy, Oakwood Manor can do that."

"I shall try to get the estate running properly, Ashley. I'm not a fool."

"And the other?"

"Agreed. I need all the help I can get," he said with resignation.

Rising, Ashley went to her room and returned with the money. "It's all here."

She felt sick as she watched him count it. If Shandal knew she was doing this, he would surely be angry. But how would he ever know? He hadn't told her to keep receipts. If he asked to see her purchases, she had enough new things that he wouldn't know the difference.

"It isn't much."

"Good Lord, Deron! It's a small fortune! It will give you a excellent start."

"Have you any jewels?"

"Only what he gave me for a wedding present. He would miss those!" So would she. He had bought them especially for her . . . for her green eyes, and he had been so charming when he had given them to her.

A lump rose in her throat. "Perhaps Eve has jewelry that could be sold."

"I hadn't thought of that," he said.

He'd catch cold at that, she thought. Unless she missed her guess, Eve Madison would leave Deron before she would sell her jewelry to help him. If he kept his promise to economize, she might leave him anyway.

"It's a good idea, Ashley. If you are right about the possibility of Oakwood Manor becoming a fine estate, she should see that she would be far better off in the long run. So I'll take your advice, and I hope you'll take mine . . . on the other matter. I may not know much about managing an estate, but I'm a man and I know what to expect from my wife."

Ashley blushed deeply. "I shall remember it."

Eight

At his lordship's normal time for rising, Lindsey knocked lightly on the door and entered. His master was sprawled out fully dressed on the bed, his clothing rumpled and reeking of drink. In fact, the entire room smelled of liquor. Wrinkling his nose distastefully, the valet crossed the room to the window, drew back the purple drapes and threw open the sash as far as it would go. With a sigh, he turned back to the marquess. Gently rolling him over onto his back, Lindsey began to pull off the scuffed and filthy Hessians.

Even with the present state of Lord Shandal's disarray, he supposed he was luckier than many gentlemen's gentlemen. His lord didn't get so terribly foxed or disgustingly dirty very often. Some valets faced this scene every day of their lives.

Lord Shandal moaned, pressing his hands to his head as though to keep his skull from bursting apart. "Leave it, Lindsey. I can't stand the torture."

"Bear with me, sir, for just a moment. I'll make you a great deal more comfortable." He removed the other boot, cast it aside and started on his master's breeches.

"Even my skin hurts," the marquess whimpered pitiously.

"Yes, sir. I'll take care." Sympathetically he finished stripping him and bundled him into his dressing robe. Turning, the valet went to a chest and drew out a vial of headache powders. He mixed a small draught in a glass of water and handed to the marquess. "Drink this, sir."

"Drink? I'll have it all back up."

"No you won't. Trust me."

"Will you then leave me alone?"

"My lord, you should know that Lady Shandal's brother is visiting. I believe that he is to leave this morning after breakfast."

Brandon groaned. "Then I suppose I'd better dress and make an appearance at the table."

"Yes, sir." Lindsey poured a steaming cup of coffee. "You'll soon feel more the thing."

The marquess gratefully reached for the coffee, while his valet began to assemble his attire for the morning. "Gave you a surprise, did I?"

"Somewhat."

Brandon grinned self-consciously. "It's been a long time since I was that foxed." He glanced at Lindsey's tightly compressed lips. "Do I detect disapproval?"

"Your affairs are your concern, sir."

"You aren't happy above half! I'll wager you'll spend the entire day cleaning my boots. I'm surprised you haven't rung a peal over my head!"

"Would it do any good?" the servant asked impertinently.

"No, it wouldn't." He stood up, stretching. "I suppose you'd best send for a bath."

"It has been ordered." Lindsey, the perfect valet, smiled smugly. "If you will sit down, sir, I will shave you. By the time I am finished, your bath should have arrived."

"You're a good man," the marquess marveled. "What would I do without you?"

"I'm sure I don't know."

His head continuing to pound, Brandon passively submitted himself to the ministrations of his man. However,

by the time he was shaved, bathed and dressed, the headache had diminished to a dull throb. Though not particularly enthusiastic about facing polite conversation,
he made his way down the stairs to the dining room.

Ashley looked up anxiously as he entered, her big
green eyes reflecting concern. Beyond a doubt, his marchioness was remembering their less-than-cordial previous meeting and was fearful of how he would treat
her. Though smarting still from her rejection, he resisted the impulse to give her a setdown and kissed her
soft cheek. "Good morning, my dear."

"Good morning . . . Brandon. Won't you meet my
brother, Deron?"

"Lord Madison," he nodded.

The young man clasped his hand. "Lord Shandal."

He turned to the buffet. "I'm sorry to have missed
you yesterday, but I had a previous engagement."

"Of course."

There was a hint of sarcasm in the viscount's voice
that Brandon disliked. He hadn't been impressed by
Ashley's description of her brother. Nor had he been
enthused about information he had gleaned on the
state of the Madison finances. Young Deron would
probably hit him up for a loan, which, in light of his
past performance, would amount to a gift. The marquess was beginning to wonder if his shy new wife was
worth her price.

He sat down at the end of the table opposite her and
began picking at his meal. Ashley looked pretty this
morning. The green sprigged muslin perfectly suited
her dark loveliness. He must remember to compliment
her.

He had to talk with her about other matters, as well.
That had been a terrible episode in her room, and they
must mend the damage. He had been and would be
patient with her, more so than he had been with any

other woman, but it was time for her to take up her duties as his wife. Her fears were beyond all reason.

Brandon looked up and caught her watching him, her dark eyebrows knitted with concern. "Is something wrong, my dear?"

"I . . . would ask you the same," she murmured. "Is something wrong with the breakfast?"

He glanced at his uneaten food. "No. I'm simply not hungry, that's all."

"I see." She brightened. "I'm so glad you joined us even if you weren't hungry. Deron will be leaving this morning, and I did so want you to meet each other."

"Leaving so soon, Madison? I had thought we might have luncheon together at my club," the marquess lied.

"Thank you! I would have enjoyed that, but I am anxious to be home with Eve. Another time perhaps?"

"Certainly."

Brandon kept up his side of the conversation, but he was glad when the meal ended. Ashley went to the morning room to go over the daily housekeeping activities with Mrs. Briggs, Deron returned to his room to see to his last minute preparations and he was able to be alone in his library. He sat behind his desk and poured himself a glass of brandy. He would talk with Ashley as soon as her brother had left. He didn't look forward to it, but it was necessary. Patience was all well and good, but he would never again feel as if he'd been driven from his own wife's bedchamber.

Ashley stood with the marquess on the front step and waved farewell as Deron mounted his horse and jogged down the square. At least that part of her problem would be eliminated for awhile. Perhaps her brother would even seize hold of his difficulties and succeed in eliminating them altogether. In the meantime she must deal with the very pressing problem of her husband.

She timidly looked up at him. "Thank you for being so kind to Deron. It is more than I deserve."

"I hardly think that. He was a guest in our house, and he is your brother. I could not be less than courteous." He presented his arm. "Ashley, I wish to talk with you."

"Very well." She sighed, resting her hand on his dark blue superfine sleeve and letting him guide her to the library.

It was her favorite room in the big establishment and the one that reminded her most of Lord Shandal. Masculine in character, it was paneled in rich walnut and furnished with dark brown leather chairs and sofa. Sporting prints hung on the walls and the massive bookcases were filled with beautifully bound volumes. Lush red velvet fabric draped the windows.

Her husband sat down behind his desk, bridged his fingers and gazed thoughtfully at her. Feeling very much like a little girl confronted with her misbehavior, she stared back uncomfortably.

"Sit down, Ashley."

"Yes, my lord."

"My lord?" he asked. "At the breakfast table you seemed to have no difficulty calling me 'Brandon.' Was that solely for the benefit of your brother?"

She studied her hands. "I suppose that it was."

"Won't you please continue doing it for *my* benefit?"

"Yes, my . . . Brandon."

"Also, won't you look at me when we talk? It seems that I have previously mentioned that, too."

Nibbling her lip, she lifted her chin and regarded him. Her heartbeat quickened. The sun streaming in the window seemed to turn his hair to spun gold. The man was all too handsome. That, coupled with his reputation, was what was so intimidating about him.

"Ashley, do you agree that we have gotten off to a bad start?"

She nodded.

"What are we going to do to remedy the situation? And don't mention annulment for I have no intention of becoming the laughing stock of all England. Have you any other suggestions?"

"No," she replied in a small voice, "except that you give me more time to become accustomed."

"Do you wish me to court you like a dazzled stripling? Shall I sit at your knee, cherish every word you say, and fall into paroxysms of delight whenever you favor me with a glance?"

She was forced to smile. "That would scarcely be in your character, would it?"

"No." He grinned briefly. "So how am I to gain your esteem?"

"I . . . I don't know how to answer that."

"Time again?" he demanded.

"I . . . suppose."

"I am not a patient man, Ashley, especially with a beautiful woman who also happens to be my wife. Your idea of time is not mine, and furthermore, I believe that the rest of the world would agree with me. Think on it." He picked up a letter and began to scan it, effectively dismissing her.

"Is that all?" she ventured.

"Yes, unless you have something else to say."

"No." She stood and made her way through a blur of tears to her own room. Closing the door, she burst into sobs.

"My lady!" Jane hurried from the dressing room to encircle her with comforting arms. "Now, now. What can be so bad as to cause this?"

"The marquess . . ." Ashley turned her face into her maid's shoulder. "He . . . he promised me patience, but . . ."

Jane held her until the tears subsided. "Has he hurt you?"

It seemed a repeat of the conversation she had had with her brother. "No . . . but he wants to claim . . . a husband's rights. Why can't he wait until we know each other better? Oh Jane, what am I to do? Please tell me what you think."

"I cannot advise you, ma'am!" the servant gasped.

Ashley collapsed into a chair. "You must! Tell me what you would do if you were in my situation."

The maid fidgeted uncomfortably. "He is your husband."

"Which gives him every right to do with me whatever he will?"

Jane stared at the floor. "If it had been me who married, I would have given no thought to doing anything other than giving him his rights whenever he chose."

"Even though he is practically a stranger?"

"It is a part of marriage, my lady."

"I see," she said shortly. "You disapprove of my actions."

"I know it hasn't been easy for you, ma'am. Not at all! But I think it might be better if you would let him have his way."

"Thank you, Jane. I shall consider it." She took a deep breath. "I think I shall lie down. My head is bursting."

She allowed her maid to assist her in undressing down to her shift and wearily crawled between the cool sheets, wishing she could quiet the turmoil in her mind.

Was no one on her side? Deron was a man, so naturally he would take the man's side. But even Jane, though sympathetic, did not agree with her actions. No matter what they did, it seemed that men held and would always hold the upper hand. They treated women as possessions to be used as they pleased. Worst of all, women supported their attitudes.

She, Ashley, was a bright, intelligent woman. She had tasted independence, living on her own with no man to care for her. She had successfully managed an estate just as well as any man could have done. She could ride as well as any man. Why then did Society insist that she be nothing more than the marquess's doll, to be dressed up and played with whenever he chose? It was unfair. She was better than that.

Rolling onto her back, she folded her hands across her ribs, and stared upward at the pretty canopy. Most women would envy her. She lived in luxury with a magnificent wardrobe, elaborate meals, and numerous servants ready to spring to action at the mere crook of her finger. Her husband must be the most handsome man in England. He was generous with her. What difference did it make if he dallied with other women? Why should it matter if he had the right to rule her like a feudal lord would do a serf? She had everything and was required to do very little in return. 'Let him have his way.' It sounded so simple.

"Oh, dear," she sighed, closing her eyes again. There was no easy solution. She would have to wait to see what he did next.

Dressed to perfection in cream-colored trousers and gold-buttoned coat of coffee brown, his Hessians returned to a mirror-like shine, the marquess sat down to dine alone in the glittering candlelight. His lady had sent word that she would take supper in her bedchamber. No excuses had been given.

Brandon frowned. This was going to be even more difficult than he had anticipated. She must be angry or frightened, or a mixture of both, to go to this length to avoid his company. Surely she should know that the servants would begin to take note of their estrangement. Even if he must enter the sacred bedroom, he must set it all to rights before the house rocked off its foundations with gossip.

Lingering over his port, he came to a decision. He must immediately seek another interview with Ashley and bring the matter to a conclusion. With determination, he ordered that a bottle of sherry and two glasses be brought to his room and, pushing back from the table, went upstairs.

Lindsey, as usual, was waiting for him. "Retiring early, sir?" He glanced at the maid following with a tray.

"I thought I would. I'll have my dressing robe, and then you may go for the evening."

The valet helped him undress and put away his clothes. "Will that be all, sir?"

"Yes."

Brandon watched the door close behind him. He drew a deep breath, picked up the bottle and glasses and tapped on the door adjoining his chamber and Ashley's. There was a lengthy pause before he heard her voice bidding him enter.

His marchioness sat, half turned towards him at her dressing table, her eyes wide with uncertainty. Her maid, hairbrush in hand, paused fearfully.

"That will be all, Jane," he said with dismissal.

The girl glanced at her mistress, who nodded almost imperceptibly, then quietly left the suite.

He set the bottle and glasses on her dresser. "I missed you at dinner. Please, Ashley, cannot we become comfortable with one another, once again?"

"Sir, I was never comfortable with you." Turning back to her mirror, she pulled her glistening hip-length hair over her shoulder and began to brush it with a trembling hand.

The sight momentarily distracted him. He had never seen hair so black or so silky. He stood mesmerized, watching the brush ripple through the glossy cascade. "I didn't remember your hair to be so very long."

"Yes, very long and very unfashionable. Will you next tell me to cut it? My aunt told me to. And so did Eve. We must be stylish, mustn't we?"

He gritted his teeth. "I like it the way it is."

"What a surprise!"

"Damme, madam! Give me a chance!"

"At what?"

"At being friends! At being a kind husband . . . I don't know!"

"Very well," she murmured.

He let out a pent up breath. "Thank you. Now will you have a glass of sherry with me?"

"Somehow I cannot picture your choosing sherry."

"I thought you would prefer it."

She shrugged her delicate shoulders.

Relieved, he uncorked the wine and filled the glasses. "Will you join me on the sofa?"

"I think not. Since you have dismissed my maid, I must braid my own hair for the night."

"Leave it loose. It is so very beautiful. Sit and talk with me, Ashley."

She considered deliberately. "If you wish."

"I do. Very much."

Tightening her new emerald silk dressing gown, she stood and faced him. He was so handsome in the sky blue robe, which matched his eyes. Ashley's irritation began to thaw. When he grinned boyishly, she couldn't help smiling ever so slightly.

"You look pretty," he told her. "Is the robe new?"

Despite the warmth of the August night, her skin prickled with goose bumps. "Yes. Francine has begun to finish some things."

She preceded him out of her dressing room and into

her chamber, sitting down on the sofa and tucking her bare feet under her. His fingers touched hers as he handed her the glass of sherry, sending a delicious tingle through her nerves. She wished she had put on her nightgown after her bath, instead of immediately slipping into the robe. The thin silk fabric made her feel exposed.

The marquess sat down, careful not to sit too close to her. He smiled. "Are you satisfied with Francine's work?"

"Oh yes!" She lowered her eyes. "You were right. I do look ever so much better in a well-cut dress of fashion. And the fabrics and colors are most flattering. Thank you."

"I shall be anxious to see you in them."

"I hope that you will be pleased."

"I'm sure I will, but we must discuss another subject. I believe you know what it is, Ashley, and I think you will find your fears to be out of proportion to what is involved."

Her eyes locked fearfully on his.

"I know it will be so." He refilled his glass and questioningly held the bottle out to her.

She shook her head, still staring into his eyes. "Is it your intention . . . tonight . . ."

"Is there a reason we should not?"

"I am frightened of you!"

"Ashley," he said gently, extending his arm along the back of the sofa, "come here."

She hesitated, the blood draining from her face.

"Please?"

Warily she moved over next to him, sitting prim and very straight.

He slipped his arm around her, feeling her tension. "I am very much aware of your innocence of men, but you are my wife, and we have probably waited longer than most newly married couples."

"I am aware of my duty, sir." She looked up at him pitifully. "Perhaps if you did it very quickly."

The marquess couldn't keep from laughing. "Like a dose of bad medicine?"

"It's not funny!" Ashley wailed. "It might work!"

He cuddled her close. "My dear, you are so preciously innocent, but surely you must know that even I cannot just . . . jump into it like a servant running on an errand."

"You cannot?" she asked candidly. "I thought that men . . ."

"No. Men must . . . anybody must . . . My God, I've never felt so inadequate!"

"I'm sorry!"

"It is due to my lack of experience, I'm sure," he said cynically. "I have never met a lady like you!"

"Somehow I do not believe that to be a compliment!" she cried heatedly.

"Ashley, you once told me that no man had ever kissed you."

"That was not a lie!"

"No, I know that it wasn't! Didn't any man even hold your hand?"

"I was busy running an estate! I had no time for that sort of thing!" She sat forward on the edge of the sofa. "And I have no time to be insulted by you. I told you not to marry me! I believe you should have married one of your mistresses!"

He grinned. "Whatever for? I find you utterly fascinating."

"You're quizzing me."

"No, I'm not. Come back here." He drew her into the circle of his arm. "Let us finish our drinks."

"And then?"

"And then, Ashley, I intend to make love to you."

Nine

Ashley awakened lying on her side with her back toward her husband, the marquess's arm cuddling her very close and his breath ruffling her hair. Fully unclothed, she looked with longing at her dressing gown where it had been tossed into a silken heap on the floor. Even after the events of the past night, she was rather abashed by this intimacy, but realized that it, like all the other, was something else she must grow accustomed to.

She had been foolish to be so frightened of their lovemaking. She hadn't particularly enjoyed every part of it, but she had the distinct impression that, when she grew used to it, she might like it very well. The thought of it warmed her body. Moreover, what she and Brandon had shared, and what she had felt, brought forth an overwhelming affection for her new husband. Shyly, she covered his hand with her own and squeezed it gently.

He stirred, mumbling. "You are awake?"

"Um."

He turned her over onto her back, propping himself on his elbow and lazily caressing her.

"I think you like this," he said.

She flushed deeply, her skin burning at his touch. Self-consciously, she closed her eyes.

"Do you?"

"Your touch is nice," she admitted.

He chuckled deep in his throat. "Are you still afraid of me?"

"Not so much."

"But a little?"

"You are so very strong and so . . . so masculine." She looked through her thick eyelashes at his bare chest.

"Would you rather I be otherwise?"

"Not at all!" Impulsively she reached up to stroke his golden hair. "I was so foolish to fear you, but I wish . . ."

She couldn't tell him. She did not dare tell him how greatly their lovemaking had changed her feelings toward him, and how much she wished it would begin to make him love her too. He had proclaimed himself immune to love. How could he engage in an act so personal and so private without feeling something of the emotion?

"Ashley?"

She met his gaze.

"You have given me a very sweet gift. I have never been . . . the first."

She hugged him joyfully. "And you shall be the only."

"I hope so."

"There can be no question of it! Surely you cannot doubt that?"

"You are a very desirable woman, my dear," he said quietly. "There will be many temptations."

Ashley eyed him with horror. "Oh, no. I shall never break my marriage vows."

Momentarily, he looked uncomfortable, then quickly changed the subject. "I am starving. Ring for your maid, Ashley, and ask that breakfast be sent up. I'm too relaxed to go downstairs."

"All right." She scurried from bed, and as quickly as possible, donned her dressing robe before jerking the bell rope.

Brandon laughed at her haste in covering herself. "Such modesty with your husband!"

"You must not expect everything at once," she retorted, smiling and handing him his own robe. "Please put this on, Brandon. The sight of you, unclothed, even under the covers, might overset Jane's sensibilities."

"Oh, but I am so comfortable! And it's hot in here."

"Please?" she begged sweetly.

"All right, madam! I can see that I must teach you to be a bit naughty. Besides, Jane is only a servant."

"A *female* servant, Brandon."

"I'm sure that it makes no difference to me, but very well, I shall do it." He took the garment and threw back the sheets.

Ashley hurriedly turned her back. "Perhaps I shall teach you a small measure of decency."

He rose to her challenge. "No! Not decency again!" Grasping her around the waist, he tumbled her into the bed. "Teach me now, if you dare!"

"Beast! Let me up!" Giggling, she struggled to escape, as Jane's knock sounded on the door.

Laughing, he let her go. "Don't you think your Jane is aware of what we've been doing?"

"Brandon, please. Behave!" Blushing vividly, she straightened her dressing gown and glanced imploringly at him.

"Only because you have been so very sweet." His eyes glittering, he got up and, with great dignity, crossed the room, to the sofa.

Ashley sighed, shaking her head. "Come in, Jane," she called brightly.

After a leisurely breakfast, the marquess excused himself to go down town to finish up his business affairs before they departed for the country. With Ashley's wardrobe nearly completed and only one more fitting required by Francine, they should be able to leave for Havard Hall within a few days. Brandon was becoming anxious to escape London's oppressive heat, and he knew that Ashley would enjoy his fine estate in Kent.

Aside from the investments which needed his attention, there were two other items he wanted to tend to. Most importantly he wished to buy his wife an exquisite piece of jewelry to commemorate their first night of lovemaking. Secondly, he hadn't forgotten her interest in hiring someone to catalog the Shandal documents. He would see to that today, and also put Reeves in search of an artist. All the Shandal women had their portraits painted upon the occasion of their marriage.

After he left, Ashley bathed, washed her hair, and sat by the window, wishing her husband would come home and knowing that his business would occupy him the greater part of the day. Now that the ice had thawed between them, she was anxious to spend as much time with him as possible and get to know him better. She'd hoped he'd put off his errands and spend the day with her, but she knew she must be very careful of making many demands on him. Just because they had spent the night together didn't mean that she could keep him in her pocket. It would take much more to make him believe that he couldn't bear to leave her for one single moment. Someday, she swore to herself, she would accomplish it. Her rakehell husband was going to fall in love with his wife.

In the midafternoon, her monotonous day was cheered by a delivery from Francine. Among the pretty garments were her riding habits, accompanied by a pair of shining boots from the shoemaker. Delighted, she pushed aside a beautiful ball gown and picked up one of the trim jackets and its matching skirt. "I shall try this on at once!"

Soon, her boredom forgotten, she preened in front of the mirror, admiring the deep green habit and appreciating how much the color brought out the green of her eyes. "Jane, think how long it has been since I had a new habit! I was little more than a child. And look at my hat!" She set the plumed creation saucily on her head.

The maid smiled at her mistress's excitement. "It's right pretty, ma'am. You'll be the most stylish horse-woman in the country."

"The country? I think I shall go riding at once!"

"Now?" Jane asked with uncertainty.

"Yes! I have never been to Shandal's mews, and it's time I did."

"Maybe you'd better wait for his lordship," her abigail advised.

"Fiddlesticks! Who knows when he'll be home? I'm so very bored and I'm going riding." With that, she tripped out of the room and down the stairs, the heels of her new boots clicking merrily.

John saw her approach in riding attire and drew a deep breath. He wished his father hadn't gone off on errands with Lord Shandal, leaving him in charge. Better still, he wished desperately that the marquess would return at this very moment.

"Hello, John," his mistress said cheerfully. "I've come to ride. May I see the horses?"

"Good afternoon, my lady." He made his bow. "Of course you may see 'em, but I'm not sure which horse his lordship would want you to ride."

"Well, he isn't here, so I shall choose." She stepped into the cool stable and breathed deeply the smell of the sweet hay.

Stableboys and grooms snapped to attention at this

very unexpected visit from their marchioness. None of the Shandal ladies had ever before entered their sanctum. Frozen with apprehension, they stood uncomfortably until she nodded and smiled at them, putting them at their ease.

"What a well-cared for stable!"

"Thank you, my lady," John replied, eyeing her with uncertainty, as he trailed stiffly in her wake.

She wandered down the aisle, seemingly happy and much at home in the country-like setting with ordinary, country-like people. The first beautiful horse she saw was a tall black with a small white star on his forehead. Flickering his ears, he blew at her and returned disdainfully to his hay. "Oh, you are so very grand," she laughed. "Much too fine to give me more than a passing look!"

" 'Tis the marquess's favorite, ma'am," John said firmly. "Definitely not a lady's horse."

"He's lovely," she breathed, "but I suppose they all are. You should have seen what I was forced to ride at home."

John shuddered, picturing a stolid, country nag, probably more at home behind a plow than under a saddle. There would be no horse in the London stable suitable to his lady's abilities. If he could only convince her to wait or somehow delay her until the marquess came home!

She moved to the next box. The pretty chestnut turned his hindquarters to the door and favored her with laid back ears.

"Temperamental, my lady. Smooth in the hunt field, but not a lady's horse."

The next horse, also a chestnut, had a friendlier disposition, as did the bay in the stall beyond. John hurriedly told her that neither were ladies' mounts.

She appeared to begin to grow frustrated, when a

fine slender gray head with large liquid brown eyes
thrust out of the last box in the row and looked curiously toward her. "A gray! I've always loved grays!"

"One of the marquess's race horses. He wasn't fast
enough, so Lord Shandal had ideas o' making him into
a hunter," John explained.

She hurried to the stall. "He's the prettiest of all,"
she said, stroking the velvety muzzle.

"But not a lady's horse. Just off the track, y'know."

"Please saddle him, John," she requested. "I shall
choose him. He seems perfectly mannered."

His heart leapt to his mouth. "He's a race horse, my
lady! He's used to running. We've only just got him
here. I don't know anything about him."

"Don't be so wary," she scoffed. "I'm a good rider."

"Maybe the bay, ma'am, would be a better choice,"
he said desperately.

"No, it shall be him," she answered briskly. "Besides,
you said that the bay wasn't a lady's horse either. What
is the gray's name?"

"Dancer," he said in a small voice.

"Dancer," she murmured. "Well then, lead him out
please."

"My lady . . ." John began, drawing himself up to his
full height and squaring his shoulders. "Per'aps you'd
better wait for my father, at least. He's head coachman.
I don't 'ave the authority!"

She cut him an amused glance. "But I do! I shall take
full responsibility. See? You have witnesses to the fact."
She gestured towards the assembled collection of wide-
eyed servants. "Saddle him at once."

Awed by her note of command, John nodded the
order. "He'll be a puller," he muttered.

"Then I shall pull back!" Leaving the stable, she
waited in the yard, impatiently tapping her knee with
her whip.

Bidding farewell to all his hopes of becoming the marquess's head coachman when his father retired, John tried once more to discourage his mistress as the gray and the bay were led outside. "My lady, if you'd reconsider. I do fear the marquess's opinion of this!"

"I shall tend to him," she said bravely. "I refuse to spend the rest of the day cooped up in the house." She stepped up to Dancer. "Give me a leg up, please."

With a vision of her crumpled body lying in the London streets, her neck broken, John took the small foot in his hand and lifted her onto the tall, restless animal. Quickly he mounted the bay and took the leadline from the stableboy.

"I shall not be led like a child," she warned. "I have told you that I am a good rider, and you must believe me."

"Let 'im go!" John rasped, exasperated.

She nodded with satisfaction, gathering up her reins and touched the horse lightly with her heel. The gray plunged forward, nearly unseating her. Regaining her balance, she settled him to a tippy-toed walk. "Ah, he feels good today!"

"Madam, he's too much!" John cried. "Please, my lady, let us wait for the marquess!"

"He is very sensitive, but I shall be ready for him next time," she said mildly, ignoring his plea. "Come, John, let us be on our way."

In hopes of stopping trouble as soon as it threatened, he rode closer to her than would have been considered proper for his position, but by the time they had reached the park, he was inclined to give her a grudging credit for her skillful handling of the beast. The gray was very fresh and skitterish to the London traffic, but the marchioness kept him well in hand, without irritating his high spirits and causing him to fight her. Still,

John could see the urge to run in the animal's taut hindquarters.

"Being turned out in the pasture would benefit him immensely," his mistress commented, as they rode through the gate of St. James Park. "He needs more exercise."

"Yes, ma'am."

"Let us trot a bit first, then we shall give him a good canter."

'More like a wild gallop', the servant thought, but set his horse after her.

Keeping her heel away from his side and letting up slightly on the reins, she eased the powerful gelding into a ground-eating trot, a little faster than she cared to be going, but still controlled. Not being familiar with the area, she kept the horse on the longest, straightest stretches she could see in an attempt to take the edge off his high spirits. In what seemed like no time they approached another gate to Hyde Park. She pulled up, looking back at him.

"John, is there any sort of circular area where I could canter him?"

"Just the bridle paths, ma'am," he told her, hoping against hope that she was beginning to weary of the high spirited horse, and, being unable to take the mettle out of him, would decide to proceed home as decorously as possible.

"Hm! I can't ride on the grass?"

"No, ma'am! There's a law."

"Well, then, I suppose I'll have to take my chances like this." Turning away from the gate, she touched the horse with her heel. The gray responded, bounding forth into a gallop, not the easy canter she had desired.

"My lady!" John cried wildly as she flew past him. "Pull 'im up!"

* * *

Knowing that it wasn't difficult to stay on a running horse, Ashley felt no fear. Indeed, what she really experienced was exhilaration. With the wind blowing in her face, threatening to blow off her well-pinned hat, and the flowing strength of the fit horse beneath her, she knew a freedom such as she had not experienced since the days before Eve had come to Oakwood Manor. It was probably unseemly to carry on so in the park, and she was frightening the wits out of John, but for the moment, she just didn't care. After all the recent upheavals in her life, this was exactly what she needed.

Unseeingly, she swept past another horseman, driving him off the path. As she careened around a corner, leaning into it to maintain her balance, she became conscious of John's cries in the background as he, riding at the bay's top speed, began to gain ground. His desperate shouts bringing her back to her senses, she pulled up.

"He's a delight, John!" she called over her shoulder. "Don't look so grim. It was a lovely gallop!"

"My lady, the marquess!" He was close to tears at the absolute horror of it.

"Where?"

"Behind us, ma'am! You ran him off the path!"

Ashley laughed, looking past him to see her husband coming at a strong canter.

"I'll be sacked!" John shrilled.

"No, you won't. I won't allow it," she airily promised, raising a gloved hand to greet her lord.

Brandon halted, concern written on his face until he saw her brilliant smile. "My dear, are you in the habit of riding down your fellow equestrians?"

"Only if they are in the habit of blocking the path, sir!" She tossed her head, unaware of how pretty she looked with her rosy cheeks and shining eyes. The powder-green plume on her hat bobbed flirtatiously.

He watched her with appreciation. "In the future, I shall take care to avoid doing so. Tell me, was that a complete runaway or a controlled runaway?" He glanced pointedly at Dancer. "I last seem to recall that animal bearing down the home stretch at Ascot."

Ashley blushed prettily. "That was a controlled, most exhilarating gallop, my lord."

"Evidently! Your cheeks are blooming beautifully."

Her fingers threaded through Dancer's steely-gray and white multicolored mane. Remembering her high-handed manner in the stable, she wondered what he had been told of her. She could well imagine the consternation which had surely greeted him when he arrived home to find her out riding.

"Brandon," she said softly, "I hope you don't mind that I took your horse. I was bored in the house, and I was so excited about my new riding apparel."

His eyes swept over her attire. "It's quite becoming."

"Are you angry with me?"

"Heaven's no! In the future, however, I would prefer to escort you myself when we are in London. I shouldn't want you to be accosted."

"It would be much more fun for you to escort me," she murmured longingly, "but am I not safe with John?"

"No." Closing his hand over her reins, he leaned over and kissed her mouth.

"Brandon!" She tapped him lightly on the cheek with her crop. "In public? In front of a servant?"

"Your groom, my dear, has withdrawn and quite deserted you. You are entirely at my mercy."

Ashley glanced over her shoulder to witness John leaving the scene at a hasty trot.

Brandon kissed her again. "You see how easy it is to accost you?"

"Oh?" She coyly tilted her chin. "What do you propose to do with me, sir?"

He raised an eyebrow. "I think I shall take you home with me, fair lady, and make love to you."

A delicious warmth swept through her body, making her wish that, instead of sitting on the horse, she was lying in his arms. "I should not object," she said shyly.

The marquess grinned. "Now you see how easy it was for me to accost you? Successfully too, I might add!"

"Oh, you!" She struck at him. "You cheated!"

He caught her whip and kissed the inside of her wrist, making the soft skin tingle. "Indeed I did. Come let us go home. You are all together too irresistible to be out with in public."

And so are you, she thought, riding quietly beside him, marveling at how he had, so easily and completely, overset her world.

Ashley dressed carefully for dinner in a new gown of creamy-white sarsonet with a deep rose, low-cut bodice and puffy little sleeves. Of her new clothes, her husband had seen only her in a dressing gown and the green riding habit. Brandon would be in for a surprise when he saw how modish his new marchioness had become.

She took great pains with her hair, having Jane brush it to a deep rich shine, then pin it up in different styles. Finally, she settled on a smooth and hopefully sophisticated version of a knotted coif she had seen in *La Belle Assemblee.* Looking at it in all different angles with her hand mirror, she pronounced her toilette complete.

"How do I look, Jane?"

"Splendid, ma'am. You'll capture his full attention."

"Only because I shall have no competition for it," she said wryly. "Oh, Jane, I wish I were a Beauty!"

The maid gave a long-tiring shake of her head. "My lady, you're pretty enough for him or any other man."

She took a last long look in the mirror. "I enjoyed his company today. He was very congenial and ever so charming." She blushed a little, thinking of how their day had started. "He wasn't angry about my riding, but he did say that he would prefer to escort me himself when we are in the city. And he gave me the gray horse! Can you believe it? Now I have a horse of my very own."

"I'm glad you're happy, ma'am. You deserve it." Jane smiled fondly at her young mistress.

Cheerfully Ashley went downstairs and into the salon to meet her husband. He was sitting in a large winged chair of gold brocade and contemplating the brandy he was swirling around in his glass. Shutting the door behind her, she paused.

Brandon looked up, his expression of meditation changing to one of pure delight. "My dear, you look lovely." Standing, he crossed the room to her and, tucking her arm in his, escorted her to the sofa.

"Do I truly?" she couldn't help asking anxiously.

"Yes you do," he firmly assured her.

"Francine has done wonders."

"Of course, but she couldn't have done it without the proper framework for her fashions."

"Nor the money," Ashley said honestly. "Thank you, Brandon. Thank you very much."

"Adorning you is a pleasure, but the dress needs something." He picked up a box from the sofa table. "I told you that you had given me a very sweet gift, Ashley. I'd like to give you one too, though not as valuable, I'm afraid."

"You have already given me so much!" She opened the box and gazed inside at pearl earrings, bracelet, and necklace with a diamond heart-shaped clasp. "How pretty!" she cried. "I shall wear them immediately."

He took the necklace and put it around her neck, his fingers warming the skin at her neck when he fastened the clasp. "I must show you the Shandal jewels. You may wear any of them whenever you wish, but most of them are too grand for anything less than a ball. Besides, I want you to have some things of your own. You haven't much jewelry, have you?"

She shook her head. "Only trifles, except for what you have given me. I once had a pretty necklace that had belonged to my grandmother. She had given it to me personally, but Eve claimed it was family jewelry and took it."

"What!"

"It's of no matter," she smiled, attaching her earrings, "and it's probably sold by now. I wouldn't have given it another thought, except that it had been Grandmother's and had sentimental value."

The marquess set his jaw.

"I do hope Deron will be successful at Oakwood Manor. It could be a fine estate." She hesitated, noting his expression. "Brandon, are you angry?"

"I do not care for your sister-in-law's treatment of you."

"You are thinking of Grandmother's necklace? Pray don't give it another thought. It isn't worth the irritation."

"Perhaps we can redeem it."

"I don't want to think about it," she said unhappily, remembering how Deron had blamed her for his difficulties and how he had approached her for money. She wanted the Madisons to stay away from her husband, and *vice versa*, for as long as possible. Any opening would give her brother the opportunity to go back on his word and ask the marquess for a loan. She needed the time to make Brandon care for her first, or he would think her nothing but a huge debit to his bank account. She herself had already cost him a great deal. She couldn't bear for her family to do the same.

"Is there something else?" he asked, as if reading her mind.

"No, I simply do not want Eve Madison to think that she has succeeded in annoying me to any great degree." She took his hand and touched it to her cheek. "Let us think of something more pleasant. Tell me about Havard Hall. When will we be able to go there? I'm very excited about it!"

Ten

The trip to Havard Hall, in contrast to her first journey with the Marquess of Shandal, was relaxed and happy for Ashley. Their days and nights together had made her comfortable and affectionate with him. Over the past few days, she had begun to learn his likes and dislikes and, though he was usually even-tempered, she could sense when a mood made him touchy and irritable.

All in all, she was happy with her marriage. Her husband was considerate, generous, and seemed fond of her. His business affairs well in hand, he went out of his way to think of things to please and entertain her. In conversation, he seemed to respect her opinion. And in their lovemaking, he brought her beyond all boundaries of pleasure.

She knew that she still had much to learn about Brandon and about her new way of life. Despite his portrayal of a kind husband, his previous reputation loomed large in her mind. She wondered if the day would come when he would grow bored with her and return to his previous ways. She didn't know what she would do if that happened. In fact, it was so painfully shattering that she couldn't even bear to think about it.

She supposed that someday she might have to face the matter, but for now, she concentrated on making herself pleasing to him. She dressed with care so as to be becoming at all times. She maintained a cheerful demeanor and listened with interest to whatever he had to say. Often she touched him as she was doing now, sitting beside him on the seat of the carriage, her arm linked sweetly through his.

"We are just now turning onto the estate," he told her, breaking their peaceful silence.

She smiled up at him. "I'm glad. I've been so looking forward to it!"

"Weary?"

"Not now. There is going to be too much to see!"

The approach to Havard Hall began with a forested area of massive trees enclosed along the public road by a tall, savagely impenetrable blackthorn hedge. The wood was clean of deadfalls and underbrush as far as could be seen, creating a cool, inviting place to walk or ride. Over all hung the lightly pungent, acidic aroma of rotting mold.

Further on, the woodland thinned to an avenue of ancient oaks, gnarled and grotesque with age. Beyond this fringe of trees lay a gently rolling greensward. Three does with their fawns, grazing in the distance, lifted their heads in dainty alarm as the carriage passed, then returned to the serious business of eating. Their seeming tameness attested to the fact that the marquess's gamekeeper was successful in his battle against poachers.

"Do you hunt the deer?" Ashley asked, feeling a touch of sorrow for the beautiful beasts.

Brandon shook his head. "I dislike venison. To my father's dismay, I never liked killing for the mere sport of it. He was an avid hunter and a keen shot. I suppose I was a disappointment to him, although I do like to bird hunt occasionally, and I foxhunt of course."

"I agree with you. One shouldn't kill for simple amusement. The deer are so very pretty! Did you please your father in other ways?"

A shadow crossed his face. "I don't know. Jamie is

more like Father. He likes to hunt and fish, and he's interested in crops and the like. A country gentleman! You should have married him, Ashley. You'd have been much happier."

"Oh no!" she squeezed his arm. "I could not be any happier than I am right now!"

The carriage clattered across a bridge over a small brook, drew up a soft rise, and came in sight of the house. Unable to control a gasp, Ashley stared open-mouthed at the magnificent structure, another testament to her husband's great wealth. "Brandon, may we stop for a moment?"

At his signal, the vehicle pulled to a halt. "Would you like to step out?" he asked.

"May we?"

"Of course." He got out and handed her down, leading her away from the drive to a an excellent vista. "Welcome home, my dear."

Havard Hall stood a full four stories high in pure Elizabethan splendor, its architecture untampered with over the years. Its central structure was flanked by massive wings, fronted with half-round towers topped with crenellation. Since there was no real need for fortification at the time of its erection, the builders had placed a multitude of long, large windows, bowed on the towers, all boasting a myriad of glittering small glass panes. Lush green terraces, complete with formal boxwood topiary, contrasted richly with the pink brick facade.

"Do you like it?"

Overwhelmed, Ashley found herself tightly gripping the marquess's arm. "It is the most beautiful house I have ever seen!"

"You said that about the town house," he laughed, kissing her fingertips.

"But I had not seen this! Oh, Brandon, it must be the finest home in all England."

"There are many who would dispute you, my dear, but look closely. Do you notice that it is designed in the shape of an 'E'? My ancestor, who built it, was a great favorite with Queen Elizabeth, and so he honored her."

"Yes, I do see it! My, this house must be noted in all the guidebooks. Do travelers stop to see it?"

"I confess I don't know. You must ask the Collinses."

"Who are . . . ?"

"Collins is the butler; his wife is the housekeeper. They've been here forever, and their fathers before them. I am afraid that you won't find this staff nearly so efficient as the one in London." He glanced at her cautiously. "Many of these people are old retainers. It's difficult to exact obedience from those who have participated in one's upbringing."

"Indeed," she replied, reading his expression of concern and wondering if it was for her or the servants. "The older servants at Oakwood Manor had a way of telling me what to do, not *vice versa*. And they were usually right!"

"Exactly, and sometimes they can be most impertinent."

"Yes. You grew up here then?"

"I was born here. Jamie was born in London, but we both lived here until we went up to Harrow. We were little devils!"

Ashley smiled, picturing two beautiful golden-haired boys darting in and out of mischief. "You were probably too adorable to be serious devils."

"Hold your opinion, my dear! I'm sure you will hear numerous tales of the outlandish rigs we ran!" Brandon escorted her back to the carriage. "I suppose we both were spoiled brats."

"If so, it is no wonder. You've had everything. What a wonderful place for children to grow up! But then, the country always is. I pity the child forced to grow up in town."

"Yes." His eyes glinted with mischievous memories. "The whole estate fell victim to our depredations. Our bottoms were often sore from punishment! Being a country gentleman, Father dealt in riding crops. What was good for a recalcitrant horse was good enough for his own roguish colts. My sister, though often equally guilty, escaped. He didn't believe in flogging fillies."

"She must have felt very superior."

"Beyond a doubt! But we would lie in wait and thrash her ourselves when first we had the opportunity. Then she would report to Father, and the whole process would begin again."

Ashley laughed heartily. "I was sorry that your sister was unable to attend our wedding. I shall be anxious to meet her, and to see your mother and brother again."

"Perhaps we can have a family Christmas here at Havard," he said thoughtfully, then grinned self-consciously. "Good God, I don't think I've ever initiated a family gathering. What are you doing to me, little witch?" he added, half to himself.

"I would like a Christmas party above all things," she smiled, "and this is the most perfect setting for it." She leaned toward the window as the carriage drew closer to the manor. "I suppose it is a tradition that the heir be born here at Havard?"

He shot her a rather wild look. "To my understanding, yes, but as I have told you, my knowledge of the family history is not extensive. By the way, I didn't forget your suggestion of cataloguing the old records. My man of business is searching for a qualified person to do it. Perhaps you will see skeletons rattling in the closet at Havard."

"That's wonderful!" Impulsively she hugged him.

"I'm so proud that I could contribute an idea that you liked!"

The marquess smiled at her girlish enthusiasm and surreptitiously straightened his mussed cravat. "My dear, I have the feeling that this is not the last idea you will contribute."

Before the horses could draw up to the main entrance, the door opened to a flurry within as the servants, who had spotted the entourage at a distance, assembled in the great hall. There was a hum of anticipation, which even reached the ears of the occupants of the carriage. The footman formally let down the steps and opened the vehicle door.

Ashley clasped Brandon's hand. "Oh, I do hope I make a good impression."

"I think they are going to love you." He stepped out first, held out his arms and lifted her down. The crowd inside surged forth slightly to catch a view of their new marchioness. Smiling he led her up the steps and at the last moment, swung her up and over the threshold. The servants applauded.

"My dear, your staff," he introduced. "Old friends, your new marchioness."

"How do you do?" she said in her soft voice, her anxiety shown only by the way she clutched his arm. "I am so glad to be here. You see, I am a country girl at heart!" She glanced up at her husband, hoping to see approval in his eyes, and received an encouraging nod. "I shan't be able to remember all of your names at once, but I promise you that I have a quick memory so it won't be long."

There were expressions of pleasure throughout the group. "Very well done," the marquess quietly complimented her, as he began the personal introductions with the Collinses.

Ashley was exhausted by the time she had spoken

with and taken the hand of each person in the hall. There were many more servants than there had been at the London house and infinitely more than there had been on the entire estate at Oakwood Manor. Her mind was boggled by all their names and duties, especially since so many of them bore the same surnames. Employment at the Hall was definitely a family affair.

Despite her weariness, she was glad to be among country people again. The staff at Havard did not act nearly so grand as the London servants did. Here, she would probably become as much involved with the matters of their lives as she had done with the Oakwood people. It would only be a matter of time before she heard of this one or that one who needed some care or assistance. She hoped that Brandon wouldn't mind.

After she had met them all, he led her to a cheerful salon, seated her and poured her a glass of sherry. "I believe that you could use this."

"I certainly could," she admitted. "Did I do all right?"

"Admirably!" He filled his own glass with his favorite brandy. "You are very patient. After the trip and all of this fuss, you would probably have rather retired to your rooms for a bath and a nap. Instead, your selfish husband drags you in here to keep him company."

"I like being with you," she protested, "and I am not at all tired!"

"Well I am." Brandon heaved a deep breath and sat down beside her. With a quick jerk he removed the intricate waterfall arrangement of his cravat. "I'm tired and these damn new boots are hurting my feet."

She set down her glass, dropped to her knees in front of him and began to tug at his Hessian.

"What are you doing?"

"Taking off your boots to ease your feet."

"You are a lady of many talents. Are you indeed a valet?"

"When the need arises." She looked up at him dolefully. "Besides, I fear you are becoming irritable so I'm going to make you comfortable."

He caught her eye, a slow grin forming at the corners of his mouth. "If you were to make me truly comfortable, you would not stop with my boots."

She ignored him, pulling off one boot and then the other. "Now, don't your feet feel better?"

"Infinitely so, but need has arisen elsewhere."

"Brandon, you are without shame!"

He sighed. "I cannot help it."

"You must," she said firmly. "I'm sure we won't keep town hours here, so our supper is probably almost ready. The kitchen staff has no doubt prepared something very special. We cannot disappoint them by being late."

"Country hours be damned!"

"Perhaps." Smiling, she positioned herself on his lap, eyes twinkling with merriment. "But you must remember that country nights are very long."

Ashley's days at Havard were filled with happiness. The marquess spent much of his time with her and when he was busy, there was still plenty for her to do.

Her first occupation was that of exploring the house. She soon realized that this was no easy task. Unlike many great country homes, Havard Hall had no closed off areas. All of the scores of rooms were kept ready for use at any time. The mammoth staff necessary to keep them well-maintained had to be a tremendous drain on the marquess's purse. When she mentioned closing the little used west wing for matters of economy, he gave her his usual bland reply, "You are the mistress; you must manage the house as you see fit," but he added, grinning, "You shall also be the one to decide which servants are to be sent away."

That, she couldn't do. Reasoning that those who were let go would probably be forced to live on Brandon's charity anyway, she decided that it was more profitable to keep them working. However, she did embark on a practice to make sudden appearances to assure herself that they were indeed earning their salaries. At first it dismayed the staff to have their marchioness popping in at any moment. Then as they grew accustomed to it, they began to enjoy the visits, for their lady always took time for a friendly chat, inquiring about the well-being of themselves and their families. If, however, she noticed dust, dirt or tarnish, she didn't neglect to mention that either. As a result, the house began to shine as it had never shone before.

There was one point of economy on which she did insist. She cut back on the elaborate meals. Seeing that Brandon was an indifferent eater, sometimes not even tasting the great variety of dishes served to him, she gave orders that the chef limit himself to a smaller sampling of honest country fare. If the marquess noticed, he said nothing, and she was far happier not to be faced with the great amount of waste. The chef, who decided that he was insulted and briefly threatened to quit, and some of the servants, who were in the habit of taking home vast quantities of leftovers, were the only ones disappointed.

Along with her household explorations, Ashley began to familiarize herself with the entire estate itself. The marquess usually accompanied her on these forays. They had begun riding together every morning after breakfast, and the event became the highlight of their day. He and John had helped her with Dancer until the gray had gained a softer disposition, and Brandon had given her some pointers on her own riding.

He was an excellent horseman, better, she had to admit, than she would ever be. She envied his ease and grace in the saddle, and the skillful way he handled the most fractious mount without ever once losing his balance. One day, coming home from a long ride, she told him so and asked, "How did you ever learn it?"

"I don't know." He shrugged. "Perhaps from riding bareback when I was a child. Jamie and I loved to do that."

"Bareback," she considered. "I would have to wear breeches."

"Which you do not have," he laughed. "Content yourself, my dear. You ride very well."

She smiled engagingly. "You could lend me some."

"I shall do nothing of the sort!" he cried, shocked.

"Please, Brandon, it sounds like fun!"

"No! Besides, your bottom is too big."

"How dare you!" she cried hotly. "My bottom is not too big!"

"Not precisely *too* big. I like your bottom! It's a lovely bottom, but it wouldn't fit into my breeches."

"Let us try. I think I could get them on."

"It is beyond all decency, Ashley," he replied a bit haughtily. "Ladies do not wear breeches. My marchioness shall not! What would people think?"

"No one need know. I can wear them under my skirt. When we reach an area of privacy, I can take off my skirt and the saddle, and you can teach me how to ride bareback." She nodded smugly. "You see? It's quite simple."

"And who, pray, will explain to Lindsey why my breeches are covered with horse hair?"

"Why, he would think you did it."

"Do you forget that my valet assists me in undressing? He would know I didn't do it."

"Oh can't you take your own clothes off?" she asked impertinently.

"Yes, my dear," he said wickedly, "and I have done so on numerous occasions. Not however, under ordinary circumstances. It's hard to get my boots off."

She flushed. "I will help you!"

"He'd still see my breeches. No, Ashley!"

"I suppose someone would catch me if I cleaned them," she mused.

"Yes indeed. Lindsey keeps good account of my clothes. He'd miss them immediately."

They rode on in silence for a few minutes before Ashley exclaimed. "I know what we could do!"

"No," the marquess said dryly.

"At least do me the honor of listening. This would work! We could ride out to a private place, you could take off your breeches, and I'll put them on. Later you can simply tell Lindsey that you were showing me how you and your brother used to ride."

"Oh? Am I to stand there in a field wearing nothing but my drawers? Or am I to put on your skirt?"

"I didn't think of that," she giggled.

"Your ideas will see me thrown in jail. Forget it, Ashley. It won't work."

"I shall think of something."

"That's what I fear the most." They pulled up at the stable. Brandon dismounted and lifted her down. Impulsively, he lightly kissed her mouth. "I think I married a hoyden."

She laughed merrily, tilting her head to study him. "And what have I married? A stuffy old marquess with no sense of daring!"

"Old? Ashley, be kind. Such a setdown!"

"That is what you get for saying that I have a big bottom!"

He slipped his arm around her waist and led her toward the house. "I also said that I liked it." Sliding his hand downward, her gave her derriere a small pinch.

She squealed. "Brandon! Someone will see!"

"So much for stuffiness," the marquess drawled. "What is next? Daring? I shall have to think on that one."

"I know how you could prove your daring."

"Yes, yes. I could lend you my breeches and allow you to ride bareback. Is there no end to this?"

"No."

"Oh very well. If they fit, I will consider it."

Ashley let out with a whoop of delight. "Come, let us try them now!" Before he could change his mind, she hurried him into the house and up the stairs to his bedroom. "Take off your breeches, Brandon!"

"My word, I don't believe I have ever been so forcefully seduced." He cocked his head toward a muffled coughing sound from his dressing room. "Lindsey, is that you?"

"Yes, sir." The valet, his expression strained, emerged.

Ashley turned crimson.

"I was just leaving, my lord. My lady." With a bow, he left the chamber.

"I am mortified!" she cried.

"That is nothing to the embarrassment you would suffer if you were caught wearing my breeches," he grinned mischievously, going into the dressing room and returning with a pair of them. "Here!" He tossed them to her. "Try them on." Draping himself into a chair, his legs dangling over its arms, he prepared to watch.

Disconcerted by his frank gaze, she fumbled at her skirt buttons. "Must you stare so?"

"I find it exceedingly enjoyable. I have never seen you undress."

The skirt fell to the floor, followed by her petticoat, leaving her standing self-consciously in her thin undergarments.

"You have the most delightful legs."

"Do not distract me." She began to tug on the breeches, a process which soon had her giggling.

"You see?" the marquess asked mirthfully. "Your bottom is too big."

"It is not!" Gasping, she managed to fasten a button. "What strange clothes! The seat is too tight, while the waist is too loose."

"Oh dear! Shall I complain to Weston?"

"But you always look as if you were poured into them."

He laughed. "Haven't you ever noticed that men are built differently than women?"

"Hm!" By sucking in and pulling the fabric taut, she finished the buttoning. "There! You see?" she asked triumphantly, turning slowly before him.

"I do. You should see too. Especially from the rear! Very indecent, madam."

"Fiddlesticks, you will be the only one to see me."

"I should hope so! Else I might find myself in a duel for your honor."

She walked toward him, the breeches enhancing the provocative movement of her hips, and seated herself on his knee. "You will teach me to ride bareback. Please?"

He drew her close. "If you will allow me to teach you something else . . . right now."

She bent her head to bestow a very thorough kiss on his lips. "I would enjoy it excessively."

Eleven

The following day dawned beautifully. Ashley, wearing the breeches beneath her skirt, rode out early with her husband, her excitement knowing no bounds. "Tell me, Brandon, how are you going to explain to Lindsey?" she asked curiously. "Have you formulated a ruse?"

"Not at all. I intend to tell Lindsey nothing."

"Just leave him wondering?"

"Exactly." The marquess shrugged. "Can you think of anything better?"

She emulated his gesture, biting her lower lip. "No. You aren't angry, are you?"

"No, Ashley." He flashed her a grin. "I'm merely looking forward to the spectacle you will make of yourself."

She eyed him suspiciously. "You will teach me properly?"

"Certainly I will! But first, if you can cease chewing your lip, let's have a good brisk gallop to take the edge off Dancer's spirits."

Ashley flushed. "I'm sorry. I know that my nibbling is deplorable. It's a nervous habit that I have been unable to break."

He cocked his head sideways, as if to analyze her state of mind. "What are you afraid of?"

"Irritating you," she answered candidly.

"Irritating . . ." He studied her for what seemed like a very long moment. "You do not irritate me, my dear. Quite the contrary."

Her heart skipped a beat. She wished he would expand the comment, but instead, he muttered, "Shall we gallop?"

"I will follow your lead."

Brandon nudged his horse into a canter, gradually extending the pace to a gallop. Ashley followed him for a brief time, then edged up beside him, casting him a brilliant smile. Returning it, he slowed the black. "Are you ready?"

She nodded.

The field he had chosen was far enough from the house and any outbuildings to avoid anything other than deliberate discovery. It was solid too, so that she would not have to be concerned about her mount's footing. She could concentrate entirely upon herself.

Halting, Brandon leapt off and, tucking the black's reins over his arm, lifted his wife down. While she was slipping off her skirt, he removed Dancer's saddle. "There's nothing to this, Ashley," he explained. "It's simply a matter of balance."

She draped her skirt across his saddle. "How shall I mount?"

"I'm going to give you a leg up."

She put her arm across his shoulders and her knee into his hand, letting him toss her up onto the horse. "Oh! It certainly feels different!"

"Just walk at first," he advised. "Think about how he moves."

Ashley followed his suggestion and soon grew bored. "May I trot now?"

"Yes, but be careful." He watched her move the gray into a trot and immediately lose her balance. "Relax, Ashley! The trot is the most difficult. Move with him."

She made one circle and pulled up. "I'm doing terribly!"

"No you're not."

"Am I making a spectacle of myself?"

He shook his head.

"Then I shall continue to try, but Brandon, his backbone is so very uncomfortable."

The marquess grinned. "So you understand why I no longer have any interest in riding bareback?"

"Yes! But I shall give it a chance if it will help me to ride better," she answered valiantly.

He would have to agree that his wife was a determined lady and a good sport. After a few rounds of the trot, she requested a canter. At this, she was much more comfortable.

"I do think this is good for me!" she called, enthused by her success. "I can feel exactly how he moves!"

"Try a figure eight."

At first, the turns adversely effected her balance, but as she continued, she improved enough so that Brandon could settle back and enjoy her fluid movements. Ashley was a good rider. Even before she had attempted this, she had shown herself to be a better horsewoman than any lady he had ever known. He wondered if she had ever been foxhunting. Hopefully she hadn't, and he could introduce her to that as well.

She halted in front of him. "How am I doing?"

"I'm impressed."

"You are?" she cried.

He smiled crookedly. "Well, I'm still not happy about you wearing my breeches, but perhaps you have learned something."

"It has taught me to feel how my horse is moving," she said honestly, "but his backbone is cutting me in two! I shall make a few more circles, then quit."

"As you wish."

She reached down and touched his cheek. "Thank you ever so much."

Absent-mindedly patting his horse as he watched her ride away, Brandon thought of how much he was enjoying her company. After a poor beginning, his marriage was turning out well. Although Ashley could be a challenge, as she had been in this escapade, she was, for the most part, very comfortable. She would make him a good wife and marchioness, and most surely, a wonderful mother for their children.

"Bran! Ashley!"

Brandon whirled to see a horseman top the rise and bear down on them at a hard gallop. Ashley wailed and headed Dancer toward him. The two arrived at nearly the same time.

"What on earth . . . !" Jamie Havard began, staring at his sister-in-law, and then he broke off laughing. "What kind of rig is this?"

"Brandon!" Ashley blushed, nibbling her lip.

He turned his attention to his brother. "This is a lesson in bareback riding, you brat! What are you doing here? Never mind! You are sworn to secrecy!"

"Of course!" Jamie's eyes twinkled. "It's a family matter, yes?" Leaping off his horse, he embraced the marquess. "I've been in the area visiting friends. I couldn't pass by without stopping. Especially to see my new sister!"

"Trust you to come at an inconvenient time," Brandon murmured. "If you had been only ten minutes later."

"Oh, what's wrong with Ashley wearing breeches? I find it charming. Come off that beast, my lady, and give me a hug!"

Smiling bravely, Ashley slipped off the gray, exhibiting her very tightly clad derriere. Brandon felt an odd stab of jealousy. Stepping between them, he thrust her skirt over her head. Ashley looked up at him fearfully.

"I think you will be more comfortable," he said quietly, turning back to Jamie and shielding her while she fastened it about her. "Certainly you couldn't go by without stopping. We hope you'll stay awhile too."

"I shouldn't want to interfere, Bran."

"Not at all! Ashley and I will be glad for your company, won't we, my dear?"

Her skirt secured, she stepped from behind him and slipped her arm through his. "We shall indeed! I am very anxious to know my new family. Brandon has told me so much about your childhood here at Havard."

"Yes, Jamie," he agreed, "and I have made you out to be the very devil. You will have to stay and redeem yourself."

"A few days then." His younger brother grinned. "I would like that above all things!"

"Good!" The marquess clapped him on the back and surrendered Ashley to his brother's hug as he turned to saddle her horse. "Let us go back to the house. If I know you, Jamie, you're probably starving!"

Luncheon was especially cheerful with Jamie's company, although Ashley wished they had returned from their ride in time for her to order the chef to prepare something more elaborate than the cold collation she and the marquess had been in the habit of taking. The thinly sliced ham and roast beef, salad, fruit, and crusty, thick slabs of French bread were delicious, but probably not quite what Jamie was used to being served. Looking at the limited variety of food gracing the buffet, she wondered if she weren't carrying her dislike of waste too far. When her brother-in-law filled his plate with twice as much food as his elder sibling, she felt real alarm. What if he found her table inadequate?

"Brandon and I have been accustomed to having a light lunch," she apologized. "I see you have a better appetite."

"Bran was always a picky eater." Jamie dug into his plateful.

"I believe that Ashley grew tired of sending untasted dishes back to the kitchen. I know I was tired of looking at them," Brandon said with finality. "Please change nothing on account of my brother, dear. He deals more in quantity than variety."

The younger man laughed. "He's right. Our father had simple tastes so we grew up on plain country fare. My word, nothing is quite so good as this mouth-watering Havard ham! Tell me, Bran, does Old Jack still rule the smokehouse?"

"I'm sure I don't know."

"Yes," Ashley answered quietly, "Jack Pollock still does, although his rheumatism troubles him greatly."

The marquess looked at her with some surprise, a question in his eyes.

"I have been meeting some of the people whenever I can," she explained. "I found Jack and his wife Betsey suffering terribly from pain in their joints, though between them, they manage to keep a neat little garden. I've had some salve made for them from an old recipe I brought from Oakwood Manor. I was to take it to them this afternoon."

"I'd like to go," Jamie declared. "I'd like to see Old Jack again. Bran?"

"No thank you. I have some paperwork which has been needing my attention. You two go."

"Are you sure?" Ashley asked. "If you had something else planned, I can send a servant with the salve."

"No, you go ahead."

They finished lunch with much laughter as the two brothers regaled Ashley with tales of their boyish exploits, leaving her in stitches as they left the table. Jamie went to arrange for a gig to be brought around, but Ashley, tucking her arm companionably through her husband's, accompanied him to the library. "It's such a lovely day. Do you really wish to stay indoors?"

He grimaced. "Yes, I've been putting this off for too long as it is."

"You don't mind my visiting the tenants?"

"Not at all. Being the mistress of an estate is something you evidently do well, and you enjoy." He turned her toward him. "So long as you don't neglect its master?"

"You know I could never do that!" Lifting her arms, she encircled his neck. "I would always rather be with you."

He kissed her deeply and thoroughly. "I suppose it is too bad that I am not more like my father. Havard is a fine estate. I hope that it hasn't suffered under my stewardship. The profits haven't, but that is as much as I know. Perhaps you can help me."

"Of course! I would like to do that!"

He grinned. "Tomorrow, I have a meeting with the steward. Perhaps you would like to join us?"

"I'll look forward to it."

"Excellent! Now go along with Jamie, my dear, and get to know him. Even though we're as different as night and day, he means a great deal to me."

"I know that!" Hugging him fondly, she departed.

Ashley fetched her straw bonnet and the basket filled with the salve and some delectable foodstuffs as well, and met Jamie in the driveway. "Had you given up on me?"

"Heaven's no! The gig has only just arrived." He handed her in, then got up beside her, taking the reins.

"I would have liked to have taken you in my curricle. Then you'd have had a grand ride! But I fear that my horses would still be a bit tired from the morning. We were on the road early."

"No matter. Another time perhaps? I've never ridden in a curricle."

"You haven't? Never been out behind Bran's famous bays?" Jamie cried with mock horror. "My dear, your husband has sadly neglected you!"

She laughed. "We've been busy with other equestrian activities."

"Such as riding bareback?" His blue eyes twinkled. "Really, Ashley, you looked marvelous in Bran's breeches, although I don't think he was very happy for me to see you in them."

"No, he wasn't," she admitted, soberly tucking a wisp of black hair behind her ear. "He wasn't very happy about the whole idea, let alone someone seeing me dressed like that. I fear my bareback days have ended."

"Surely he wasn't angry with you?"

"No, not that. I believe he takes more of an 'I told you so' attitude." She shrugged delicately. "It really was a silly scheme, but I made him allow it."

Jamie chortled. "No one *makes* Bran do anything! He was amused by it!"

"He was that," she smiled.

"And entranced," he mused. "He can scarce keep his eyes off you."

"He probably looks at me in disbelief that his life can have altered so," she said dryly, but she had begun to wonder if Brandon was beginning to develop a fondness for her. He seemed to enjoy her company. Now, he had asked for her assistance in matters concerning the estate. And since their first night of lovemaking, he had no longer gone to his own bed. He slept with her.

"You're smiling," Jamie teased.

"I am?"

"You're happy with him, aren't you?"

"More than I ever dreamed of," she murmured, half to herself.

"You're good for him." Jamie reached out to squeeze her hand. "My brother has long needed a settling influence. Maybe you'll make a country gentleman of him yet."

"I rather doubt it. More like, he'll change me into a London lady!"

"I have an idea that you can play both roles with equal success."

"My dear Mr. Havard!" she cried, tossing her head. "You have a most inflated opinion of me. I am not at all sure that I can live up to your ideal."

He laughed, pulling up outside the cottage of Jack and Betsey. "You will, though. In fact, I believe that old Bran is going to lead a very interesting life with you, Ashley."

Jamie was sure that his prediction would come true by the time he and his sister-in-law had visited the elderly retainers and he had taken a circumnavigous route home past some of the favorite old scenes of his childhood. Ashley was nothing less than a sweet, caring, fun-loving lady, with a rich sense of humor and a head on her shoulders. He hoped when he married, it would be to a woman like she.

She had talked kindly with Old Jack and his wife, patiently listening to their stories of Havard Hall and the Havard family. Genuinely complimenting the old man on his skill in the smokehouse and her delight in the product, she cajoled him into agreeing to take on an apprentice to share the labor and to learn the secrets

Cathleen Clare

of his trade. The young man to fill the position would be his choice alone.

When they left, Old Jack drew Jamie aside. "Our new mistress is a special lady, Master James."

"Yes, I believe she is," he enthusiastically agreed.

Turning for the hall, Jamie was sorry that their afternoon was ending, but he was glad that Bran had allowed them that time to get to know each other. Ashley had been so nervous and shy at the time of the wedding that he had scarcely received any impression of her, at all. She was easier in his company now, too, probably because of their afternoon together and also because Bran had evidently talked a good bit about him. He liked his new sister-in-law. He liked her exceedingly well, and he hoped that his brother realized what a priceless gem he had wed.

Brandon's choice of women seemed to lean toward the sultry, petulant sirens. Jamie wondered how anyone could be happy with that sort of woman, but to give the marquess credit, he had to admit that Bran was choosing a mistress instead of a wife when he selected one of those sensual skylarks. Perhaps his brother's ideas were closer to his own when it came to marriage. Maybe he would change his ways as well.

All too soon, he drew up in front of Havard Hall, where a groom rushed to take the horse and a footman assisted his lady from the gig. Still laughing at one of his inane childhood adventure stories, Ashley slipped her arm through his as they went inside together. "Collins," she asked the butler. "Where is my lord?"

"In the library, madam, having tea."

"We are late." Hurriedly she propelled him down the hall and flung open the door.

The marquess looked up with a grin as they entered the room. "Well, James, I had begun to wonder about you. I knew you couldn't be lost, so I was deciding that you had run away with my wife."

Laughing, Jamie raised an eyebrow. "I would like to."

"Oh Brandon," Ashley fluttered, "we've had a wonderful time!" Happily she sat down to pour the tea. "Cream or sugar, Jamie?"

"My brother will probably wish to join me in a glass of brandy, my dear," the marquess said, "although I can see that you have been liquor enough to his head." Standing, he crossed to the sideboard to pour the drink.

Jamie followed. "She's wonderful, you know," he said in an undertone. "You're lucky, Bran."

"I've often thought that she should have married you. She deserves better than me, doesn't she?" he murmured offhandedly.

"I don't think so," he replied urgently. "No one does. What a thought!"

"You're too loyal, little brother." Abruptly, he turned away, then hesitated. "I am glad that you approve."

Jamie nodded emphatically. "I do. One hundred percent!"

Twelve

It rained all evening and night, soaking the dry ground and giving the crops a much needed watering. Brandon awakened to cloudy skies, with the scent of rain and wet, rich earth in the air. The change in weather was welcome, but it just might make them miss their early morning ride together.

Shifting slightly to ease the numbness in his arm where Ashley lay on it, the marquess lazily stroked his wife's soft bare back. With a sleepy, unintelligible murmur, she nestled closer to him, her head snuggling against his collarbone. Lord, she was a little charmer, he thought. Despite all her growing experience, she retained a certain trusting, youthful innocence.

He kissed the top of her head. "Good morning."

"Um . . . is it? Already?" she murmured, hugging him. "It looks so gray outside. Will we ride?"

"I don't know. Let's decide after breakfast."

"I hope we can. The air always smells so fresh and good after a rain."

Turning her over onto her back, he kissed her and swung out of bed, shrugging into his dressing robe. "I'm starving."

"You had a late night, my lord," she teased laughingly.

"As did you, madam." Leaning over the bed, he

kissed her again and pulled the bell rope to summon Jane. "I'll see you at breakfast."

"Shall I dress for riding?"

"Yes, do. We'll go, if at all possible." Passing through the connecting doorway, he entered his own bedroom and greeted Lindsey. "Is it raining?"

"No, sir, not at present."

"Then I shall dress for riding."

"As you wish." While the marquess was washing, the valet laid out his master's undergarments and retrieved a pair of buff breeches and a pristine white linen shirt.

Brandon dressed himself, allowing Lindsey to help him pull on his shining black Hoby boots, and tied his cravat successfully in one try. Slipping into a blue superfine coat, he left the room and descended the stairs to meet Jamie, also dressed for riding, in the breakfast room. "Good morning, little brother."

"Morning, Bran. Be sure to try these muffins. They're light as a feather."

Helping himself to the offerings on the sideboard, he sat down at the head of the table. "For once, Jamie, I think I'm going to eat as much as you."

"Oh, I doubt that. Where's Ashley?"

"She'll be along."

Jamie smiled. "She's a lovely lady. You're growing very fond of her, aren't you, Bran?"

"I suppose one should be fond of one's wife," he answered noncommittally. "Eat your muffins, Jamie, and quit prying. You're going to ride with us, I see."

"Not if you don't want me to. I don't want to get in the way."

"Nonsense!"

"Nevertheless, I hope you'll tell me when you and Ashley want to be alone together."

"We both enjoy your company. Enough said!" He

and Jamie stood as Ashley entered the room, clad in her entrancing green habit.

"Well, gentlemen, it is not raining and shows signs of clearing. So we ride?"

"We ride," Brandon said, "but we'll stay nearby so we can make a dash for home if it starts up again. I'd hate to see you soaked to the skin, my dear."

"Right!" said Jamie cheerfully. "It wouldn't be at all the same as dampening your petticoat!"

"What? Why would I do that?"

He colored. "Many ladies," he began, "dampen their petticoats to . . . uh . . . enhance their appearance."

She curiously tilted her chin. "It sounds rather soggy to me. Why would they do that?"

Jamie glanced helplessly at his brother.

"It makes their dresses cling to them." Brandon grinned. "It shows off their figures to greater advantage."

"Even in the winter?" Ashley asked incredulously. "It seems like a good way to catch cold. I should never do it."

The men laughed. "My dear sister," Jamie smiled, "you have no need to resort to such tricks. Your beauty alone is enough! If you dampened your petticoat, you would have men falling dead around you."

"Fiddlesticks." She applied herself to her breakfast. "Brandon, do you wish me to dampen my petticoat?"

"I wish you to do as you please. As for me, I know quite well what your figure is like!"

"Then that is all that matters," she said with finality.

Brandon felt a selfish pleasure in the fact that she didn't seem to care to attract other men. When he took her up to London during the Season, he didn't particularly relish the thought of having others swooning over his marchioness. It was the custom for a lady, even a married one, to have gentlemen admirers, but he didn't look forward to having his salon filled with a young herd of moonstruck calves.

Finishing breakfast, he called for their horses and gallantly offered her his arm as they left the breakfast room.

"It looks as though it's going to be a nice day after all," he said, as he tossed her up onto Dancer's back. "Perhaps you'd like to plan something for the afternoon."

"I believe you have an appointment with the steward."

"I'd forgotten." He sighed. "You won't let me put it off, will you?"

"I don't think you should. Perhaps it won't take long."

"Hopefully." He swung up onto the black. "But I do want to discuss buying some new mares."

"Racing stock?" asked Jamie.

"Yes. I've a good stallion I'm taking off the track, but we need some new bloodlines to breed him to. I want to expand the stable."

The equine conversation continued until they had topped a rolling hill some ways from the house. "I think I shall have a canter." Ashley, slightly ahead of them, looked back. "Oh look! There is a carriage pulled up in front of the house."

The marquess turned, suddenly staring with disbelief.

"I can't recognize it this far away," Jamie murmured. "Probably some neighbors come calling."

"I'll go and see," Brandon said hastily. "You two enjoy the ride. I'll join you later." Filled with dread, he spurred the horse for home. Unlike Jamie, he had recognized the commodious, closed carriage. Last year, he'd had it built specially for Lady Alicia Milton. It, with the team of matched golden chestnuts, had been his birthday gift to her. There was none other like it in the country.

So she had come here. It was a brazen act, but boldness would never stop that high spirited, thoughtless Beauty. He could have kicked himself for not going to see her. A visit from him might have forestalled this outrageous move on her part. He simply hadn't realized that so much time had passed since he had shown her any attention.

As a result, he was now in the very devil of a predicament. He would have to send her away before Ashley returned, and it probably would not be easy. If his mistress had gone to this extent, she would not willingly be put off. She would be angry.

Dismounting, he tossed his reins to a footman and went inside. "Have we a guest, Collins?" he asked the aged butler.

The man bowed stiffly with an air of disapproval. "I have shown them to the drawing room, sir.

"Them?"

"Lady Alicia Milton," he said, as if it pained him to utter the words, "and Lord Hayworth."

"Thank you, Collins." So Alicia was escorted by her cousin, no doubt to lend respectability to her mission. Frowning, he entered the drawing room.

"Brandon!" Alicia cried, skipping across the floor to place her hands in his. "How I have missed you!" Looking at him longingly with large aquamarine eyes, she turned up her chin to be kissed.

He saluted her cheek instead of her mouth, the heady scent of her perfume floating over him. He couldn't keep from lowering his eyes to her deeply cut bodice. God, she was desirable, he thought wildly, stepping backwards. He glanced at Lord Hayworth. "Hello, Freddy."

"Bran." The acknowledged male paragon of outrageous fashion fluttered his fingers and re-applied himself to the brandy he was drinking.

"You've been ignoring me, darling," Alicia purred, demanding his attention. "How very naughty! You see how desperate I became? I had to cajole Freddy into bringing me to visit you, and a very long trip it was! Most distasteful on all accounts." She pursed her lips into a delicious pout.

"You shouldn't have come," he said quietly.

"Tried to tell her so myself," Lord Hayworth ventured, "but she'd have none of it, don't you know? Stubborn lady!"

"Oh, drink your brandy and be still!" she snapped. "It's all you've done since we left. I'll not have your comments! You were glad enough to come. 'The marquess keeps the best wines and brandy,' you said, 'and sets the finest table.' Well, Freddy, you may shut up and enjoy it. Your mute presence is all that is necessary."

"I'm sorry." Brandon shook his head. "You must know that you cannot stay."

"Toss us out, will you?" Hayworth laughed.

"I'm sorry," he repeated, "but you must leave before my wife returns. This is beyond all bounds of decency."

"Now, what is indecent about a visit from two old friends?" Alicia slipped her arm through the marquess's and drew him through the French doors and onto the terrace. Once outside, she enfolded herself in his arms, leaning her golden head against his chest. "Please don't be angry with me. I had to come. I had to see you!"

"It isn't proper!"

She laughed throatily, smiling up at him. "Since when have you and I ever concerned ourselves with proprieties, darling?"

He extricated himself from her embrace and walked to the stone railing. Leaning on it, he gazed out at the brightly blooming rose garden. "Dammit, you should have known I would come to you as soon as I could."

"No, I didn't. I thought it was over between us. I had to find out for myself. After all, you didn't even answer my letters," she complained petulantly.

"I sent you money."

"That isn't good enough, Brandon." She joined him at the railing, once more filling his nose with her exotic scent. "Have you any idea how people have laughed at me?"

"They'll do more than laugh, if they hear of this escapade," he warned, "and I don't want my marchioness to be a part of it. You must leave at once. Go up to London. I'll see you when I get the chance."

"You are giving me my *conge,* are you not?" she wailed.

"No, I am not. I'm simply trying to avoid scandal."

"You must love that woman very much to send me away so exhausted and so overset by my cousin's misplaced wit. I only brought Freddy to lend legitimacy to the situation, but he has behaved so horridly to me." She fluttered her lashes. "Please let me stay for just one night so that I may refresh myself. It is the least you can do!"

"Alicia . . ."

"I shall keep to my room. No one need even see me, though I wish you would. You cannot know how painful it has been to lie alone, remembering, and wanting you to desperation! I have been living in agony!"

He couldn't keep from grinning with disbelief. "Alone, Alicia?"

"Alone. I swear it!"

"I always thought that Sammy Wentworth had a *tendre* for you, and I know he's in Brighton."

"I didn't go to Brighton; I stayed at home. People in Brighton are laughing at me," she whined. "Don't tease me, Brandon! My nerves are raw. I am quite overset by all of this! Let me stay. At least for one night! After that, I shall do as you wish."

"No!" Brandon gripped the railing. "It's impossible!"

"Your wife probably doesn't even know of our relationship. I hear she is merely an ignorant country girl, probably too naive to realize—"

His temper flared. "I won't have you discussing Ashley!"

Alicia laughed. "Don't enact the role of a doting husband with me, Brandon. I know you too well, remember?"

Resisting the impulse to strike the smug smile from her face, he turned on his heel. "Goodbye, Alicia."

"Just like that? No parting gift?"

He paused. "You and your worthless cousin will be gone from this place in five minutes. If you wish to see me again, you will wait for me in London."

"Well, we shall see about that, *Lord Scandal.*" Lifting her chin angrily, she brushed past him and entered the drawing room. "Come, Freddy, we are leaving. I am sure that I cannot bear to spend another minute in the midst of all this charming domesticity!"

"I wonder who our guests are," Ashley mused cheerfully, peering into the distance. "I believe we had best return. If they've come any distance, they'll no doubt be staying for luncheon, and I wish to make sure that something suitable is prepared."

"Surprise visitors should have no qualms about sitting down to cold beef and ham. I did not!" Jamie grinned, turning his horse toward the mansion. "I thought your cold collation was excellent."

"You are family. You do not count." She laughed.

"You are such an easy guest, but you must remember that I shall very definitely be judged on my abilities as a hostess."

"You'll do splendidly, I'm sure."

"I hope so! Pride of position means a great deal to Brandon. Perhaps more than he realizes."

Jamie nodded in high approval. "You're good for him. Bran has needed someone like you for a long time. I'm glad you're a part of our family. I only wish I'd found you first."

She reached over and squeezed his hand. "Thank you. That's a kind thing to say."

"Kind, but true." He playfully lifted her hand to his lips and kissed it.

Ashley smiled and turned her head, again squinting at the distant vehicle. "I can see it better now. It's a very fine black carriage trimmed in yellow."

"What!" he shouted.

She blinked with surprise. "Do you recognize it?"

Jamie stood in his stirrups. Ashley watched his jaw clench and his lips press into a fine line. He resumed his seat, his face growing taut and pale.

"Who is it?" she cried. "Is there danger? You must tell me!"

"Danger, yes," he hissed, "but not the kind you are thinking of. My God! It is beyond all belief!"

"Please, Jamie, tell me! Who is it?"

He took a deep breath, exhaled it noisily, and studied the withers of his horse. "No."

"Jamie!" Ashley grasped his arm and gave him a shake. "Tell me! I demand it!"

Slowly, he turned to face her. "It's . . . Lady Alicia Milton."

Pain stabbed her breast, nearly taking her breath. She clenched her fingers into fists to still their trembling. "I see," she managed to answer quietly.

"She is . . ."

"I know who she is." Inhaling deeply, she dropped her hand from his sleeve and returned it to her reins. Raising her chin, she bit the inside flesh of her lower lip. "Well, I hope she likes cold beef and ham."

"A dead cat would be more suitable fare!" he thundered. "Let us go as slow as possible and give Brandon a chance to get rid of her before we return."

"Do you think he will?" she asked in a small voice.

"Ye Gods, Ashley! Of course he will! He wouldn't house his wife and his mistress under the same roof!"

"I wonder." Heart aching, she rode on in silence, unable to keep her gaze away from the unmoving carriage in the drive.

Lady Alicia Milton. His mistress! Of course, she had known about her, and Brandon had said that he didn't intend to give up his women. She should have no complaints, other than the unsuitability of this visit. A man's mistress should remain elusively in the background of his life. She should never come calling on him at his home! Lady Alicia must be very sure of the marquess's fond regard.

An agonizing hollow formed in the pit of Ashley's stomach. Even at this moment, Lady Alicia might be in her husband's arms, enjoying his kisses. Blinking back tears, she gnawed harder on the inside of her mouth and tasted blood.

What would she do if she had to meet the woman face to face? At a ball in London it would have been an easy matter. She would have been a lady, polite but distant. But here? In her own home? What rules of etiquette applied to this?

Ashley sighed. Hopefully Jamie would be right, and Alicia Milton would be gone by the time they arrived home. If not, there was nothing she could do but act the lady and leave the whole embarrassing situation to her husband. The mistress was Brandon's business, and he must handle it. Surely, he would know that the woman's remaining at Havard was impossible.

"What does she look like, Jamie?" she asked, not even wishing to hear the answer.

"Medium height, blonde, stylish," he said shortly.

"And very beautiful?"

"Yes."

She sighed. "Of course she would be. Brandon would choose the best."

"That is a matter of opinion!" he growled.

"You do not like her?"

"I find her a demanding, vicious shrew." He violently shook his head. "Please, Ashley, this is not a proper subject for us to be discussing."

"I know." She gritted her teeth. "I am not comfortable with it either, but you are the only one I can ask. You are the only one I can trust to tell me the truth, or to give me advice."

Jamie frowned. "You're in love with Bran, aren't you?"

She nodded miserably.

"Damme, I wish you weren't!"

They were closely approaching the house and still the carriage stood in front. Suddenly, a very angry lady stalked out. Without waiting for the footman, she flung herself into the vehicle. The chuckling gentleman behind her climbed in, and the coach moved slowly away.

"Thank God," Jamie breathed. "You see? You had nothing to fear."

"No. Not at the present, I suppose." But she had a very great deal to fear in the future. She had given her heart to her husband and could never expect to have his in return. She must share it with such as Alicia Milton and no doubt with others she didn't even know about. But he had told her so. She had known she would have to face it eventually. Why, then, did it hurt so badly?

Luncheon was a miserable affair. After a futile attempt at conversation with Ashley and a few less than successful exchanges with Jamie, Brandon gave up and ate his meal in silence. There was something very wrong with his wife. She was always animated and happy with him, but not now. There could only be one explanation. She knew about Alicia Milton. Jamie must have told her.

His anger flared at his brother. Why had Jamie done that? Any fool should have realized that he would hurry Alicia on her way before she ever came into contact with his marchioness. There was no need for the dolt to identify the visitor. And Lord knew what else he had said!

After lunch, he turned cold blue eyes on his younger brother. "Jamie, I would like to see you for a moment in the library."

Leaving Ashley to her own devices, he led the way and shut the door behind them. "Well! Are you pleased with yourself? You've upset Ashley."

"I? It wasn't *my* ladybird." The younger man crossed the room to pour himself a glass of brandy.

"You didn't have to volunteer information!" Brandon shouted.

"What makes you think I did? I recognized the carriage. Ashley realized it and pried out of me whose it was. No explanation was necessary. She already knew about the Milton."

"Knew about her?"

"Why shouldn't she?" Jamie snapped. "You've never been discreet about your affairs!"

Brandon flexed his fists.

"Get rid of that woman!" his brother burst forth.

"You don't need her! Not when you have a lady like Ashley!"

"You mind your own business," he snarled. "You know nothing about it!"

"I know enough to realize that you had best watch your step. Ashley is worth ten Alicias. And she loves you!"

Brandon gulped. "She told you that?"

"Good God, she didn't have to! Anyone with half a brain can see . . . but yes, she did."

"I told her not to," he muttered.

His brother looked at him as though he'd taken leave of his senses.

"You know how I am," he meagerly explained. "I didn't want her to expect more."

"But aren't you happy with her?"

"I suppose. However, that doesn't mean I'm going to sit in her pocket!" He stood. "I have an appointment with the steward."

"Bran?"

"What is it?" he asked brusquely.

"Why don't you give up whatever it is you're trying to prove? Just because you earned the nickname of 'Lord Scandal' doesn't mean that you have to live up to it."

"I'll thank you to mind your own business." Irritably, he strode toward the door.

"Bran?"

He paused.

"Be careful. Ashley is very hurt."

"As I told you," he said coldly, "she has no right to be. Also, Jamie, I believe that your visit has come to an end."

Thirteen

Re-arranging a bouquet in the main hall as an excuse for her lingering presence there, Ashley watched for Brandon to leave the library and quickly caught up with him as he turned into the side corridor. "I remembered our appointment with the estate manager," she declared. "Did you think I had forgotten?"

"I don't wish you to forego your own pleasure in the management of the estate," he said, slightly guardedly. "It isn't necessary, I assure you. Havard is quite well run."

"I'm sure it is. If you would rather I didn't . . ." she began stiffly.

"No," he assured her, "I value your opinion."

"I don't wish to interfere." Miserable, she avoided looking at him, wishing he would hold her in his arms and comfort her pain. But how could he do that when he was the cause of it? Ever since Alicia Milton's appearance, he had seemed like a stranger to her. The warmth they had developed between each other had fled, leaving her feeling much as she had on her wedding day.

"You are not intruding," said the cool, distant marquess, offering her his arm. "I'm glad you are taking an interest."

They walked stiffly and silently to the office and entered. Evans stood, greeting them pleasantly.

"I've asked Lady Shandal to join us." Seating Ashley and waving the steward to his chair, Brandon sat down behind the desk, shuffled through several documents laid before him, and set them aside. "My lady has had experience in these matters and has agreed to lend us her expertise."

Evans looked at her in some disbelief. "Very good, my lord. Lady Shandal is well liked by the tenants." He pointed toward the papers that Brandon had moved away. "I have prepared a list of items for purchase immediately, and those which we'll need by next spring."

"All right, Evans, but first I wish to discuss the stables."

"Yes, sir."

The marquess leaned back, tenting his hands. "I want you to erect a new broodmare stable, behind the present one, with facilities for twelve mares. I want it to match the old one in architecture and design, but I want the boxes to be larger. Can you see to this?"

"Certainly, sir." Evans busily began jotting down notes. "When would you like me to begin?"

"As soon as you can find a builder. Spare no expense of course."

"Yes, sir."

"Good! Now that that's settled, what is this?" He absently leafed through Evans' notes. "I know little of plows or hayrakes. You must do whatever you think is best."

The man nodded pleasantly. "Yes, sir. This is what I have in mind. I am proposing several changes in the way we've been doing things. I'd like to replace all the old plows with a newer version, which will—"

"Let us all have a taste of wine," Brandon interrupted, reaching for the nearby bottle and glasses.

"Thank you, my lord," the steward replied patiently.

"You see, plowing in the same manner over the years causes a shelf of hard earth to be created——"

"One moment, Evans."

"Yes, sir?"

He smiled at Ashley. "Wine, my dear?"

"Yes," she agreed quickly, wishing he would let the man get on with it. Her husband obviously had little interest in farming. Evans must have been handling things at Havard much on his own. He seemed to be doing an excellent job of it too. It was a miracle that he hadn't quit and taken employment with a landowner who took more of an interest in his labors.

"I believe I shall walk out immediately to look over the area for the stable." Brandon rose, pointing to his vacated chair. "Sit here," he said to Ashley, "and go over these things with Evans. You have my full authority to do whatever is necessary. You know more about it anyway." He hastened to the outside door. "Good day, Evans."

"Sir." The steward rose, looking hopeless, as a bewildered Ashley took the master's seat.

"I fear he has little interest in farming," she apologized, then couldn't help laughing to ease her own tension. "Poor Mr. Evans! I am sorry, but I assure you that I have had experience in managing my brother's estate while he was in the Army. Oakwood Manor wasn't nearly so fine as Havard, but I doubt that you shall find me entirely lacking in knowledge."

"No, ma'am." The steward shifted uncomfortably, crossing and recrossing his legs. "About the plows . . ."

"I fully understand what you are saying, and I quite agree that we should have them. I confess that I am surprised that we haven't purchased them already. I had thought that this estate was much more modern." She frowned. "We must modernize as quickly as possible, but I don't wish to make a huge dent in this year's profits, especially with the new building to be accomplished. Perhaps we may make a plan, which will be carried out over the next several years."

"Yes, ma'am!" The steward's hazel eyes began to glow with appreciation. Busily, he shuffled his papers. "May I call your attention to this?"

She looked on the list at the item he indicated. "A new bull?"

"Yes, and not just any bull," he enthused, "but one of impeccable bloodlines. Our bull is old, and the herd is becoming inbred. We need fresh blood."

"You'll also cull some of the less desirable cows and replace them?"

"Yes, ma'am, the herd needs new vigor." He gazed at her with appreciation.

"Begin looking at once, but remember my guidelines," she cautioned.

"Certainly! Perhaps you would like to view and approve each purchase, my lady!"

Ashley laughed. "I doubt the marquess would wish me to hang about cattle markets. Not that I haven't, mind you! No, I shall trust your judgment."

"You'll not be disappointed, ma'am. Now, about the sheep!"

By the time she left the happily planning steward, it was growing late in the afternoon. As she climbed the stairs to her room, the pleasure of her new responsibility departed and a pall of unhappiness settled over her. At least her meeting with Evans had taken her mind off Alicia Milton for a short while.

Jane, with sewing in her hands, stood as she entered. Her expression told her mistress that she knew of Lady Alicia Milton's visit and that she was well aware of the woman's despicable role.

"I am completely exhausted," Ashley sighed. "Please

call for a bath. I want a good, long soak, and then perhaps a short nap before dinner."

"Yes, ma'am."

While the maid went to do her bidding, Ashley flung herself, fully dressed, across the bed, wondering if she'd ever felt so weary in all her life. Closing her eyes, she visualized the events of the morning, and worse still, her conjured image of the beautiful mistress. Pressing her face to her pillow, she loosed the sobs that she had been holding back all day.

"Oh, my lady!" Returning from her mission, Jane rushed to the bed and gently patted her shoulder.

"I'm sorry," Ashley stammered, "I shouldn't take on so."

"No, no. Anyone would," the maid soothed. "Damn him!"

Snuffling, she tried to control her tears. "It isn't as if I hadn't known." Turning on her side, she reached for the handkerchief in Jane's hand. "He did warn me."

"But for her to come here!"

Ashley blew her nose. "I know. At least he had the decency to get rid of her as quickly as possible. Did you see her, Jane?"

"I caught a glimpse of her," the abigail said, unimpressed. "You are just as beautiful."

"You're very loyal." Ashley laughed cynically. "Tell me the truth. What does she look like?"

"Stunning, ma'am. She is very blond and has big blue eyes. Her figure . . ."

"Yes?"

"It is . . . well, it's ample." With relief, she moved to answer the tap on the door. "It must be your bath."

Ashley rose, going to the window and standing with her back to the servants who brought the tub and water. Looking down on the front lawn, she saw a rider approaching. Even from a distance, she recognized his faded livery. It was Walters, one of the grooms at Oakwood Manor. Panic seized her. There must be trouble there. Either something had happened to Deron or Eve, or . . . or her brother was making another plea for money. Dear Heavens, if it was the latter, it couldn't have happened at a worse time.

"Jane!" she cried, pulse pounding in her temples. "There's a messenger from Oakwood! Run down and see what he brings!"

"Ouch!" The sting from her cut lower lip forced Ashley to abandon her attempt at nervously nibbling, but nothing could stop her hands from trembling as she opened the missive that bore Deron's handwriting and seal. She scanned the preliminary greetings and got to the heart of the matter. He badly needed money and was applying to his 'loving and very fortunately placed sister.'

Eve had remodeled the house and bought fashionable new furnishings, as well as a new wardrobe for herself. As she had pointed out, it was all very reasonable that she should do this. With a fabulously wealthy marquess and marchioness in the family, she and Deron must keep up appearances. Ashley must not be shamed by her closest relatives.

Since it was really his sister's fault that this situation had come about, Deron felt it only reasonable that she should accept the responsibility for the debt. Pin money wouldn't do, though she had been kind to give him that. He had followed her advice and was setting Oakwood Manor to rights, but surely she must realize that her marriage had forced the Madisons to assume a prominent social position. Ten thousand should be adequate for now.

Heart beating painfully in her throat, Ashley folded

the letter. Ten thousand! He may as well have asked for the moon. The marquess had generously replenished her purse when they had left London, and she had spent little of it, but it certainly was pin money compared to what Deron asked. Only her husband had control of that amount of money, and she could never ask him for it. My goodness, Deron wasn't even asking for it as a loan! He wanted it as an outright gift!

Nor was there any logic behind it. The unfortunate situation wasn't her fault, no matter what Deron might think. The blame rested on Eve's shoulders. Her greed had caused this downfall.

And what could she do? She couldn't stand by and watch her brother jailed for debt. Despite whose fault it was, Deron was caught in the middle of it, and he would suffer the consequences.

A day ago she felt she could have thrown herself into Brandon's arms, sobbed out the problem, and asked him to help her handle it. She couldn't do that now. Alicia Milton had forcefully driven home the reminder that her marriage was really just one of convenience. Ashley occupied only a small place in her husband's life. She could never hope to gain his love if she became a burden. He would not take kindly to a wife whose relatives tried to milk him dry. She must think of something else.

"My lady?" Jane interrupted gently. "It is time to bathe and dress for dinner."

"Very well." She woodenly went through the paces, scarcely noticing the tepid water or the gown Jane had laid out for her to wear. The horrible day had ruined her appetite, anyway. Nausea stirred her stomach at the very thought of food. How could she eat when her mind was in such a turmoil?

The maid looked searchingly at her. "Is something wrong at home, ma'am?"

"Deron's debts." She pushed back the tears. "He'll never be able to pay them, and I can't ask the marquess for help. Not now!"

"No," the abigail commiserated, "it would probably not be a good time."

Ashley shook her head. "Think, Jane! Have I anything to sell that Lord Shandal wouldn't miss?"

"Only dresses, ma'am, and used clothing brings very little."

"Yes. Well . . . I must think of something else."

Jane removed her mistress's dressing robe and slipped a sheer white silk gown over her head. "Maybe Lord Madison will come up with a way to solve his own problems."

"No," she said sadly, "I don't think that anyone but a rich man can overcome this. He's in far too deep."

Supper was a repetition of their silent luncheon. If anything, Ashley seemed more strained and preoccupied. After watching his wife pick disinterestedly at her food, Brandon decided that he had had enough. They would have a frank talk and clear the air between them. His wife had uncommonly good sense. She must realize that he was fond of her and that no other woman could threaten her place. Damme, she was his marchioness! Couldn't she understand that females like Alicia provided only brief pleasure?

When she rose to leave him and Jamie to their port, he stood as well. "Ashley, I must talk with you."

She looked at him worriedly. "All right."

Giving her his arm, he led her to the library and firmly closed the door. "Won't you sit down?"

"If you wish."

"I do." He waited until she had sunk to the edge of the sofa. "My dear, what happened today was very unfortunate. I understand that you are aware of the identity of our visitor?"

"Yes." She bit her lip and winced, ceasing the gesture.

Brandon raised an eyebrow. "Ashley, are you in pain?"

"Yes. No." She lifted her hands and abruptly dropped them in her lap. "Please go on."

"I was speaking of our visitor," he muttered awkwardly. "You know who . . . er . . . what . . ."

She lifted her eyes to meet his. "She is your mistress."

Her outspokenness made it difficult to continue. He strode to the desk and poured himself a glass of brandy. "You must know that I had nothing to do with her coming here. I would never be guilty of something like that."

"I believe you to be honorable."

Brandon heaved a sigh of relief. It was going to be easier than he had thought. Despite her naivete, he would make her perfectly aware that no woman like Alicia could ever threaten her position in his life.

"You see, my dear, the 'act of love' means nothing but pleasure. I think that, by now, you yourself realize—"

She gasped. "It means more to me than that!"

"Ashley, it—"

"Is it nothing more to you than that? Oh, I have been so wrong! Lately I thought that . . . for you too . . . Oh, I cannot bear another minute!" Bursting into tears, she leaped to her feet and whirled through the door, slamming it behind her.

"Ashley!" Dashing after her, Brandon took the steps two at a time, tried her bedroom door and found it locked.

Damn! She had really done it this time! Within minutes, if not already, the household would be rocking

with gossip. It had been a terrible enough day without
her adding a great quarrel to it. Why couldn't she simply have cried, let him reassure her, and be done with
it? Damn women! Why couldn't they just be sweet and
understanding, without being so difficult? She hadn't
even allowed him to finish the discussion.

He entered his bedroom and strode to their connecting door. Luckily, it hadn't a lock or she would probably
have barred his entrance there. Without ceremony, he
flung it open.

His wife lay on her bed, head buried in her pillow
and weeping wildly. Walking to her bedside, he hesitated, helplessly looking on. He touched her back.

"Ashley?"

"Go away!" she gurgled.

"My dear, you must stop this," he tried to say calmly,
wishing he could pick her up and shake her back to
her senses. Without speaking or looking, she swung
hard at him. The marquess jumped back out of range.
"Madam, you must get hold of yourself!"

"Get out! Get out! Leave me alone! Go to your doxy
and your damn pleasure!"

"Ashley!" He moved forward, caught her shoulders,
and pulled her up to a sitting position. "Please!"

She struck at him again, but this time he wasn't quick
enough. Her hand caught him across the face, dealing
him a smarting blow. "There you are, you . . . you . . .
libertine!"

"Hell!" the marquess shouted, rubbing his burning
cheek. "Now do you feel better? Now are you satisfied
with yourself?"

"I hope it hurt!" She drew back again, but this time
he caught her wrists and jerked her to her feet. "Let
me go, you brute!"

Looking into her defiant green eyes, his own anger
flared higher. "How dare you cause me this embarrass-

ment! Everyone in this house must have heard that door slam!"

"I?" she cried. "*I?* Cause *you* embarrassment? No, my lord! I shall not take the blame for everyone's misdeeds! This whole sordid situation is no one's fault but your own!"

"Not entirely! I certainly did not send for Alicia! What do you take me for? I'm not a fool!"

"You are a low, disgusting wretch! Neither your looks, your wealth, nor your title gives you leave to trample people's feelings and to fly in the face of decent behavior! I have never been so mortified!" She crumpled a little, her strength fading.

His own temper subsided somewhat as he saw her exhaustion. Taking his chances, he let go her wrists and enfolded her in his arms. "Please, can't we speak of this as adults?" He took her muffled response as agreement. "Come sit on the sofa." Gently, he piloted her across the room and sat her down. "Let us have a drink and calm ourselves a bit. Have you any spirits in the room?"

"I always do . . . for you. It's in the cabinet over there." She lay back her head and closed her eyes.

The marquess poured a glass of brandy for himself, and for her, one of sherry. "May I sit down?"

"If you wish to do so, there is little I can do to prevent it."

"Dammit, Ashley! Can't we discuss this matter without cutting up at each other?"

"Apparently not."

He sighed, sitting down and taking a long draught of the liquor. "Let us begin again," he murmured, placing her glass in her hand. "I'm sorry that you became involved in this. I didn't intend for it to happen. You see, Alicia Milton has been a part of my life for quite awhile. She is—"

She eyed him wearily. "I have told you that I know who she is, Brandon. She's your whore."

"So much for genteel conversation!"

"I see nothing genteel about this entire matter," she said shortly. "I am perfectly mortified to be a part of it."

"I'm sorry," he repeated, taking a deep breath and exhaling it slowly.

"You may have laughed at my upbringing and called me a simple country girl," she continued, "but I was taught early on to be decent and moral."

"My conduct over the years has indeed been reprehensible," he admitted, "but may I remind you that I told you of my interest in women before we were married? No doubt your aunt did too, and I imagined that she counseled you to look the other way. You're overreacting to this."

Ashley sniffed deprecatingly.

"Good God, woman, you are my marchioness! Alicia is nothing but a passing paramour. You are behaving like a silly child."

"Perhaps I have learned it from you! Brandon Shandal, you are a spoiled brat! Have you no thought for anyone's feelings but your own?"

"Damn!" He threw his glass into the fireplace where it shattered into thousands of glittering slivers. "Is there no reasoning with you? Lord, but I'm sick of women! I'm sick to death of them! I'll tell you what, my dear wife. I am going to London. I'm going to London where I can get drunk every night with my friends, and I'm not even going to look at a woman! Now how's that for 'Lord Scandal'?"

She stared at him speechlessly.

"If you need anything, you may write to me there." As he stalked toward his bedroom door, he heard her glass join his in the fireplace.

Fourteen

Ashley awoke after a miserable night of blaming herself for the marquess's anger. If she had kept her feelings to herself, listened quietly, and held her temper, her husband most likely would be lying beside her at this moment, cradling her sweetly in his arms. But already he had left for London. Earlier, she had heard the horses' hooves in the drive.

She was wrong in the way she had behaved. In the very beginning, he had explained it to her. She could still hear his voice in her aunt's drawing room, telling her that he liked lots of women and that she shouldn't expect him to give them up.

But last night, it had hurt so much when he'd said that their tenderest intimacy was only an act of pleasure. It seemed to hold no more significance to him than a play, or a ballet, or an evening of drinking and card playing with his friends, while it meant such a great deal more to her. When he made love to her, she felt as if she were joining her whole soul with his. In her blossoming love for him, she had forgotten that he was the dashing 'Lord Scandal', a man who was skilled in the art of *pleasuring* women. In the future, if there was one, she must not fail to remember that. The feelings he gave her were all merely artful illusions.

Neither had Deron's letter aided her in rising to the demands of the situation. If it were not for her worry about her brother, she might have been able to come to grips with her standing with her husband. As far as that problem was concerned, by striking out at the nearest object, which happened to be Brandon, she had made matters worse than if she had blurted out the truth about her family. Now, she couldn't help Deron. She couldn't even help herself. She would send him her pin money and explain that the marquess was away from home. Later perhaps, when she could think more clearly, she could devise a way to assist him. Above all, she must prevent Deron from appealing to Brandon. If that happened, nothing she could do would mend matters with the marquess.

With a light scratch on the door, Jane entered her chamber. "Good morning, my lady. I thought you might like your breakfast here this morning."

Her stomach rolled. "Just tea if you please. I am too ill at ease for anything more. Jane, you must know that the marquess and I had a slight altercation. Tell me, are all the servants gossiping about it?"

Eyes downcast, the maid sat the tray onto the tea table, poured her mistress a cup of steaming brew from a silver pot, and brought it to the bedside.

"Jane?" Ashley prompted.

"Well, ma'am," she sighed, "they are talking, of course, and everyone is unhappy for you. They blame Lord Shandal."

"It is not all his fault. Part of it lies with me and my inability to hold my temper." She slowly sipped her tea. "You, of all people, know that he made no secret of his activities when I accepted him, so I want no one to feel sorry for me."

"They'll do it no matter what. They've been wanting a mistress for Havard Hall, and they're afraid you'll go away."

"Well, I won't do that. Where would I go?" Ashley

picked up a piece of toast, then set it aside after only one bite. "I shall carry on as normally as possible. I can't hide in my room, though I would like nothing better than to do just that!"

"You don't look well." Jane frowned. "Under the circumstances, my lady, no one would begrudge you a day in bed."

"No," she said bravely, "it would only make me more miserable. I'll go outdoors. That will revive me. I must have a clear head, so that I may think of some way to resolve this dilemma."

Rising, Ashley dressed with less care than she had when Brandon was at home and went downstairs. Passing through the service area and into the flower room, she picked up a knife and basket, and went out the door to the garden. Snipping a brilliant selection of roses for the Chinese bowl in the hall, she tried to push her troubles from her mind, but found that it was almost impossible to do. Thoughts of Lady Alicia Milton kept crowding out any pleasant reflections. Would that woman be in London? No matter, Ashley had no doubts that Brandon's mistress would would seek him out as soon as she heard he was in town.

Setting her basket aside, she sank down on a stone bench. Did Brandon's statement about being tired of women really include the Milton female or did it apply only to herself? How long would he feel that way? Considering her husband's reputation, it wouldn't be very long at all. And who would be there waiting? Alicia.

Ashley couldn't follow him to the city. He had as much as told her so, when he had instructed her to write if she needed anything. She could do nothing but remain here, penning him cheerful, newsy letters, until he either came back or sent for her.

Tears sprang to her eyes. She *must* stop thinking of all of this. She would make herself ill with worry. Passing a trembling hand across her damp cheeks, she took a deep breath.

"Ashley, are you all right?"

She whirled. "Jamie, you startled me! Yes . . . I just felt bad for a moment." She forced a bright smile. "I'm better now."

"Are you sure?" He sat down beside her, watching her with concern.

"Oh yes. Quite sure." She nodded briskly.

"Well, if you are feeling more the thing, there are two men from London who wish to see you. One is an archivist hired to catalog the family documents, and the other is an artist engaged to paint your portrait."

"An artist? I knew about the archivist, but not about the other."

"Both were sent by Bran's man of business," he explained. "They apologize that they have not attended you at an earlier time, but they were engaged with previous contracts."

She slowly shook her head, lowering her gaze. "I'm not so sure I'm anxious to have my portrait painted."

Jamie took her hand and brought it to his lips. "It's customary that we have a portrait of every new family member. Actually, I think it's a good idea, Ashley. It will help occupy your mind."

She shrugged. "I fear that I'm not in my best looks, but I suppose it must be done. I wonder where Brandon will hang my portrait?"

"In London with his, I imagine. Mama's is still there, you know. He'll probably have hers sent here, and yours put in its place."

"If he isn't too weary of seeing my likeness," she grimly quipped.

"Ashley, don't be sad. Everything will turn out all right." He picked up her basket and offered her his arm. "I'm glad these people have come. I'm going to be leaving, myself, so I'm relieved that there will be activities to entertain you."

"Must you leave?" she cried, turning toward him. "Oh, I know I shouldn't be selfish. You have your own life, of course, but I do so enjoy your company."

"As I enjoy yours," he said quietly, "but I think it would be best if I left. My presence might cause gossip."

"Did Brandon tell you that?"

He lifted a cynical eyebrow. "Not in those exact words."

"I see." She tried to smile. "Where will you go, Jamie?"

"To my estate in Derbyshire, I think. I like to be there for the harvest. Then perhaps I'll go to London. Mustn't stay out of circulation too long! I might miss the bride of my dreams," he laughed.

"I hope that you find her, for you will make the most perfect husband." Taking his arm, she walked in silence to the house, almost wishing that she had wed him instead. Life would be so much simpler for the lucky lady who married Jamie Havard.

"You won't be leaving today, will you?" she asked.

"No." He opened the door for her. "I'll stay for a few more days. I want to make sure that the estate is running well before I go."

"Brandon didn't even give a thought to that," she mused.

Jamie shrugged. "Not to defend my foolish brother, but Evans runs the place so well that it truly isn't necessary for Bran to concern himself with it."

Ashley smiled wistfully. "The people wish he would."

"Certainly, but it's just not in his personality. I do, however, hear that you have taken a hand in beginning some improvements."

"Yes," she said, flushing. "I hope you agree."

"Indeed I do."

"Really, I did nothing more than approve what Evans had already planned."

"You showed an interest," he insisted. "That matters a lot to a dedicated man like Evans." He beckoned to a servant. "Please put these flowers in water. Lady Shandal will arrange them later."

When they were alone again, he took her hand. "If Mama could help, I'll be glad to seek her out. Bran does listen to Mama's opinions . . . sometimes."

Ashley felt a stab of horror. "Goodness no, please don't! I don't wish your dear mama to know of any of this. It would be too mortifying! I must simply learn to . . . to know my place."

He irritably pressed his lips together. "Come now, Ashley, you're better than that."

"Brandon did warn me of his propensities. Last night, my behavior with him was inexcusable. He had every right to be angry."

"I can't believe that you are defending him in that matter!" Jamie cried.

"He is my husband," she declared.

Her brother-in-law clenched his jaw, his mouth drawing a fine line.

"Don't be angry with Brandon." Ashley lay her other hand on his and gently squeezed it. "I know that you care, Jamie, and that you wish to help, but the matter must rest with Brandon and me. Let us not discuss it any further."

He shrugged. "As you wish. But if you ever need me, I'll come as quickly as I can."

"Thank you, dear friend."

They strolled down the hall toward the library. "I'll have plenty of things to keep me busy," Ashley noted, "but I suppose I must still find time to sit for my portrait."

"I shall look forward to seeing it. With your black

hair, be sure to wear something vivid. You would look magnificent."

"The artist, no doubt, will advise me."

"Also have a miniature done for Bran," he suggested. "You can give it to him for Christmas."

She stared with surprise at him. "Do you think he'd want one?"

"Yes I do. By then, he'll probably be very glad to have it. Old Bran is going to miss you, Ashley. It won't be long before you see him again."

"I hope not. I surely hope not." She paused at the library door, then squared her shoulders and walked forth to meet her new employees.

Brandon pushed his team hard throughout the day, making only brief stops to change the animals and to have a hasty drink and a bite to eat. Still, no matter how fast the speed or precarious the turns, his anger remained. All he could think of were those two beautiful, willful women and the havoc they had wrought with his life.

Alicia Milton had stepped beyond the pale in coming to Havard. She might be bold as brass, but even she knew better than to flout convention. She must have felt very, very sure of herself, else how could she have been so stupid?

He remembered her plunging neckline, her sensual fragrance. The voluptuous decolletage of her gown had caught his attention as it was meant to do, but there his interest had stopped. If she wished to put forth the image that she claimed, that of an old friend come to visit, why did she dress herself up like a courtesan? Furthermore, even the mere remembrance of her heavy application of *eau de cologne* made him want to sneeze. And the way she had draped herself all over him, caring little whether they were seen? He should have given her a good strong setdown.

He suddenly realized that in coming to Havard, she had forced her own dismissal. He couldn't risk having her involve himself and his marchioness in scandal. He would have to get rid of the woman. Strangely enough, he didn't really care. He was suddenly very weary of her.

Actually, in everything but bedsport, Alicia was tiresome. She couldn't sustain any conversation that did not center about her personal attributes. She didn't like horses. She was spiteful if she didn't get her way. A man's mistress should be interesting out of bed as well as in it. What had he ever seen in her? Old Milton must have died of boredom, instead of gout.

Banishing her from his mind, he turned his thoughts to Ashley. He should have tossed his marchioness over his knee and given her a thorough thrashing to bring her to her senses. So she considered him a spoiled brat? In her own way she was spoiled too. He had done it himself by giving her too much of his attention for far too long. The silly, romantical chit! He had warned her of what it would be like to become his wife, and she had chosen to ignore him. Any emotional upheaval on her part was her own fault.

Hell! Why couldn't she be more reasonable? They had enjoyed their time together, even that foolish plot of hers to ride bareback. Together they had talked, laughed, explored the estate, and in bed, she had responded so very passionately to his lovemaking. He was fond of her, wasn't he? He was an indulging, affectionate husband. Dammit! He'd given her more than he'd ever given any woman. What else did she want?

Gritting his teeth he urged the team to greater speed. She wanted him. She wanted his total commitment.

Well, she wouldn't get it! She could adapt herself to his way of life, or she could spend the rest of hers in misery.

Sparks flashed from under the horses' hooves as the curricle spun through the streets of London. Young bucks out late on the town jumped to the safety of the sidewalks. Painted Cyprians screamed and clutched their bosoms, hoping that their feigned terror would attract the attention of well-heeled gentlemen. The Watch, seeing immediately that the disrupter of the peace was undoubtedly a nobleman, turned their backs and pretended not to notice.

Brandon drew the curricle to a skittering stop in front of Shandal House. Since he was unexpected, there were no lights in the windows, but he knew that his staff had long since returned from their holiday. The house would be in order. Giving the reins over to John, he felt in his pockets for the key.

"I have it, sir." The wavering voice was a bare whisper.

"What is it, Lindsey? Speak up!"

"I have the key," he breathed.

"It sounds as though you also have the sore throat."

"No, my lord."

"Well then, where is it?" the marquess asked irritably. "What's the matter with you? Are you half-asleep?"

"Oh, God, no." The valet unclenched his trembling hands from the side of the curricle and fumbled in his pockets. He handed a set of rattling keys to his master.

"I see." Brandon grinned for the first time that day. "You became unhinged by my driving, didn't you?"

Lindsey nodded weakly.

"Sorry, I forget your dislike of excessive speed." He hopped down from the vehicle and started toward the door.

"Lord Shandal's a dab hand at the ribbons," John observed airily.

"You just go to Hell." The gentleman's gentleman

jerked the marquess's portmanteau from the boot and hastened after him.

It was still dark outside when the bubbling nausea awakened Ashley. In seconds she knew that this attack was no mere queasiness. Hand over her mouth, she ran to her dressing room to vomit into the chamber pot. Spasm after spasm boiled through her stomach until there was simply no more to come. Weakly, she stood, rinsed her mouth in tepid water and crept to her bed.

She couldn't remember ever being so sick in her life. Tearfully, she turned on her back and breathed great gasps of air. First Brandon and Alicia, then Deron and Eve, and now this. Dear Lord, how much more could she take? She had enough trouble without being ill on top of it all. She hated calling Jane at such an hour, but she needed her. She tugged at the bellpull.

"My lady!" It seemed like no time before her abigail bustled into the room, clad in her night clothes and cap.

"I'm so sick," Ashley moaned.

"Poor lady," Jane said soothingly, sitting down on the side of the bed. "What can I do?"

"Could you," she asked plaintively, "find me a glass of cold water?"

"I'll fetch it straight from the well."

"Oh, I do hate to ask you to do anything for me at this time of night!"

"Now never you mind. Besides, it is nearly morning." She patted her mistress' shoulder. "Did you throw up?"

Ashley nodded.

"I thought so." Jane brought the bowl from the dressing room and set it on the bedside table. "Just in case . . . while I'm gone."

Merely the thought of the receptacle standing in

readiness increased Ashley's distress. Taking it in both hands, she leaned over the side of the bed and heaved until her stomach muscles ached. She had only just laid back when the maid returned.

"It's nice and cold, ma'am." Jane poured a glassful from the sweat-beaded pitcher, wet a cloth with the cold water, and sat on the edge of the bed.

"I'm afraid I'll have it up again," Ashley sniffled.

"Take very tiny sips, my lady."

She complied. "Oh, that's good. Thank you so much."

"I wondered when this would start." The abigail wiped her mistress' brow with the cool cloth.

"When what would start?"

"The morning sickness."

"Morning sickness?" Ashley forced a hollow laugh. "Look outside, Jane. It isn't morning."

" 'Tis close enough."

"No, I don't think it's that. You see, I've scarcely eaten in the past two days. That, and everything else, has upset my stomach."

" 'Tis a babe. my lady. Haven't you noticed? You haven't had a monthly since the very first week we came here."

Ashley mind raced backwards. It was true. Brandon had laughed at what she called her 'infirmity' and had slept with her anyway, cuddling her close and rubbing her aching back. He hadn't seemed to care about his own desires. He had wanted to be with her.

Tears sprang to her eyes. "Do you think it's true?"

"I know so!" Jane laughed.

"A baby." Ashley set aside her glass and leaned back on the pillow, folding her hands protectively across her abdomen. "Can it really be happening to me?"

"It can. It is!"

"So wonderful . . ." She sat up suddenly. "I must

have a doctor to advise me, Jane. I must take very good care of him. Nothing must go wrong!"

"You're right, my lady, but shall we allow the man his last hour's sleep before we send for him?"

Ashley giggled girlishly. "You're right. We'll have him here today, though. Oh, I feel ever so much better just knowing what is going on! I hated waking you, Jane, but now I'm ever so glad. Why didn't I realize?"

The abigail settled her mistress and drew the sheet over her. "You realize it now, so try to get a bit more sleep. I know that's good for the babe. And don't you worry about anything. I'll be right here in the chair."

"You'll be uncomfortable."

"Not for the short time left of the night. Go to sleep, my lady," Jane ordered.

Obediently, Ashley closed her eyes. A baby! A little life growing within her! Pray God it was a boy. Brandon's first child simply had to be a son.

Fifteen

"Congratulations, Lady Shandal." The young physician smiled broadly. "What you have suspected is true."

"There is no doubt?" Ashley asked anxiously.

"I hardly think so. You may inform the marquess."

She sighed. "Thank you, Doctor. I am so very happy! Now tell me what I must do. I want nothing to go wrong."

"I recommend fresh country air and fresh country food. You should be active without straining yourself, but discontinue horseback riding." He shrugged. "My colleagues in London may dispute what I prescribe, but I've seen more healthy babies born to strong, well-fed farmer's wives than to the poor or the wealthy indolent. These women have easier births as well."

She nodded.

"Lord Shandal, of course, may have other ideas. He might wish you to see one of the fashionable physicians. After all, I'm just a country doctor," he admitted, though with pride.

"But your advice makes sense," Ashley supported. "If I am not healthy, my baby cannot be healthy either."

"Exactly. Eat plain food: meats, vegetables. Stay away from sauces, gravies, and sweets. I'm leaving you a medicine which should help control the morning nausea, but even if it doesn't, you should be feeling better for luncheon and supper. I also wish you to exercise daily.

You have a beautiful estate, Lady Shandal. There should be many walks you can take without overdoing it."

"I like to walk," she acknowledged.

"Good! Birthing a baby is work. It goes much easier for a mother who is in excellent physical condition."

"Like training a horse."

He laughed. "Yes, you might say so. You are training for a great event, Lady Shandal."

"I shall be ready," she said confidently.

"With your attitude, ma'am, you cannot fail!" he approved. "There is one more thing."

"Yes?"

"It's best to live a life of serenity. Let Lord Shandal handle any problems that may arise."

Her smile faded.

"Is something wrong?"

Ashley forced her cheerfulness. "Oh, nothing more than the usual dilemmas that arise on an estate this large."

"Don't be a worrier, my lady." He winked, snapping shut his bag. "What seems to be a problem today is usually forgotten by tomorrow."

Spirits sinking, she hollowly agreed, thanked him, and bid him good-day. *Serenity.* How could that effect her baby? The good food would make him grow healthy. The exercise would help her bear him easily. But serenity?

There was no serenity in her life. Her husband was angry with her. Her brother was head over heels in debt and would soon be furious with her, too, because she couldn't help him. And this little life inside her needed serenity? How could she give him that? With a wrenching sob, she turned over in the bed and buried her face in the pillow.

What would Brandon think of this? He would be happy because he had sired a child, who would hopefully be the next marquess. He would have done his duty and need not bother with her again, until the baby was born and she was ready to conceive another. He would go about his pleasures, and she would be left alone. It was almost too much to contemplate.

She wouldn't tell him. No one could write such news in a letter, anyway. She would bide her time and keep the secret of the baby to herself. Of course, Jane knew, and the servants would guess, but with the marquess away, she was safe. If and when he returned, the news might be so old that he wouldn't find out. But she hoped he wouldn't stay away *too* long. Perfect timing was what she needed, time to attach him to her side before her pregnancy began to distort her body.

She was beginning to be able to view the situation more level-headedly. Looking back, she could see that she had gained a large measure of Brandon's attention. They had been nearly inseparable since coming to Havard. She felt sure that he enjoyed her company or he could have easily come up with a thousand excuses to avoid her. He seemed to relish their intimacies. If only Lady Milton had not appeared on the scene!

Why had the woman done something so utterly unacceptable? She didn't think that Alicia was so dim-witted. To remain in her position she must be very cold and calculating. Therefore, she must have been so desperate that she had lost all sense of reason. She must have been convinced that she was losing Brandon to his new wife.

Ashley smiled. Her husband would have to come home sometime. When he did, she would make very sure that he never wished to leave again. She would become everything that a man like Brandon could want, mistress, wife and mother to his children, all rolled into one.

Still, there was the knotty problem of Deron looming

in the background. Uncle Sheldon was a wealthy man. Perhaps he would be willing to help. After all, the Sheldons had been so wonderful to her. The next time Deron applied to her, she would make that suggestion.

Jane returned from showing the doctor out. " 'Tis nice to see you with a smile on your face, ma'am."

"I'm feeling much better. I'll get up now." She swung out of bed. "Everything is looking up. I feel that all will work out well!"

Brandon spent his first morning in London tending his accounts. Next, he called for his curricle and embarked for Rundell and Bridge's, the city's most fashionable jewelers. There, he selected a valuable diamond necklace, placed his card with it, and ordered it delivered to Lady Alicia Milton. She would understand its parting message.

He lingered over a lovely ruby and diamond set. Ashley would look well in red as well as green. That woman! When he'd awakened that morning he had, in his foggy state of half-sleep, reached for her and wondered where she was. She'd become a habit. He cursed himself for even thinking of her now, but he bought the jewels anyway and slipped the case into his coat. If he didn't give them to his wife, he would present them to his next mistress.

The future ladybird would not be hard to find. There were any number of women in London who would be only to willing to be a marquess's mistress, but he would have to choose carefully. He couldn't afford the risk of another confrontation.

That ruled out any woman who moved in Society. Even if they were very discreet, there would still be whispers. The lady would likely meet up with Ashley at social affairs. He would have to look lower.

He would choose an actress or an opera dancer, but he didn't savor the idea. He'd always had women of the upper class as his mistresses. The other choices were sometimes not as clean as they could be. Their voices were not as pleasing. Their conversation was often crude. Still, he must make do. By damn, it was his right and practice to have a mistress, and no one was going to tell him differently! He was not the type to be a family man, contented with only one woman. It would be boring.

Leaving the jewelry shop, he drove to Michael Hinckley's house. If he was in, he'd take luncheon with Michael. He hadn't seen his best friend since before his engagement.

"Welcome, my lord," the footman greeted him cheerfully. "Lord Hinckley has just sat down to luncheon."

Brandon nodded. "I'll find my own way."

"Bran!" The earl rose from his chair as he entered the dining room. "You'll join me?" He motioned his servants to set an extra place.

"Thank you." He sat down comfortably.

"What brings you to London? Really, Bran, you surely did set us on our ears when we heard the announcement. My God, I'm your best friend, and I didn't even know that anything was brewing!"

"It happened rather quickly."

His friend eyed him suspiciously.

Brandon laughed. "No, it wasn't something that *had* to happen. It just turned out that way. Both of us preferred to have a quiet wedding."

He had been remiss in not inviting his friends, especially Michael, to his wedding. At the time, however, the publicity was just not something he was willing to face. He wasn't even sure he was ready to discuss it now, but the time had come.

"Well, congratulations anyway! Tell me about the new

Lady Shandal. Have you brought her to town with you? We're all anxious to meet her."

"She remained in the country."

"Oh," Michael said with disappointment, "so you won't be here very long."

Brandon shrugged casually. "I don't know about that."

At that remark, his friend was wise enough to discontinue his questioning. The servants brought the main course, and Brandon applied his attention to the choice, rosy beefsteak. He hadn't considered what people would think of his leaving his new marchioness behind in the country. Well, it was no one's damn business but his. No one had the right to question what he did.

"Just because I have wed does not mean that I must change my whole way of life," he acknowledged aloud. "I intend to do as I please."

Michael looked at him strangely.

"You don't think that's right?" he challenged.

"I didn't say that, Bran. I didn't say anything."

"You thought it! You think I should be riding along in my wife's pocket. Well, I won't."

Michael lifted his hands in surrender. "How you and your marchioness conduct your marriage is not my affair."

"You have thoughts on the matter," he prodded.

"Good God, Bran, are you trying to provoke me to argument?" the earl demanded. "I'm your friend, remember? We've been through a lot together."

He caught himself. Michael was right. That was exactly what he was trying to do . . . start an argument so that he could defend his actions. "I'm sorry. This isn't an easy adjustment."

"I shouldn't think so, especially for you."

"I had to get away and think about it."

The earl nodded politely. "Reasonable."

"All of us must set up our nursery sometime. How many times have you heard that?" he rambled. "Ashley seemed to be the right young lady. I explained my idea of marriage to her and she accepted it."

"Then you have everything exactly as you want."

Brandon laid down his knife and fork and took a long drink of wine. "That's the problem. Nothing turned out as it should. I feel responsible, not just for her security for she asks very little in the way of money, but for her happiness. She doesn't seem to care whether she's a marchioness, or whether she has all the luxuries to go with the position. She wants me, too. She's in love with me, and I don't know what to do about it."

Michael's eyes narrowed. "How do you feel about her?"

"I don't know that either," he said slowly. "She's sweet, and fun, and lovable, and infuriating, all rolled up in one."

His friend grinned.

"Don't laugh," he protested. "It's true."

"I believe you. She sounds like she is the right lady."

Brandon glanced at him sharply. "What do you mean by that?"

"Oh . . . nothing. Is she pretty?"

"She'll do, especially with her new wardrobe. She's been buried in the country all her life. She'd never even seen London, until I brought her here to dress her properly."

"An innocent lamb?" The earl's grin widened. "I wouldn't have expected you to discover a lady like that."

"I didn't. Mama set the whole thing up." He was forced to smile. "You couldn't expect me to find a suitable marchioness, could you?"

"Certainly I could, if you turned your mind to it."

"Well, I didn't have to, and Ashley is perfect for the role. She's attractive; her manners are perfect; she takes an interest in the estate; the people love her. She's a nice wife, Michael."

"I'll look forward to meeting her." He hesitated. "When did you say you were bringing her to London?"

"I didn't." Brandon set his jaw. "I'll bring her sometime, of course. I'm just not sure when."

"The Little Season is starting. Not everyone is in town, but it won't be long before they are. You'll wish your marchioness to be in residence before long."

"What difference does it make?" he asked stubbornly. "Besides, Ashley prefers the country."

"People might talk, Bran."

"I don't care," he said coolly. "As you yourself said, however Ashley and I handle our marriage is *our* business."

Lady Alicia Milton was not in a good mood. First, she had broken a fingernail while grasping a vase to throw at her awkward abigail, then her obnoxious cousin Freddy had turned up for lunch and proceeded to laugh at her foolishness in visiting Brandon's estate. Now, right in front of him, she had received a parcel from a deliveryman which contained a beautiful diamond necklace and the marquess's impersonal calling card. It was her farewell gift, and Freddy took more delight in it than he would a bottle of fine French brandy.

"Should've known, coz," he chuckled.

"Oh, shut up so I can think!" she snapped.

"Nothing to think about. Over and done with. Go back to the chase, cousin. Start anew."

"What do you know about it?" she asserted. "You are nothing but a parasitic fribble."

"Might be able to set you up with someone. Family favor, don't you know?"

"Keep your favors to yourself! I can just picture the fop you would come up with. Go away, Freddy. I have to think."

But her relative was too obsessed with her liquor cabinet to leave. In the end, Alicia did. She went to her bedroom and tore through her massive collection of nightwear. She would fix Brandon. When he caught sight of her once more, attired in her most arousing negligee, he would come to his senses. Not taking the time to ring for her moronic maid, she ripped off her clothes and dressed in the sheerest, lowest-cut night gown she owned. Over that she slipped an acceptable day dress, fastened the diamond necklace around her neck, called for her carriage and departed for Grosvenor Square.

The marquess was not at home and the butler did not wish to permit her entry, but Alicia sailed past him. "You will do as I say. I have business with Lord Shandal. It will go ill with you if you turn me away."

His nose as high in the air as was humanly possible, he showed her to an attractive salon.

It was Alicia's first visit to Shandal House, but she didn't take the time to survey her surroundings. Hurriedly, she shed her outer dress and slippers, poured herself a glass of sherry, and stretched out seductively on the sofa. Draping the hem of her gown across her knee, she lowered the narrow strap from her shoulder, letting it hang enticingly down her arm. Brandon would not be able to resist. He would forget all notions of living without her. The diamond necklace would become the gift of a man to his beloved mistress, not a *congé*.

Her heart thumped with excitement as she heard his arrival in the hall. Soon, she would be in his arms once more, and it wouldn't matter whether the artless little marchioness was in residence or not. She looked toward the door through her luxuriant lashes.

"What the hell are you doing here?" he demanded, entering.

"I've come to be with you," she purred.

Eyes fixed on the diamond necklace, he slammed the door behind him. "How plain must I make it, Alicia? You are no longer a part of my life."

"Let us not allow a small misunderstanding to ruin what we have together. I'll admit that I was in error. It will not happen again."

He shook his head. "No."

She moved her knee so that the gown rode higher. "Do you not like what you see?"

"Not particularly," the marquess said coldly.

Fear twisted her stomach. She rose quickly and hurried toward him, throwing her arms around his neck. "But I love you!"

He disengaged himself, stepping away from her. "You know nothing of that emotion, Alicia."

"And do you, *Lord Scandal?*"

"Maybe."

Her anger overcame her. She had been his paramour for two years. Did he think that he could dispense with her so easily? "Do you think you love that silly chit you married?" She sat down, crossing her legs and indignantly swinging her foot. "What pleasure can she give you?"

"A great deal." He sighed. "Give it up, Alicia. Find yourself another protector. Try Sammy Wentworth. He likes flashy blondes."

"I don't want Lord Wentworth. I want you!"

"I'm sorry."

"You owe me an explanation!" she wailed.

"I owe you nothing, Alicia. You've been well paid. You can't accuse me of penury."

She could not. He, along with her deceased husband, had made her a wealthy woman. But he owed her something more. Hadn't they been together for a very long time? Hadn't he given her hope of someday being his wife?

"Brandon, you and I have been together for a very long time. You gave me expectations . . ."

"I'm sorry," he repeated, his voice calming. "You must know that there could have been no 'expectations'. You are not a child, Alicia. You were well aware of the game you've been playing and that someday it would be over."

She stamped her foot. "You led me on!"

"I did nothing of the sort."

"You did!" she shrilled. "You made me think that I would eventually become your marchioness!"

"Don't be ridiculous, madam. It's a pity that you cannot end our affair in an honorable manner." He set his jaw. "This conversation has come to a close. I don't know you anymore." Turning on his heel, he left the room.

"Dammit!" she shouted.

"Get that woman out of here!" he ordered his footmen and disappeared.

Alicia shrugged into her dress as a grim brace of servants entered. "Don't you lay a hand on me! I am a lady! I shall leave under my own power. You won't toss me into the streets."

A grin tugged at the corner of one man's mouth. "Just do it quickly, ma'am. His lordship don't like disobedience."

"Cheeky clod!" As she fastened the final button, a fingernail snapped. "Go to Hell, all of you!" Tossing her golden curls, she swept past them grandly, ignoring the chuckles and whispers.

Sixteen

Keeping the news of the baby to herself wasn't as easy as Ashley anticipated. The difficulty began on the very day of the physician's visit. When she descended the stairs for luncheon, she noticed an unusual cheerfulness in the house that had been missing since Brandon's departure. Collins and the footmen greeted her with knowing smiles, and Mrs. Collins practically turned herself inside out in seeing to her comfort while she waited in the salon for the meal to be announced. Of course, none of them made mention of the doctor or of Ashley's condition, but the speculation was there just the same. Jamie, too, was extremely solicitous of her well-being, but he was more blunt about it.

"The estate is in order. I was going to leave in the morning, Ashley, but I won't do so until I am reassured of your health."

"I don't wish you to go for I'll miss your company, but I am much better now." She helped herself to a sizable portion of green beans, roasted potatoes, and prime beef, looked longingly at the sweet muffins, and selected a slice of bread instead. She was absolutely ravenous after her fast. Glad that she had ordered a more substantial luncheon to be prepared during Jamie's stay, she felt as though she could eat it all single-handedly.

"What did the doctor say?"

"He said I would be just fine."

"Be or are?"

"Both." She popped a forkful of beans into her mouth and savored their fresh, wholesome flavor.

He had yet to pick up his flatware. "I am your brother-in-law, so I don't believe I'm stepping out of line in asking what the trouble is."

"Jamie, this food is delicious," she enthused. "There is nothing like vegetables straight from the garden. Think of what the city people are missing! I can scarcely believe that *you* have not begun to partake."

"Don't try to distract me, Ashley. It won't work."

She laughed lightly. "I tell you, I'm fine."

Jamie ignored her assurance. "You barely ate a bite, yesterday. Understandable, perhaps. This morning you took no breakfast and had a visit from the doctor," he went on. "Now you're eating like a half-starved climbing boy. I won't leave until I've reached the bottom of this. Better still, it might be a good idea to send for Bran."

"Don't you dare!" she gasped.

"He would wish to know if his marchioness was ailing."

"If you do that, Jamie, I shall never speak to you again! When Brandon comes home, it will be by his choice, not because anyone summoned him. He would despise me for it."

"Well then?" He waited.

Ashley pursed her lips. "You are blackmailing me!"

He grinned, picking up his fork, at last. "Indeed so. In fact, the more I think about it, I believe that Mama, also, would wish to know. She used to pride herself on nursing the bunch of us when we were sick."

"You wouldn't!" she cried.

"Just wait and see. Think of it, Ashley. If she found out that you were in an interesting condition, she would be on your doorstep in no time and would hover over you for all the remaining months. Then, of course, she'd stay longer to help with the baby." He grinned wickedly and began his meal.

Amazed, she shook her head. "How did you know? The doctor didn't tell you, did he?"

"No. I guessed," he admitted. "After what has happened, no lady could look as contented and happy as you do, unless she had received extraordinary good news. That, coupled with your appetite and the doctor's visit, makes it rather easy to surmise what's going on with you. I'm sure that everyone knows."

"They may guess, but only you and Jane know for sure." She intently leaned forward and clasped his hand. "You must tell no one, Jamie. I don't want anybody to know until I tell Brandon."

"Certainly. You'll write him of it, of course."

"I will not," she proclaimed.

"Ashley! Even my recalcitrant brother deserves to learn that he's to become a father!" he asserted.

"It's not something that one writes in a letter."

She lowered her eyes and continued with her meal. Jamie dived into his. They finished the main course in silence. When dessert was served, Ashley turned down the rich apple dumpling and chose plain fruit instead. Her brother-in-law raised an eyebrow.

"If I recall, the apple dish was one of your favorites. The doctor must have advised you against it."

"Yes." She sighed. "No sweets! It will be hard, but it's worth it. I am determined to do everything perfectly."

"Then you should let Bran know immediately," he said quietly. "If you were my wife, that's the way I'd wish it."

"You are very different from your brother. I know what I am doing, Jamie," she adamantly stated. "Brandon and I have had difficulties. These must be sorted out before I add any more to it."

"Knowing you were to have a child might make a difference to him."

"Yes! He would probably decide that he had done his duty, and I'd never see him again until after the baby was born. Please do not tell anyone! I must handle this in my own way."

He eyed her with misgiving. "You have my promise."

"Thank you." She smiled fondly at him. "I think you are the best friend I've ever had."

He pretended to consider her statement. "You do me honor, dear, but I believe that this time next year, my misguided brother will play that role."

"I hope you are right." She reached out again to squeeze his hand. "I do *so* hope you are right."

The subject was not mentioned again that day, nor during the evening. Before supper, when Jamie walked with Ashley through the woods, they talked only of Havard Hall and the improvements that were to be made. After the meal, they played piquet until bedtime. As he bid her good night, he took both her hands in his.

"I won't expect you to see me off, tomorrow. I know that mornings are not your best of times."

"No, but it's a happy reason why." She leaned forward to place a chaste kiss on his cheek. "I shall miss you."

"And I, you." He grinned and hugged her. "Remember, if you ever need anything . . ."

"Don't worry so. I'll be fine!"

She bid him good night instead of farewell and proceeded to her bedchamber. She almost seemed to miss him already. With his departure, her days would fall into a dull, endless routine.

Her prediction was correct. In the mornings, she sat

for the artist, who insisted on working outside whenever possible. He was painting her dressed in her scarlet riding habit and standing on a rise overlooking the place where she'd had her lesson in bareback riding. She thought it unusual for him to paint her thus. Every previous marchioness was portrayed inside, dressed in formal attire. But she didn't question the decision. No doubt the painter and Brandon had worked out the details in advance.

She was glad to have the reason to get herself up and outside in the early hours of the day. The fresh air helped her morning queasiness and sharpened her appetite for lunch. The nausea sometimes made her late for her appointment with the man, but he did not complain. No doubt, like the others, he had guessed her condition.

In the afternoons, she either met with Evans or assisted the archivist in his sorting of papers. It was fascinating to see the bare bones of the Havard family gain flesh through documents and diaries. She was deep into a household account book belonging to Brandon's great-grandmother when Collins came for her.

"My lady, you have received a message from your brother. It appears that a quick reply is necessary."

"Oh dear." She stood, hastily dusting her hands together. "I shall tend to it immediately."

Excusing herself, she took the missive from the butler and sought her desk in the morning room. She knew, before she even opened it, what the letter would contain. Deron was making another plea, and he hoped that the oft absent marquess would be home this time. The situation could not wait any longer. His sister must help him, and she must do it now.

Ashley made a mew of distress. It seemed that her brother's debts had increased, instead of lessened.

What was wrong with Deron? Couldn't he see that he could no longer continue in this fashion?

"Is something wrong, ma'am?" Collins cried, nearly falling over his feet as he hastened to her side.

She started. She hadn't realized that the butler had remained in the room. "A slight problem with my brother," she murmured, eyeing him curiously.

"You are all right?" he asked worriedly.

"I am fine." She tilted her chin to look up at him. "Everybody seems so suddenly vigilant as to my well-being."

He flushed.

"Tell me, Collins, does everyone know?"

"We have guessed, my lady," he said candidly, "and if we are correct, we couldn't be happier."

"Well, whatever your assumptions may be, please bear in mind that it isn't a thing that can be told to Lord Shandal in a letter. He shall know when I tell him myself."

"Of course, ma'am. None of us would dare to presume!" he gasped.

She smiled. "I know, and I do thank you for your concern."

"This is a very special thing, my lady." He bowed. "May I bring you refreshment?"

"A cup of tea would be welcome."

"As you wish." He bowed again and departed.

Ashley returned her attention to her task, taking paper and pen from her drawer. She would direct Deron to apply to Uncle Sheldon, as she had done with Aunt Rose. The earl might or might not agree to help his nephew, but it would buy some valuable time for her. She hoped that her brother's situation could stand the wait. Her dilemma demanded it.

* * *

The dowager Lady Shandal could scarcely believe the piece of scandal that her good friend, Lady Corley, had dropped on her in her own drawing room on her very first day back in London. Her son could never be so depraved. She had brought Brandon up to respect the important values of family honor and loyalty. Despite his sad reputation of womanizing, he had always seemed to accept this responsibility. True, he hadn't always been as discreet in his liaisons as she would have preferred, but surely he hadn't sunk as low as this! Could his years of rakehell and revel have effected his sensibilities?

"Are you certain?" she almost whispered.

"Mandy, I would never lie to you about such a thing," Lady Corley said earnestly. "I saw her with my own eyes. Alicia Milton was coming out of the front door of Shandal House. Her attire was disheveled, and her hair was rather mussed."

"You're sure it was she?" the dowager repeated. "You're sure that her hair was blonde and not dark?"

"I am acquainted with Lady Alicia. She is the same bold blonde she always was."

"Merciful Heavens. What shall I do?" she lamented.

"You should give him a good, solid scold!" the countess expostulated. "You should have spanked his bottom more often when he was a boy."

"His father did that."

"Well, his father is not here now. It is up to you," she said flatly.

"I can't spank him!" the dowager cried, aghast. "He's much too old!"

"Admonish him, Mandy, reproach him! You always spoiled your boys too much."

Lady Shandal lifted an expressive eyebrow. "And your Jonathan was not spoiled?"

"Jonathan has never done anything like this."

"He isn't married!" her friend defended. "You cannot compare."

Lady Shandal's shoulders slumped. "Yes, you're right. I must confront Brandon. Dear me, Caroline, this will be difficult to do."

Her friend's eyes twinkled. "For you? Ha! Once you have made the approach, you are always devastating. He doesn't stand a chance against your tongue!"

Brandon studied himself in the full length mirror in his dressing room. Clad in snug buff pantaloons, shining Hessians, and a blue coat that matched his eyes, his cravat tied with precision, and his guinea-gold hair slightly ruffled, he looked very much the sophisticated gentleman. The perfect man on the town! That was exactly what he intended to be tonight. He would spend a part of the evening at his club, then proceed to Vauxhall Gardens where he would survey the *wares*. Perhaps a new mistress might turn up among the delectable, little ladybirds there. It was time he ignored his mental disturbances and returned his life to normal.

Alicia was securely gone at last. Her last ditch effort had terminated any fond feelings he might have retained for her. The woman had been impossible. He would take much greater care with her replacement. His next mistress would be well aware of her place.

Nodding with satisfaction, he left his rooms in time to hear a visitor arrive in the hall below.

"Lady Shandal, how pleasant to see you once more," his butler intoned.

Ashley? His heartbeat quickened with shocking excitement. Had she driven up to London? Then remembering their parting, he sternly set his jaw. Did she think that she could come here and force him to do her bidding? If so, she was very, very wrong. Not his marchioness, nor any woman, would tighten the shackles on him.

Stalking down the stairs, he observed the new arrival. "Mama!"

"Brandon, dear."

He hurried to her and caught her in his arms. "I didn't know you were in town."

"I arrived last night," she said tautly.

"And didn't send me word? Shame on you!"

"Well, I am here now and I am well pleased with my rented house. The furnishings aren't quite what I would have chosen, but it will do. I have no desire to own a place in the city."

He detected an unusual irritability about her. Did she feel unwelcome at Shandal House? "You could have stayed here, you know."

"No, no. Ashley is now the mistress of this house and of Havard. She should be allowed to rule them on her own, without the ghost of my past authority haunting her."

"As you wish."

Removing her gloves, she walked toward the salon. "Will you offer your mama a glass of sherry?"

"Of course." He opened the door for her, frowning slightly as she sailed through it. "I would ask you to stay for dinner, but I made plans to dine at my club."

She airily waved a slender hand. "Ashley has chosen to dine on a tray tonight? No matter, I shall join her."

"Mama . . ."

"She isn't ill, is she?" The dowager turned to him with concern written on her innocent features.

"Ashley did not accompany me to the city."

"Oh."

His mother's lack of expression in that one syllable set his defenses rising. He closed the door and went to the sideboard. Pouring a glass of the sweet wine for her and a hefty draught of brandy for himself, he took a deep breath and whirled around to serve her.

"Perhaps it is for the best." She regally lifted her chin. "At least she was spared the indignity of Alicia Milton's visit here."

On the one hand, Brandon was relieved. Since his mother was referring only to Alicia's visit to Grosvenor Square, she couldn't know about the travesty at Havard. On the other, how could she know about that most recent incident? Someone had seen, and that person must have rushed to tell her. How many others knew?

"I am disappointed in you, Brandon." Her voice was calm, but the words lashed him like a whip. "I thought that any son of mine would be more honorable than this."

He exhaled with a whoosh. "You don't understand."

"I hope not. I most sincerely hope that a gentleman of this family would never do such a humiliating thing to his lady wife."

"Please sit down, Mama."

"I should faint," she dryly stated.

"But you won't." He sat across from her, leaning forward. "I did what you wanted me to do. I gave Alicia her *conge*. Unfortunately, she didn't want to accept it. She came here attempting to entice and cajole and implore herself back into my good graces. It didn't work. Whoever saw her departure from here witnessed her final expulsion."

The dowager marchioness sighed with relief. "You are done with her?"

"I am," he vowed.

"Thank the Lord. She wasn't good for you, Brandon. Her pretensions were beyond all belief. She was a loose, foolish girl, and she is a loose, foolish woman. I shall never understand why old Milton put up with her. Nor you either, for that matter."

"She served her purpose," he said blatantly.

His mother raised an eyebrow. "At least, all of that is now at an end."

"Alicia is no longer in my life." He drained his glass and went to the sideboard to refill it. "How did you find out about what happened?"

"Caroline Corley was driving past when the Milton appeared. Of course she came to me first with the news. We needn't worry about Caro. She won't slip her tongue. Unless others saw, no one will ever know."

"There is little we can do about it if they do, but the *ton* will know very quickly that I am no longer involved with her."

"I am so relieved! Now there need be no other woman," his mama continued. "You are satisfied with Ashley."

Brandon glanced over his shoulder at her. "She is a most talented marchioness. I'm fond of her."

Lady Shandal clapped her hands with delight. "I knew as soon as I saw her that she would remove your obsession with multitudes of women."

"Multitudes?" he asked evasively. "Surely not droves!"

She narrowed her eyes and slipped to the edge of her chair, studying him intently. "You cannot be thinking of setting up someone else?"

Here it was again. People trying to force him into fitting their mold! She had better realize that he wouldn't take it, not even from her!

"Before our betrothal, I explained my way of life to Ashley. She is aware of matters," he said coldly, returning to his seat.

"How could you!" she shrieked.

"Mama, lower your voice," he begged.

"If you may do as you please, so may I! I shall lower my voice when *I* wish to lower it!"

"This is ridiculous," he groaned.

"It certainly is! Really, Brandon, this is outside of enough!" she shrilled. "This family has put up with your peccadilloes for far too long. We are all heartily weary of it!"

"Mama!"

"I have not finished!" Her eyes flashed with uncommon anger. "Ashley is the most superior young lady who has ever come into your life, and you are ruining it all! You are going to lose her, if you don't take care!"

"I doubt that." He grinned flippantly. "She loves me."

From her enraged appearance, if his mama had been a man, she would have called him out. He didn't care. Watching her spring to her feet and swish angrily from the room, he downed his brandy. So be it. She would learn that she could not tell him what to do. They all would learn! Even Ashley.

He was quick to follow in her footsteps, snatching his hat and cane and hurrying to his carriage. Once inside, exhaustion flooded over him. Damme! Why couldn't everyone leave him alone? First Jamie, then Ashley herself, and Michael and Mama.

Of them all, it was Ashley's face which floated through his mind. She had been hurt and angry and hadn't given him the opportunity to explain, but the time would come when he could. Then she would understand and accept him just as he was. Of them all, she was the only one he could rely on.

Seventeen

For several days after she had replied to Deron's plea, Ashley waited anxiously for a further response. When none came, she began to breathe more freely. Her brother must have followed her advice and appealed to Uncle Sheldon. Hopefully, the earl had agreed to assist, and all was now well at Oakwood Manor. She hoped that their uncle had administered his counsel, too. Deron and Eve might listen to the older man and change their spendthrift ways. Eventually, she would hear of the outcome. In the meantime, other matters demanded her attention.

The artist had concluded his work and returned to his London studio to put the final touches on the portrait. She hadn't seen what he had completed thus far, for he had been so very protective of the canvas. No one, not even a marchioness, was allowed to view any of his accomplishments until he was finished.

It was well that he had gone, for harvest had begun and Havard Hall became a beehive of activity. In the mornings, Ashley walked or drove a gig to the fields to watch and encourage the tenants in their labors. She spent the afternoons in the stillroom, overseeing the bottling of produce and the making of pickles, relishes, and preserves. By day's end, she was ready to sit back, put up her feet, and take her ease. There had been a time when none of this would have wearied her. The baby was sapping her strength. But the doctor had said that exercise was good, and she wasn't overdoing it. Besides, the work took her mind away from thoughts of Brandon for a large part of the day. Only at night and on the way to and from the fields did she experience the empty feeling of loneliness.

She wondered how long it had been since the marquess was present at harvest time. From several comments she had heard, it must have been many years ago. She wished he would take more of an interest in the estate. At least, he should attend the harvest feast on the final day, but she was scarcely the one to tell him that. It was, however, time that she send him one of her cheerful little notes. She would mention the harvest event, and perhaps he would take the hint. Before supper, she had just sat down to do so, when she was interrupted by Collins.

"Madam, you have visitors. A Lord and Lady Madison."

"Oh dear." A heavy sense of foreboding chilled her veins. She stood, hastily putting away her writing materials. "They are my brother and his wife. Please show them in and see that rooms are prepared. I'm sure that they will be staying."

Heart in her mouth, she waited by the desk. A visit from the Madisons spelled trouble. No doubt they were destitute and had come in person to beg for money. Uncle Sheldon must have turned Deron down.

There was nothing she could do to help them without Brandon's assistance. Nor could she prevent them from seeking him out themselves. Apparently, the time had come when her family's debts would be exposed. Most likely, the marquess would be furious and wish that he'd never laid eyes on her. He had bargained for a wife, not a liability. From now on, he would see her as nothing but a great drain on his purse. Their happy time together would be forgotten. He would begin to despise her.

All was finished. There would be no hope now for her marriage, her happiness, nor her love for him. Unable to keep her shoulders from slumping slightly, she forced a smile as her brother and his wife entered the room. She must keep her chin up. She was a marchioness, and she must behave like one.

"Deron, Eve, how nice it is to see you." She saw the lines of worry in her brother's face and knew that she was right. He was unable to salvage himself.

"It's pleasant to be here," Eve exclaimed brightly. "What a lovely house, Ashley. Why, it's almost like a palace!"

"Havard is beautiful." She eyed her sister-in-law's fashionable dress and wondered if Brandon would pay for it. "I shall enjoy showing it to you."

"Your butler has informed me that the marquess is not at home," Deron remarked.

"No. He'll be sorry he missed you."

"He is in London?" The tone in his voice held more of a demand than a polite inquiry.

Ashley took a deep breath. "Yes."

"I see."

"Since I am alone, I shall doubly enjoy your company," she said hurriedly and rang the bellpull, "but I shall not keep you here chatting when it's almost time for dinner and I know that you are probably wishing to change. Collins will show you to your rooms."

As her relatives departed, Ashley poured herself a glass of sherry and leaned against the sideboard. She had to have time, time to mull over her next move. Wearily, she closed her eyes, wishing that she had someone, anyone, that she could discuss this with.

What on earth was she to do? Nothing . . . besides tell Deron of her quarrel with the marquess and throw herself upon his mercy. Perhaps things weren't as bad at Oakwood Manor as they seemed. Maybe Deron had exaggerated. She drank deeply of the wine. Somehow, there must be a solution.

But by dinnertime she could come up with no remedy. As Jane put the final touches on her hair, Eve entered the room.

"Ashley, you live so splendidly. I do envy you." She glanced around the dressing room and sighed. "All these lovely clothes . . . Do you have jewels to match each gown?"

"Not hardly," she said dryly. "My husband isn't that much of a spendthrift."

"But surely he has given you some."

"Yes, he has. For our wedding he gave me a set of emeralds. And . . . and later, pearls." She felt like crying when she remembered the occasion when he had given her the pearls, and how he had said that her gift had been more precious.

"I would love to see them! I do so appreciate fine jewelry. Please won't you show them to me?"

She reached into her dresser drawer and withdrew her jewelry box. "I keep these here. You'd enjoy seeing the Shandal jewelry, but the marquess keeps that locked away in the safe."

"Ah . . ." Eve lifted the emeralds to her throat. "You are so very lucky."

"There is more to life than jewels. Let us go now. It's almost time for dinner." She took the necklace back and put the box away.

Deron joined them in the hall. His troubles soothed by the wine he had drunk, he made a cheerful evening companion until Eve, pleading weariness, went early to bed. Then he came immediately to the point.

"I won't mince words, Ashley. I'm head over heels in debt. The day doesn't pass without creditors banging at the door. I'm lost. There's nothing I can do but beg for help. I think you know that's why we're here."

She nodded miserably. "Didn't you contact Uncle Sheldon?"

"There's no need. He lent me money some time ago. He won't loan more."

Ashley gasped. "How could you get in so far!"

"It's Eve. She's ruined me. I wish I had never . . ." He angrily gulped his drink and poured himself another. "What did I ever see in her? What a fool I was!"

"Don't say any more, Deron. Eve is your wife. Her spending habits are outrageous, but you did love her at one time."

"Maybe," he said morosely, walking to the window. "*Besotted* might be a better word."

Ashley joined him, staring out at the dark expanse of Havard's parkland. "You must not question your marriage, now. It is done."

He shrugged. "What about you and the marquess?"

She swallowed, blinking back tears. "I love him."

"Good for you."

"I don't know if it is or not," she murmured. "We have had the most dreadful quarrel. That's why he is in London."

"I'm sorry, Ashley, but I have to see him."

She lowered her head so that he would not see her shining eyes. "You must do what you have to do."

"Then you give me your permission?"

"I can do little else." Ashley sighed with resignation. "Of course, I wish you would not. Remember, he was very angry with me. He might refuse to help."

"I'll have to take that chance. The matter won't wait long enough for you to patch up some silly lover's spat."

"It isn't silly!" she cried. "I am miserable, Deron!"

He rubbed his forehead as though it ached. "I shouldn't have said that. I really do want you to be happy." He squeezed her hand. "I wish I didn't have to add to your troubles."

She sighed. "I suppose it can't be helped. When will you go?"

"In the morning. As I said, the matter won't wait."

"Then the sooner the better!" She laughed with false gaity. "Perhaps all will turn out well in the long run."

"I hope so, Ashley. I certainly do."

Brandon didn't find a mistress at Vauxhall Gardens. Nor did he find one at the theater. The ladybirds seemed to have lost their appeal. He couldn't keep from comparing them with Ashley. All of them finished a poor second to his sweetly passionate, infuriating marchioness. No woman he'd seen in London was as beautiful, as exciting or as companionable as she. What was wrong with him? He couldn't force her from his mind. His own wife was becoming an obsession.

Whenever he wasn't thoroughly occupied, he thought of her. He even dreamed of her at night, waking himself up in a hot sweat of desire. She had bewitched him. Was he never to be himself again? Perhaps he just needed more time.

Without a mistress for the first time in many years and with the family disapproval, the only good company he had was with his old friends. The three of them had gotten into the habit of meeting once or twice a week at each other's houses for dinner, drinking, and cards.

This evening was the marquess's turn. After his French chef had stuffed the guests full of sumptuous offerings, they retired to the salon for port and brandy. Sitting by the fireside with their drinks, Michael Hinckley, Sammy Wentworth, and Brandon were chatting about the latest *on dits* of the *ton,* when the butler chose that moment to interrupt.

"My lord." He bowed. "There is a Mr. Trumbull to see you. He claims to be an artist and is carrying what appears to be a painting."

"Send him in." He turned to his friends. "It must be the portrait of Ashley that I commissioned."

"Excellent! We'll see your marchioness at last!" Michael exclaimed.

The marquess met the deeply bowing Trumbull at the door. "Have you finished the portrait?"

"Yes sir, I have, and if I may say so, it represents Lady Shandal perfectly. Such a kind and delightful model!"

"Has she approved it?"

He shook his head. "No, sir. I did the basic work at your estate, then returned to London to my own studio for the final touches."

"Let's see it then," he enthused, as his friends gathered round.

The artist leaned the large picture against a chair and carefully drew off the wrappings. "The Marchioness of Shandal, gentlemen," he announced with pride.

Brandon's eyes riveted on the portrait. Ashley stared back at him, but it was not the Ashley he remembered. The artist's rendition had made her haughty and challenging.

Dressed in a scarlet, black trimmed habit, she was standing on a rise with a stormy sky as a backdrop, her black gloved hands clutching a riding crop. Clouds of black hair billowed around her shoulders. Her firm chin was uplifted with her lips sensually parted. Her eyes glowed with a strange mixture of invitation, desire, and command. Beside her stood a large Irish Wolfhound.

Brandon caught his breath. It was not his innocent, sweet, little Ashley. This exquisite creature was a very mature woman with a mind and a sexuality all her own.

She was the kind of daring Beauty a man dreamed of conquering in his bed.

"The dog was supplied from my imagination, sir," Trumbull volunteered. "It seemed right."

A low whistle beside him startled the marquess from his reverie. "My God, Shandal," laughed Sam Wentworth, whose prowess with women, the marquess privately admitted, was nearly equal to his own. "You left *her* alone in the country?"

Brandon favored the artist with a scorching frown. "The whole thing is from your imagination! That doesn't look like my wife."

Trumbull stood his ground. "It is how I saw her, sir. Lady Shandal is very beautiful. She is a marchioness and the mistress of a great estate. This is how she looks."

"I don't like it."

"If you do not care for it, I shall keep it myself, my lord, as I believe it to be the best work I have ever done. There are art collectors who would pay far more than I have charged you for this work. It is a valuable painting, no matter who is its subject."

"Blackmail," Wentworth grinned, "but perhaps he is right. I myself have always appreciated fine art. Name your price, man. I shall buy it."

The marquess flashed a hot look at his friend. "I'll keep it myself. Go along now, Trumbull. You'll be paid." He continued to stare at the portrait. It wasn't her, and yet it was. Why had the artist seen this view of her, while he himself had not? Did she look this way to everyone but him, or had she changed when he left?

Lord Hinckley came up beside him for a closer look, favoring Ashley Shandal with an appreciative gaze.

"It doesn't look like Ashley, Michael, does it?"

"How would I know? Remember, none of us have ever seen her."

"I think you're hiding her from us, Bran!" Sammy

clapped him on the shoulder, poured himself another brandy and raised his glass. "Gentlemen, a toast! To the lovely and luscious Ashley, with the beautiful bedroom eyes."

Brandon whirled on his heel and started toward his friend, but Michael caught his arm. "Don't, Bran."

He stopped, but Wentworth had caught the motion. Raising a dark eyebrow, he lifted his glass again. "To her very jealous husband! We must beware." He drained his glass, refilled it, and sat down, crossing his long, elegant legs. "Sorry, Shandal." He shrugged. "Didn't mean to turn you up nasty. You of all people should understand my appreciation of a beautiful woman."

"Yes, yes, Wentworth. Of course." He turned back to the portrait. " 'Bedroom eyes' indeed!"

Michael grinned.

"You too, old friend?" the marquess demanded.

"My honest opinion?"

"Yes."

"Well, the artist has depicted her as being rather seductive. Challenging, but seductive."

"But she isn't," he protested. "Hell, I was the first man who ever held her hand!"

Michael shrugged. "Don't ask me. Maybe she learned it from you. Come on, let's refill our glasses. You can't expect me to make a decent critique if I haven't seen the original."

"I should bring her to town," he mused, crossing the room with the earl.

"Definitely! Especially after this. We're all curious, you know. After all, you're the first one of us to be led up the aisle."

"I'll think on it."

"You should. If she looks anything at all like she does in the painting, you shouldn't leave her alone in the country, Bran," Wentworth said drolly. "She might become tired of waiting for you."

The Dowager Marchioness of Shandal studied the portrait of her young replacement. Ashley had changed since she had seen her at the wedding. She had matured into a woman, and she was outlandishly beautiful without the little girl air. There was a leashed passion in her that should set Brandon's blood racing. She was exactly what that foolish boy needed. Oh, what fun it was to watch him pace the floor as he was doing now! How long would it be before he dashed off to Havard?

Brandon paused. "Well, what do you think?"

"I think it's quite lovely. What do *you* think?"

He snorted. "It doesn't look like Ashley."

"No?" She appraisingly tilted her head.

"No!" he snapped. "It looks like a portrait of someone's mistress."

His mother choked back a laugh. "How can you say that? She isn't indecently attired. My goodness, Brandon, a ballgown reveals more than a riding habit!"

"I'm not speaking of her clothes. It's her expression. It's . . ."

"Yes?" she trilled.

He set his jaw. "It's wanton."

"Oh I don't think so. She looks rather commanding, but not wanton. She looks like a marchioness."

"She looks like she wants . . ."

The marchioness swallowed hard against her bubbling mirth. It was delightful to see Brandon so overset. What had happened to her cool, sophisticated son?

He pushed a hand through his golden hair and frowned. "You don't suppose that Ashley and that artist . . ."

"Not at all." She saw his frown replaced by relief. "If

Ashley wished to take a lover, she would set her sights higher than that," she couldn't help adding.

He strode to the sideboard to pour himself a glass of brandy. "She wouldn't dare," he said under his breath.

"What was that? I didn't hear you."

"Never mind, Mama. It wasn't important."

"Well then, I shall be on my way. I'm to play cards this afternoon at Lady Corley's." She stopped at the door. "It's a very good portrait, Brandon. I shouldn't hesitate to hang it."

"Thank you, Mama, for your opinion." He downed the liquor and reached for more.

The marchioness left the house and gleefully entered her carriage. He was in love all right. He was so besotted with Ashley that he could hardly bear it. It wouldn't be long before he would be forced to admit to it. She loosed her laughter and was forced to wait ten minutes in front of Corley House before she regained her control.

Eighteen

"Good morning, my lord." Sammy Wentworth's stiff butler, framed in the doorway of the exquisite town house, bowed deeply to Lord Shandal. "I'm very sorry, but his lordship is not at home."

"Gone out early?" he questioned. "Perhaps I'll catch him in the park. He had a new pair of horses he was most interested in my seeing."

"He is out of town, my lord," came the stentorian tones. "My Lord Wentworth left yesterday for his estate in Kent."

"In Kent!" the marquess cried. "Yesterday!"

"Yes, my lord. My lord owns a small estate in Kent. No doubt he has gone for a bit of hunting."

"Yes, and I know what he hunts," Brandon muttered.

"Sir?" The aged retainer stared at his master's friend as though the young peer had bats in his belfry.

"Never mind!" Brandon hurried off the stoop and leaped into his curricle. "We're going to Havard, John!"

"Now, sir?"

"Yes . . . no. I've a stop to make first." He dashed the horses a short way down the street and pulled up at Lord Hinckley's house. Speeding to the door, he let fall the heavy brass knocker.

"His lordship is still abed, sir," explained Michael's butler.

"It's time he got up." Brandon pushed ungracefully past the amazed servant and darted up the stairs, unceremoniously entering his friend's bedroom. "Michael! Wake up! It's late."

"What the . . ." The earl blinkingly struggled out of a heavy sleep. "Bran. Why . . ."

"Get out of there." He caught the corner of the covers and stripped them from him.

Lord Hinckley grabbed for his comforter. "Dammit, Bran! What's the meaning of this?"

"How would you like to go to Havard?"

"Havard?" Michael fell back on the pillows. "Of course I'll go, but what's the rush?"

"Get up!" The marquess tossed him his dressing robe. "I want to leave immediately. Sammy's gone to Kent."

"So? He inherited an estate there. Didn't you know that?"

"No I didn't and, furthermore, I don't trust him. Ashley's in Kent too, you know. Get dressed, Michael! Where's your valet?"

"After this rude awakening, I'm sure he'll be right along." He got out of bed, stretched, and yawned. "Sit down, Bran, and stop moving about. It's going to take me a short while. I'll have to dress, and David will need time to pack my clothes."

"David and Lindsey can follow later in the carriage. We'll take my curricle. It's faster."

"I need my coffee." Michael yanked the bell rope. "A few more minutes won't matter."

"They might where Wentworth's concerned," Brandon said ominously.

"Good Lord! Is that what you're so concerned about? Sammy and Ashley? Come, Bran! Doesn't your little wife know enough to keep her skirts down?"

"Of course she does!" he said hotly. "It's Sammy I'm concerned with. Sammy and his silver tongue!"

Michael's valet swept into the room with a pot of coffee and two cups. With a flair that Lindsey would have approved of, he served the two gentlemen and disappeared into the dressing room.

"Please hurry, Michael," Brandon pleaded.

"If you want me to go, you have to let me wake up properly. Why are you up so early to start with?"

"I was going to look at Wentworth's new team. I assumed he'd be out at the first crack to exercise them. That's how I found out that he was in Kent. Hunting? Ha! He won't be hunting birds. He'll be hunting women!"

"I wouldn't worry about it."

"That is very easy for you to say."

Brandon sat down, drinking his coffee and fidgeting, while his friend joined his valet in the other room. Even now the seductive Lord Wentworth could be riding down the oak-lined avenue to pay a call on the lady with the 'bedroom eyes'. Brandon wasn't at all sure that Ashley could cope with that suave libertine. She was innocent of such men, and friend though he might be, Sammy was enough of a devil to delight in cuckolding the famous 'Lord Scandal'. Brandon should have gone on, instead of waiting for Michael.

But his friend would lend moral support. Ashley had been very angry with him. It was true that her letters had been charming and pleasant, but that didn't mean that she would receive him with open arms. Then too, Michael would provide assistance if Sammy became a problem. The earl was level-headed, much more so than he. It was well that he was going.

"How long will we be gone, Bran?" Michael called from the dressing room. "Will we be bringing the lady to London?"

"Yes, I think we will. We'll be away for just a few days, a week maybe."

That was what he would do. He would bring Ashley to London. These past weeks, he hadn't really enjoyed his pretended bachelorhood. He had to admit that he missed her, particularly in the mornings. It had been nice to wake up with Ashley in his arms. And as for the nights . . .

What was keeping Michael? Standing, he walked to the dressing room door and saw that his friend was having difficulty with his cravat. His valet hovered beside him, collecting the wrinkled ones that Michael discarded.

"Oh for God's sake!" the marquess cried. "Let David do it! I'm in a hurry!"

"Very well." He nodded to his man. "Go ahead, David. I suppose I'll have no breakfast either?"

"No!" Brandon watched the earl's valet tie a neat oriental in one deft effort. "You can make it till lunch."

Michael shrugged into a light olive jacket that complimented his hazel eyes. "Ready then."

"At last!"

"I wasn't so very long, Bran. Besides, I couldn't just throw myself together and ride alongside you. You're always so elegant."

"In this?" He looked down at his deep blue Weston coat, simply tied cravat, buff breeches, and shining black boots. "I look more like a country squire."

"No, you're top drawer. Always are. I envy you! Quiet elegance, that's the thing."

"Just like you." They trooped down the stairs and left the house. The marquess dropped John at Shandal House with orders to follow with the two valets, then set off speedily for Havard Hall.

Michael propped up his leg and leaned back. "I think you're worried all out of proportion. Of course, I don't know Ashley, but I doubt that Sammy would try to seduce your wife. Damme, he's your friend! Would you try to bed his wife if he had one?"

Brandon grinned. "It might be a challenge to see how far she would go. Sammy's always been somewhat of a rival, you know."

His friend rolled his eyes skyward. "I'd hate to be married to either one of you."

"I'd hate it too!" the marquess laughed. "But seriously, Michael, Ashley is young and inexperienced. She wouldn't know how to handle Sammy's advances. He could sweep her off her feet, using only a tenth of his charm."

Ashley had seen few gentlemen of class. What if she preferred Wentworth's dark, good looks to his own fairness? She was black-haired herself. She might like that best.

"We don't even know how distant his estate is from yours. If it were close, you'd have known about it."

"I suppose so, but after all that talk of 'bedroom eyes', nothing could be far enough away!" As if to emphasize, he pushed the horses to greater speed.

"You're in love with her, aren't you?" Michael asked suddenly.

"I've never been in love with anybody!"

"You are now. You're in love with your wife. What an *on dit!* 'Lord Scandal' fell in love!"

"Don't be ridiculous!" he cried. "I'm fond of her, that's all!"

Michael chuckled. "Think on it, Bran."

"I don't have to! I know myself better than that."

They continued on in silence. The earl finally got a bite to eat and a tankard of ale, while the horses were changed at an inn. Brandon joined him in the drink, but not in the luncheon. His desperation to get to Havard had taken his appetite. Prying his friend away as quickly as he could, he set off again, taking every shortcut he knew and arriving at his estate in the late afternoon.

As they rolled up the neatly trimmed drive, butterflies assailed the marquess's stomach. How would Ashley receive him? Truly, he had treated her so very shabbily. Would she be cool and distant? Would she cut up at him? Perhaps even lock herself in her room again? That would hurt, and Michael would see it all. He suddenly wished he had come alone.

As he pulled up in front of the hall, he noticed the large number of trestle tables set up in the parkland. Servants were moving among them, arranging things for what seemed to be a large party. Was Ashley entertaining? Without even informing him? What a setdown! But that was a matter that could be tended to later.

He slowly stepped down from the curricle as a footman hastened to take charge of the horses. He turned to his friend. "She was angry when I left," he said quietly. "We both were. We exchanged some words that were better left unsaid. I don't know how she will greet me."

He hadn't long to wait.

"Brandon!" Ashley hesitated only briefly at the door before dashing forward past an astonished Collins to throw herself into his arms. "Oh my darling, what a wonderful surprise! You're just in time for the harvest feast! Everyone will be so pleased!"

Heart leaping with relief, he lifted her into the air and crushed her to him. "A warm greeting, pet."

"I have missed you so!"

"And I, you." He hadn't realized how much until he felt her soft body against him. Reluctantly he set her away. "We have a guest, my dear. This is my best friend, Michael, Lord Hinckley."

"Lord Hinckley," she smiled.

"It's Michael." He kissed her slender fingers.

"Then you must call me Ashley." She turned to her husband. "How very coincidental! I met another one of your friends today. Lord Wentworth."

"I told you so," the marquess said irritably to his friend. "I knew that Sammy would waste no time in coming here. What did he do, Ashley?"

"Do?" She frowned. "He had tea with me. Is something wrong? Isn't he your friend?"

"Yes he is. We'll talk of him later." He protectively tucked her arm through his and started into the house. "Right now, I believe that Michael and I would delight in a glass of brandy."

It had been a long time since Ashley had thrown her heart into dressing for dinner. Even last night in the company of Deron and Eve, she had not been at her best. Without the marquess to see her, it didn't seem to matter.

How glad she was that her brother and sister-in-law had left Havard before he arrived! She was also thankful that they and her husband had apparently missed each other in town, or on the road. If they hadn't, Brandon would surely have told her, and he wouldn't have been in such a good a mood either.

She sighed. Of course, that left it to her to tell him of Deron's trouble. It couldn't be avoided now, but it would wait until morning, after she'd had a beautiful night in his arms. Perhaps, his reaction to Deron's woes wouldn't be so bad after all. He had come home to her and had told her that he wished to take her back to London with him. He must care for her. At least a little!

She pushed her brother from her mind and smiled at her reflection in the mirror. She was pretty tonight in the shimmering deep green gown with its handsome decolletage. Perhaps, she was even a little bit elegant. Brandon had never seen her in this dress, but she knew he would be pleased. She hoped that he would find himself unable to pull his attention away from her.

Her dark-fringed eyes sparkled. "Jane, would I appear overly grand if I wore the emeralds at the harvest feast? I don't wish to flaunt myself before the tenants, but I want to look nice for him."

"They would be perfect, ma'am. Everyone will be honored that you took particular effort in dressing." She hastened to remove the jewel box from the drawer.

"I don't wish to be overdressed, but this is a special occasion."

Jane wailed. "My lady!"

Hearing the hysteria in her maid's voice, Ashley turned. "What is wrong?" She stared at the empty box. "Oh, no, it can't be!"

The two women gazed silently at each other. The abigail found her voice first. "My lady, I would never do such a thing as to take your jewelry."

"I know that, Jane. No one in this house would!" She leaned her elbows on the dressing table and put her head in her hands. "Dear God, now I will have to tell him this as well. You know of course that it had to have been . . . my brother."

"Lord Madison would not!"

"He was very desperate." No wonder the marquess had not seen the Madisons. They were not going to London. They were probably fleeing the country, escaping their debts and the Marquess of Shandal's certain wrath. They could live for a long time on the proceeds of her jewelry. But what would happen then? More theft? Until one day when they would be discovered?

"Lord Madison would never do such a thing," Jane said firmly. "It was that woman."

"It doesn't matter now," she said sadly. "I must think of what to do. You mustn't tell anyone of this, Jane, until . . . " She drew a deep breath. "Until I tell my lord."

"He'll be awfully angry!"

"He will be beyond anger. He may even toss me out."

"Oh, no, ma'am, not if you tell him of the baby! And he does care for you. I know he does! He wouldn't send you away."

"I suppose not, but that would almost be preferable to his anger and his disgust." She shook her head wearily. "But I'll not tell him until morning. I will have one last wonderful night before he begins to despise me."

Pinching some color back into her cheeks, Ashley rose and walked to the door, pausing. She touched her lower lip. "That is strange."

"My lady?"

"Through all of this trouble, I haven't once nibbled my lip, not since I bit it so hard I cut it, over that horrible incident with Lady Milton." She shook her head wonderingly. "Brandon will be glad . . . if he stays long enough to notice."

With that, she swept from the room.

The harvest feast was a great success. The tenants enjoyed the great quantities of food and ale, the games and prizes, and the presence of the marquess and marchioness. The party would continue into the wee hours, growing a little rowdy, now that Lord and Lady Shandal had bid them good evening.

Knowing that Brandon and Ashley wished to be alone together, Michael retired early, pleading weariness. Shortly after, they followed him, arm in arm, up the stairs. At her bedroom door, the marquess paused, lifted his wife's chin with one finger and kissed her lightly.

"I'll return soon."

Even this very non-passionate kiss sent tremors of excitement coursing through her veins. "I shall be waiting," she whispered, determined to think only of the night ahead.

Entering her bedroom, she smiled brilliantly at her maid. "Hurry and help me undress, Jane, then I shan't be needing you any more tonight." She stepped from the dress and removed her undergarments while her abigail brought out a soft peach negligee. "Everything went so well. The people were pleased to have the marquess in attendance. Perhaps he is taking an interest at last."

"I'm glad."

She slipped the gown over her head and sat down at her dressing table, peering closely at her image in the mirror. "Do I look all right?"

"You're beautiful," Jane replied confidently, removing the pins from her mistress' hair and letting it fall lushly over her shoulders. "You'll leave it long?"

"Yes. Thank you, and goodnight. I'll brush my hair myself."

Jane left only moments before the marquess arrived. Walking up behind his wife, he lifted her hair and kissed her neck. Sighing, Ashley gazed at his handsome face in her mirror.

Leaning over her shoulder, Brandon opened his eyes, caught her look and grinned. "Studying my style?"

"Perhaps." She leaned her head back against him.

"Shall you use it on me?"

"I might do that."

"There will be ample time," he promised wickedly. "I don't think we'll be bothered tonight." With a flourish, he picked her up and carried her to the sofa, sitting down and settling her on his lap.

Ashley snuggled comfortably against him. "No, we

won't be disturbed, but we have been a very poor host and hostess. Poor Michael! I cannot believe he was as tired as he professed. He is probably sitting in his room, just as bored as he can be."

"He can fetch a book, or return to the party. Don't worry about Michael, my dear. He knows exactly what he is doing. I would do the same for him."

"Still we must think of some entertainment for him. A dinner party, perhaps? We can invite Lord Wentworth and some of the neighbors; that is, if you intend to stay for awhile."

"Actually I had planned that we leave immediately for London," he suggested. "Would you like that?"

"I like to be with you," she murmured.

"Ashley, there is one thing I wish to ask you," he said, a little stiffly.

"Yes?"

"It's about Sammy Wentworth. Did he behave . . . uh . . . properly, when he came here?"

"Yes of course." She eyed him curiously. "Why do you ask that?"

He shrugged uncomfortably. "Sammy is well-known to be . . . Well, with women, he . . ."

Ashley laughed lightly. "Do you mean that he has a way with women?"

"He most often has *his* way with women! He is the greatest womanizer in all England."

She smiled mischievously. "Ah, my love, have you a rival for your title?"

"Ashley! You should not . . ."

"I know." She giggled. "I couldn't help it!"

"For that, you shall pay!"

Ashley shuddered deliciously as his mouth descended on hers. Parting her lips and slipping her arms around his neck, she gave herself up to him, her body molding to his.

The intensity of the marquess's kiss increased. Picking her up, he carried her to the bed. Poised above her, he let his gaze ripple slowly over her body. "You are so very beautiful," he murmured.

"Am I?" She looked into his darkened blue eyes. "Am I really?"

"You are the most beautiful woman I have ever seen." He caressed her cheek. "The artist was wrong. He didn't capture your sweetness, but your eyes . . . Ah yes, he succeeded there."

"My eyes?"

"They are full of wanting."

Her whole body was full of wanting. His languorous touch was sending boiling spasms of desire coursing through her blood.

"Brandon," she murmured and reached for him.

Nineteen

Hoofbeats in the drive awakened Ashley. Fearfully remembering the events of the past few days, she slipped from under the warm covers, donned her gown, and hurried to the window. Could it be a message from Deron? Shivering, she looked out, but the horse and rider were now blocked from her view by the portico.

"What is it, darling?" The marquess tossed on his dressing robe and joined her.

"I thought I heard someone coming."

"You're freezing." Brandon swept her into his arms and returned her to bed, tucking her gently beneath the comforters. "I'll stir the fire."

She watched him rekindle the coals, his hair brilliantly shining in the firelight when the wood ignited. It would be a sight she could remember when he discovered Deron's activities and no longer came to her room. Nausea assailed her, but she determinedly pushed it back. She must tell him everything . . . now . . . before he learned all her secrets from others.

She drew a deep breath. "Brandon, I must talk with you."

He grinned over his shoulder. "So serious this early in the morning?" Standing, he came to her and slipped into the bed, taking her into his arms. "Are you warmer now?"

Ashley nodded. "It must have gotten very chilly last night. Brandon . . ."

He drew her onto his chest, stroking her back. "I missed you in London," he said softly. "Quite a bit actually, but most of all in the mornings."

She blinked back tears. "Brandon, I must tell you something. First . . ." She moved his hand to her stomach. "I know you cannot tell yet, but . . ."

A knock at the door interrupted them. The marquess swore. "Who is that to disturb us?"

Ashley struggled to move, but he held her tight.

"Come in, dammit!" he ordered.

A quaking Jane emerged halfway through the doorway with a helpless glance at her mistress. "Sir, madam, I am sorry to disturb you, but my lady's brother is here. He insisted on her being roused. He said—"

"To Hell with what he said! Who is the master of this house? Who?" the marquess demanded.

"You are, my lord," Jane stammered, "but he was so awfully forceful. He said—"

"You shall tell him that we will see him when we are ready to see him! Until then, he can cool his heels!"

Ashley touched his cheek pleadingly and looked at her maid through long wet eyelashes. "I will come."

"No you won't. If you insist on someone greeting Deron now, it will be me!" Brandon leaped out of bed and stormed toward his room. "I don't care if he is your brother. We shall see who gives orders in this house!" he shouted, slamming the door.

"Oh dear God!" Ashley pressed her face into the pillow. The moment she had dreaded had finally come, and it couldn't be happening in a worse fashion. Why had Deron come back? If only she could have had time to talk separately with both her husband and her brother first.

Now there would be a great confrontation between

the two men, and she would be caught in the middle. She hurriedly sprang from bed. "Jane, help me. I must get dressed as quickly as possible, so that I may be prepared for any eventuality. The time has come. He's going to hear it all, and it will be in the very worst way!"

The marquess, hastily but impeccably attired in Weston coat and breeches, flung open the drawing room door and faced Deron Madison. "Who are you, sir, to get me out of bed and to overset your sister?" he challenged. "Brother-in-law or not, you shall refrain from giving orders to my servants which run counter to my own wishes! You shall never disturb me when I am with my wife, except in dire emergency, nor shall you command my presence before I've had my breakfast! Do I make myself clear, Lord Madison?"

"Yes, sir." Avoiding his glare, Deron shifted uncomfortably from foot to foot. "I'm sorry, sir. I did not know that you were in residence. I asked only for my sister."

"A pretty way to ask for her!" he snapped. "Your sister is my marchioness. As such, she quite outranks a mere viscount, even if he is her brother! In the future you will show her more respect, or you will deal with me!"

The younger man took a deep breath. "Yes sir. I'm sorry, sir."

"Well, what is it you want that is so damned important that it cannot wait?"

"It was . . . some business with Ashley," Deron stammered. "I won't waste your time, my lord. I'll wait for her."

Brandon's temper reached a greater height. Ashley had been prepared to share a confidence when this puppy had interrupted the mood. Moreover, she had been obviously distressed when she heard of her brother's arrival. For that and all else, he wasn't about to let Deron off the hook.

"What concerns my marchioness concerns me!" he spat out. "I won't have her overset. Now what is it?"

Deron shrugged with dejection and reached into his pockets. Withdrawing emeralds from one and pearls from another, he deposited the precious jewels on a table. Stepping back, he walked stiffly to the windows and waited, almost cringing, for his brother-in-law's reaction.

Brandon's eyes widened. "It's Ashley's jewelry!"

"You recognized it," Deron breathed.

"Of course, I recognized it, you dunderhead! I bought it for her! What are you doing with it?"

The young man turned, clenching his teeth. "I wish I could say that my sister had lent it to Eve, but you wouldn't believe that."

"No, I would not." He softened his voice. This was going to be awkward. Much as he disliked Madison's behavior toward Ashley, he had to admire his sense of honor. It had taken great fortitude to come here in person to rectify the matter.

"Am I correct in assuming that Lady Madison stole these pieces?" he asked quietly.

Deron nodded miserably, a deep flush crawling up his neck and suffusing his face. "When I discovered what she had done, I sent her on to Oakwood Manor and came at once to return Ashley's property."

Feeling sorry for his brother-in-law's embarrassment, Brandon nodded kindly. "That's exactly what you should have done. Frankly, Deron, I've never cared a great deal for your wife, but I would not have thought her to be a thief. What brought this about?"

"I suppose she did it to help me. I'm in the suds. My creditors have closed in, and I've no hope of paying my debts. In fact, that's why we were here in the first place.

I came to beg a loan. Eve must have slipped into Ashley's room and stolen the jewelry while we were discussing it."

Brandon sat down heavily. "You came to beg a loan you cannot expect to repay."

"But I think I can! I've seen how I can improve Oakwood Manor, and Eve has promised to stop her spending." Eyes shining once more, he stepped forward eagerly. "If you'll come to my rescue, I'll promise to work my hardest and pay back every guinea you loan me and Ashley's pin money too!"

Brandon lifted an eyebrow. "So my wife gave you her pin money?"

"Yes. Twice. It was a generous sum, but not enough to turn the tables."

"She didn't tell me." He sat down, wishing he'd requested Collins to bring coffee. At the time, he hadn't wished for Deron to be welcomed with any kind of civility. Now, he wanted the strong morning bracer for himself.

Why hadn't Ashley told him of her brother's plight? If she had twice given him money, the first time must have been in London. They had been on such good terms after that. Why hadn't she shared the dilemma then?

"Please don't blame my sister," Deron implored. "She only wanted to help me."

"Ashley's money is hers to do with as she pleases," he said. "She isn't required to answer to me. But tell me, Deron, you must have known at the time that the pin money wasn't enough. Why didn't you come to me before now?"

"Ashley begged me not to."

"I wonder why . . ."

Deron uncomfortably glanced at him. "She was

afraid you would hate her for it. She loves you very much, my lord."

Brandon thoughtfully stroked his chin. "I also wonder if she knows that the jewels are missing."

"I don't know."

"Well then . . ." The marquess eyed him steadily. "I'll help you, Deron, but we'll do it my way, under my terms."

Ashley's brother hung his head. "I haven't a choice."

"I suppose not. You sit here and think about your needs while I breakfast. We'll discuss this matter later."

In the hall, he relented in his mistreatment of the guest and ordered Collins to provide him with refreshments. Entering the breakfast room, he greeted Michael, who had already filled his plate and was eating calmly. "What a morning! Whoever said that the country was peaceful?" He shook his head.

"I did overhear you ripping it up at some poor fool as I came downstairs."

"It was Ashley's brother. Came here high-handedly demanding to see her and found me at home instead."

Michael chuckled. "How unfortunate for him. Is he joining us for breakfast?"

"No, I left him in the drawing room, deciding how much money he's going to try to attempt to extract from me," Brandon said grimly.

"Oh, one of those kind of brothers! Are you going to lend it to him?"

"Yes," he muttered, helping himself to the buffet. "I don't want Ashley overset."

"Anything I can do?" Michael asked.

The marquess shrugged. "I need to come up with a solution to his difficulties that will set him on course, once and for all. I don't intend to spend my life and my fortune bailing him out."

"Sounds like a matter for your man-of-business."

"I intend to send him there, but first I must convince him that he is going to have to change his ways. And the ways of his wife! I think that she is probably his major problem. She's a spendthrift."

His friend winced. "Mercenary females are the very devil! Whom did he marry?"

"Eve Trehorne. Beautiful widow. Not quite the thing if I recall, though she was considered a member of the *ton*. Do you remember her?"

Michael grinned. "I certainly do."

Brandon shot him a questioning look. "Should I ask how well you knew her?"

"Well enough to form the impression that she would not be averse to becoming a man's mistress," he revealed.

"Did you . . ."

"No." Michael laughed cynically. "I also had the idea that she would be a great expense."

He smiled ruefully. "That's exactly what Deron is discovering. Well, the lady will have to learn to live without her luxury."

"Good luck."

"I'll need it." He pushed away from the table. "I hate to leave you on your own again, Michael. I'm not being a very good host."

"No matter! I think I'll take a ride over the estate. It's a nice morning."

"Yes, I wish I could go with you. Choose whichever horse you want and treat the place as if it were your own. Shall I see you at luncheon?"

"I'll be back," he promised.

Brandon rolled his eyes and shook his head. "I hope to have this business concluded by then."

"Don't concern yourself with me," Michael cheerfully assured him. "I'm perfectly comfortable."

"Thank you, friend." He left the breakfast room and

went to the library, sending a footman to fetch Lord Madison. Settling himself into the deep winged chair behind the desk, he thought back over the events of the morning. Deron was a problem, but he was only a minor irritant in comparison with Ashley.

Why hadn't she told him of the problem? Dammit, he was her husband! If something was wrong, she should have come to him. He thought of her bare neckline last evening. He had been surprised that she hadn't worn any jewelry. She must have discovered that it was gone.

"Lord Madison, sir."

Brandon looked up. "Come in, Deron. Sit down."

The young man did as he was bid, resting uneasily on the edge of his chair. He deposited the jewelry on the desk and looked sheepishly at his brother-in-law. "You forgot these."

"So I did." He fingered the heart-shaped clasp on the pearls. "How bad is your situation?"

"Very bad, sir." Deron spread a small sheaf of papers before him. "It's all here."

The marquess glanced briefly at the figures, blinking with surprise. "Are you sure?"

"Yes, sir."

"Who made this accounting?" he challenged.

Deron quaked. "I did."

Brandon picked up the papers and studied them more seriously. "This record seems very thorough."

"I was always good at figures, sir."

He disapprovingly clicked his tongue. "You appear to be equally good at spending what you don't have. This is a lot of money, Deron."

Ashley's brother leaped to his feet, his restraint breaking. "Don't you think I don't know that? Dammit, do you have to rub it in? I'd have been better off shooting myself than coming to you!"

"Don't be ridiculous," the marquess said mildly. "I don't want you dead. It would disturb my wife. Sit down." Leaning forward, he poured two glasses of brandy. "Here. Drink this and calm yourself. I have some questions to ask you."

Sighing explosively, Deron flopped down and gulped the brandy.

"Your income, it appears, is based on proceeds from your estate, yet you seem to have spent little cash in developing it. Why, pray tell, did you redecorate your house? Plows would have been a better expenditure."

Deron groaned. "It was my wife's idea."

"And all these expensive clothes? Your wife's idea too, I assume." Brandon pounded on. "Just look at these hideously high food and liquor bills. Life at Oakwood Manor must be top-of-the-trees! I'm surprised I haven't been invited to a house party."

"Eve did want to invite you, but I was afraid that Ashley would be . . ."

"Angry? Overset?"

"Both," Deron murmured. "My sister is a pinchpenny."

"My wife is intelligent enough not to overspend her means," Brandon contradicted. "Now, tell me why you think it's necessary to live on so grand a scale when your estate is falling to pieces around you?"

"Eve believes that since you are in the family, we must adopt a certain standard," he muttered.

"Even if you can't afford it?"

He shrugged. "She insists."

"Dammit, man," Brandon exploded, "can't you control your own wife?"

"Can you?" Deron fired back. "No man can control a woman once she's got her head set on something!"

"What I can do has nothing to do with you, but *yes, I can!* Now, in regards to you, you are going to have to do so, too, because the first thing I require will be for you to put a period to your wife's spending!"

Deron shifted nervously in his chair. "She has promised, but I don't expect it to be easy," he answered honestly. "Still, I'll have to. You're my last resort."

"Excellent. Next, you will work with my man-of-business in drawing up a budget, which you will adhere to. He will assume control of your income and will give you a quarterly allowance. Agreed?"

"It makes me feel like a child!" he protested.

"When it comes to spending, you are. My God, I can't believe you have the audacity to argue with me when I'm trying to save your reckless hide!"

"A man has to act like a man," Deron mumbled.

"Oh, hell." Brandon set his jaw. "Are you ready for more?"

"Yes, sir," he sighed. "This isn't easy, you know."

Brandon refrained from comment. "My next condition is that there will be no credit, you understand?"

"All right," Deron said numbly.

"You'll be set upon a schedule to repay me, with interest. This isn't a gift, unless perhaps I see you doing so well that I decide to reward you with a cancellation of the debt. Finally, you'll obtain a dealer to buy as much of that fancy furniture and baubles that he will, and you'll bring down the old things from the attic."

"I'll take a loss!"

The marquess shrugged. "I won't have you living in such a style on my money. Take it or leave it, Deron."

"You know I'll have to take it!"

"Then I want you to go to London, tomorrow. My man of business will draw up an agreement and begin paying off your debts." He stood up. "In the meantime, feel free to enjoy the hospitality of Havard Hall." He rose and extended his hand, which Deron shook. "Col-

lins will show you to your room. I shall see you at luncheon. And Deron?"

"Yes sir?"

Brandon eyed him piercingly. "You know that these
jewels could have saved you?"

"Yes I do." Ashley's brother grinned lopsidedly. "I
may be a lot of things, but I'm not a thief."

Watching the young man leave, Brandon refilled his
glass and sipped thoughtfully. It remained to be seen
whether Deron would keep up his side of the bargain,
but there was no other choice than to lend him the
money, even give it to him if it came to that. Ashley
would be devastated if he did not, and she was what was
the most important of all.

Now he must deal with her. Wondering what would
have happened if he hadn't come to Havard when he
did, he reached for the bell rope.

Her heart in her mouth, Ashley entered the library
and stood stiffly, as Collins closed the door behind her.
"You wished to speak with me?"

"Yes, I do." Brandon smiled grimly. "Will you sit
down?"

She obeyed, poising on the edge of her chair like a
recalcitrant schoolgirl ready to receive a scold. "Is it
about Deron?" Her gaze fell on the emeralds and pearls
on the desk. "Oh!"

He nodded. "Indeed."

Lightheadedness nearly overcame her as the blood
drained from her face, leaving her pale and stricken.
"I believe I know what you wish to speak of." She looked
at him through her eyelashes and waited for the storm
to burst.

"Why didn't you tell me of his problem?" the marquess asked gently.

"I was going to," she whispered, "but I wanted him to solve it by himself."

"Didn't you realize how much money was involved?"

She trembled. "Yes."

He frowned. "Ashley, do you think I am such a great brute that you cannot confide in me?"

"Not at all!" she blurted, then managed a fearful glance at him. "Mostly I think you are wonderful."

"You do?"

She bobbed her head.

"Then why didn't you trust me to help?" He came around the desk and took her hands. "I would have, you know. Indeed, I have done so, even though your brother's wife is a jewel thief."

It was too much for her to bear. Ashley burst into tears. "Why can't he have solved his own problems? Why must he come here with them? How could he do this to me!"

The marquess gathered her up into his arms and forced her against his chest. "He couldn't solve them, Ashley. He had to have help."

"How sorry you must be that you married me!" she wept, breast aching. "First, you had to buy me a complete wardrobe; now you must be saddled with the debts of unwanted in-laws, and theft, and—"

"No, it's not like that!"

"I hope that an heir is worth the great price you are paying!" she sobbed wildly.

"Don't do this!" he found himself shouting. "You are wrong! I don't mind it!"

"You couldn't help but mind it! You would never have chosen any of this! I am a rock around your neck! No, far worse than that! I am like some horrible medieval penance!"

"No, Ashley, I care for you! Will you give me a chance to do so!" He caught hold of himself and lowered his voice. "Please calm yourself, my dear. It isn't at all as you think."

"I am not pretty enough for you, and I am not as exciting as . . ."

"You are perfectly exquisite, dear," he reassured, "and you are very exciting."

His words finally penetrated her agony. "Do you really think that?" She couldn't be understanding him correctly! Lifting her head, she searched his eyes. "Do you really, truly, think I'm pretty?"

He nodded solemnly. "I wouldn't have married you if I hadn't. You did give me the opportunity to cry off." Bending his head he kissed her. "I wouldn't have married anyone I didn't think I could grow fond of. Now is that settled?"

"But Deron . . ."

"Deron and I have come to an agreement, a solution to his problems. I believe that he will try to hold to the letter of it, and that he will pay back what he is borrowing. He's an honest man, and he knows I won't frank him for the rest of his life. Please put it out of your mind."

"I shall talk to him," she vowed desperately. "I shall make him—"

He interrupted her with another kiss. "You shall not. This agreement is between gentlemen, and it is concluded. I know that you have long managed your brother's affairs, but trust me to do it, this time. I don't want you to give it another thought."

"I do trust you," she swore, "and I do so hope your plan will work out."

"Then not a word to him about it?"

"No." She let her head drop to his shoulder. I'm sorry I was so overset. I want things to be as you wish."

Brandon removed his handkerchief, wiped away her

tears, and bid her to blow her nose. "I only wish you to be my sweet wife and to be happy."

"I am." She smiled. He still cared for her, no matter what her relatives had done. There was yet a chance for her to gain his love!

"Now I have to ask this," he said, setting her back. "Are you sorry that you married me?"

"Oh, Brandon, how can you ask that when you are well aware of your effect on me?" she laughed.

"Don't answer frivolously."

"I didn't mean to sound so." She slipped her arms around his waist. "I am happy that you are my husband, and I love you most dearly. When I married you, I knew I would fall in love with you, even though I would have to share your affections with others. It's all right, Brandon. I shall grow accustomed."

He pressed her head to his chest and laid his cheek against her hair. "It's rather one-sided, don't you think?"

"I like to love you," she said dreamily, relaxing against him. "I believe we're friends too, aren't we? We like some of the same things, especially horses and riding."

"Yes, darling, we're friends."

"And I believe you're fond of me?" she asked, all her hopes riding on his answer.

The marquess took a very deep breath. "I'm in love with you, Ashley," he confessed quietly.

"What!" she cried, lifting her head to stare at him.

"I'm in love with you." He grinned with open relief. "Good God, Ashley, I've never been in love with any woman! I scarcely know how to act."

"Oh, Brandon." Her eyes glazed with tears. "I think you'll figure it out."

His lips met hers in a breathtaking kiss, that deepened until her mouth felt as though it were on fire. She knew from his own response that he must be experiencing much the same. Her heart soared.

He finally raised his head, caressing her cheek. "Since we have been married, there has never been another woman."

Ashley took a deep breath. "Alicia Milton . . ."

"I administered her *conge,* when I arrived in London. I don't need her or anyone like her again. Not when I have you."

"I do love you so," she told him with heart-felt devotion.

"I hope you always will, for I intend to love you very much, for a very, very long time." Brandon lifted her chin and looked deeply into her eyes.

Ashley slipped her arms around his neck, sliding her fingers caressingly through his guinea-gold hair. "And I intend to do the same."

The next long kiss was interrupted by a sudden question from the marquess. "What was it you were going to tell me, this morning?"

"Oh yes!" She laughed saucily. "I almost forgot! You are to be a father."

"Almost forgot?" He stared open-mouthed at her. "Ashley!"

"Do you like it?" she asked eagerly.

"Certainly!" He hugged her close. "But I don't know that I'll be very good at it."

"You will," she said confidently, her heart swelling with love for him and confidence for their future. "You will be wonderful at it! Just as you are at everything else."

Epilogue

The afternoon sun cast long shadows over the thin crust of snow. Unamindful of the chill, Ashley stood with Brandon on the portico of Havard Hall, watching their guests arrive. She was dressed appropriately for the holiday season in red velvet, a sprig of holly in her dark hair. Clasping her hands together in anticipation, she glanced up at her husband to find him looking at her with fond amusement.

"Happy?" he asked.

"Oh, yes!" Her green eyes glimmered. "Thank you for what you've done for Deron."

Her brother had arrived earlier . . . alone. Angered by his strict economy, Eve had left him for greener pastures. Deron had been very downcast until Brandon had taken him into the library for a long talk, after which they had both emerged cheerfully.

"He'll do all right now," the marquess said. "He sees that he's well rid of her. And I gave him a Christmas gift."

"Oh?"

"I canceled his debt to me, and gave him an extra five thousand."

"Brandon!" Tears filled her eyes.

"He'll use it wisely. He's learned from all this."

Ashley flung herself into his arms. "This is the happiest Christmas I've ever had!"

He held her close and dropped a kiss on her head. "For me too."

"Brandon! Ashley!" the dowager marchioness cried laughingly from the arriving carriages. "Cease this indecent display and come greet us!"

Giggling, Ashley dashed down the steps to embrace her mother-in-law and Jamie, and to meet for the first time Brandon's sister Mary Anne, her husband, and their brood. "I'm so glad that everyone could come!"

"We wouldn't miss a Christmas at Havard for anything," Jamie grinned, escorting her into the house.

They proceeded to the drawing room where servants served brandy to the gentlemen, sherry to the ladies, steaming chocolate to the children, and a large tray of refreshments for all. Deron joined them and was quickly accepted with no questions asked concerning the absence of Eve.

Observing how Brandon hovered about his wife, Mary Anne remarked dryly. "I never thought to see my brother become the April gentleman."

But the dowager marchioness was thoroughly studying Ashley. "My dear, aren't you gaining weight?"

Flushing, Ashley looked up at her husband.

Brandon lay his hand on her shoulder. "That is our Christmas surprise, Mama."

"That Ashley's gaining?" Deron asked, puzzled. "Why should . . ." He broke off as his sister burst into laughter.

"Damme, now I see!" He clapped Brandon on the back. "Congratulations, man!"

"What about me?" Ashley reminded pertly.

He grinned fondly. "Why, you always accomplish whatever you set out to do."

She smiled. So she had. She had a home, a child on the way, and a husband whose love enveloped her like a warm cloak. No one in the world could be happier than she.

"Let us drink a toast!" Jamie cried. "To Bran and Ashley, and," he added wickedly, "to the demise of *Lord Scandal!*"

"Jamie, really," his brother said with disgust.

"Well, isn't it?"

The marquess grinned self-consciously at his marchioness. "Yes, I suppose that it is. She has tamed me."

"Have I really?" Ashley asked him later, when they found a private moment when their guests were engaged with chattering conversation, refreshments, and overexcited children.

"Have you what?"

"Tamed you?"

Her husband gathered her into his arms and lowered his head.

"Brandon!" she cried, feeling all eyes surveying them. "Not in front of everyone! I can see that I haven't tamed you at all!"

He pointed upward. "Mistletoe. I have an excuse."

"Oh, very well." She laughingly lifted her lips to his and received a rather shameful, but very satisfying kiss. "On second thought, I wouldn't wish you to be *entirely* tame, so long as your mischief is directed totally at me!"

About the Author

Cathleen Clare lives with her family in Ironton, Ohio. She is the author of seven regency romances, including *An Elusive Groom* and *Lord Scandal's Lady* (both available from Zebra Books). Cathleen is currently working on her next Zebra regency romance, *A Priceless Acquisition,* which will be published in November 1997. Cathleen loves hearing from her readers and you may write to her c/o Zebra Books. Please include a self-addressed stamped envelope if you wish a response.

YOU WON'T WANT TO READ
JUST ONE—KATHERINE STONE

ROOMMATES   (0-8217-5206-5, $6.99/$7.99)
No one could have prepared Carrie for the monumental
changes she would face when she met her new circle of friends
at Stanford University. Once their lives intertwined and became
woven into the tapestry of the times, they would never be the
same.

TWINS   (0-8217-5207-3, $6.99/$7.99)
Brook and Melanie Chandler were so different, it was hard to
believe they were sisters. One was a dark, serious, ambitious
New York attorney; the other, a golden, glamourous, sophisticated supermodel. But they were more than sisters—they were
twins and more alike than even they knew . . .

THE CARLTON CLUB   (0-8217-5204-9, $6.99/$7.99)
It was the place to see and be seen, the only place to be. And
for those who frequented the playground of the very rich, it
was a way of life. Mark, Kathleen, Leslie and Janet—they
worked together, played together, and loved together, all behind
exclusive gates of the *Carlton Club*.

*Available wherever paperbacks are sold, or order direct from the
Publisher. Send cover price plus 50¢ per copy for mailing and
handling to Penguin USA, P.O. Box 999, c/o Dept. 17109,
Bergenfield, NJ 07621. Residents of New York and Tennessee
must include sales tax. DO NOT SEND CASH.*